SOMEONE ELSE'S CHILD

NANCY WOODRUFF

SIMON & SCHUSTER

New York London Toronto Sydney Singapore

SIMON & SCHUSTER
Rockefeller Center
1230 Avenue of the Americas
New York, NY 10020

Book design by Ellen R. Sasahara

Manufactured in the United States of America

1   3   5   7   9   10   8   6   4   2

Library of Congress Cataloging-in-Publication Data

Woodruff, Nancy.
Someone else's child / Nancy Woodruff.
p. cm.
1. Friendship—Fiction. 2. Middle-aged women—Fiction. 3. Teenage boys—
Fiction. 4. Traffic accidents—Fiction. 5. New England—Fiction. I. Title.
PS3573.O62645 S66 2000
813'.6—dc21   00-028185
ISBN 0-684-86507-6

The author would like to thank this book's first readers,
Denise Dailey, Ann Darby and Sandy Tyler, for their
early encouragement and continued support;
Paul Elie for his unparalleled criticism midway;
Renee Bacher for her energetic readings in the final stages;
Ann Rittenberg, Marysue Rucci and Nicole Graev for
expertly turning half a manuscript into a real book;
Fred Carl III for some tiny plunders;
and Mark Lancaster, with love,
for absolutely everything else.

FOR MY PARENTS,
WITH LOVE

SOMEONE ELSE'S CHILD

PROLOGUE

I F THIS WERE the small town Jennie had always imagined existed somewhere in the Midwest, she might have heard about the crash at the hospital that very night. Whispers of horror and shock would have passed through the corridors—"all young kids, such a heartbreaker," "the Linders girl," "Kevin Cleary's daughter," "that new boy, family came from out west." The staff would have hurried to attend, the whole place holding its breath until they knew whether the girl they'd brought in with a heartbeat was going to make it or not.

It seemed to Jennie that that's how it should be—a car accident calling on everyone in the town to help, all collectively hoping or praying, as beliefs allowed, waiting and knowing and mourning. But this wasn't a small town. It had been once, and some of the older residents remembered it as such, though it had grown into a suburb—68,000 at last census, a place where people mostly got the news from TV or the morning paper, not from one another. And geographically, it was huge, twice as big as the Manhattan island where so many of its residents made their living. The town's fifty square miles began at the ocean and stretched inland, from beachfront houses through the offices and boutiques of the town center, past older neighborhoods of colonials and capes and tudors out to back-country acreage, old stone or clapboard houses with their own streams or ponds or studios, bordering nature preserves, horse farms, forests. That was where it happened—out there on the back roads, where there weren't even road signs because the town council insisted they would mar the beauty of the landscape. There were miles and miles of roads back there. Curvy. Heavily shaded. At night, pitch dark. Jennie had lived in this town all her life but wasn't able to picture the stretch of road where it happened until she actually drove past.

She wondered later if it would have truly made a difference, knowing about the accident that night, instead of the next morning. Her proximity was to make her breathless later, for Jennie was on the fourth-floor maternity ward when they brought them into the emergency room, a fifteen-year-old boy and two girls, each just sixteen. That's when the large suburb revealed its intimacies, created by children carrying news and goodwill across lawns and streets. Jennie knew all three of the teenagers who had been in the car: Rachel and Erica were her daughter's best friends, and Matt was the boy it seemed they had all begun to love.

JENNIE

S HE HAD HER LUNCH early that Friday, just after 11:30, the thick
stack of envelopes she'd picked up from her post office box on the
table next to her. She meant only to sort them while she ate, then take her
requisite nap before sitting down at the computer. Daily updating, that
was the key to her business. If she missed even a day she felt swamped, the
work piling up so much that she would return to the computer at 3:00
A.M. when the baby's punches and thumps kept her awake.

Jennie ran a one-woman business organizing high school reunions.
She called it My Old School, and she liked its orderliness, its neat stacks
and growing lists, detective phone calls trying to track down lost alums.
She even liked finding banquet halls and choosing menus—planning it all
and then sitting back to see how it turned out.

She had taken an interest survey back in high school. *Would you: a)
strongly like, b) somewhat like, c) somewhat dislike, or d) strongly dislike the
following tasks: Sorting tobacco leaves by size and color. Separating nuts from
bolts. Transporting boxes from one shelf to another.* How she and her best
friend Elizabeth had laughed then. Jennie had expected to be doing research in Africa or writing her way through Europe, undertaking some
exciting, successful endeavor that would be hers for the asking. No one
then would have predicted that Jennie Northrop, valedictorian of the
Class of '83, Most Likely to Succeed, would have left college after a semester to come home and marry her high school sweetheart, have their
baby, and sixteen years later, still be here.

Even her strange little business had come to her without planning.
She'd done so much work on her own ten-year reunion that Sheldrake
High had hired her to do the next year's, and now she was handling
schools all over the area. Her income probably wasn't equal to the hours
she spent fiddling with databases and envelopes and menus, but it was

more than she'd made at any of the other jobs she'd held over the years to put herself through college and grad school.

Jennie took bites of her tomato and mozzarella sandwich and immediately felt hot. It was one of those early May days when it is warmer outside than in, the kind of day when ladies in their eighties would still wear turtlenecks and cardigans while college students at the end of their semester might put on shorts and polo shirts. Jennie, nine months pregnant, wearing only a tank top and huge cotton stretch shorts, couldn't get cool enough.

Her July reunion, little more than two months away, was a twentieth reunion from her own high school. It was her sister Stephanie's class, and though it was a big class—576 graduates—Jennie recognized many of the names. Steph's friends, kids who had been seniors when Jennie was a freshman. Responses were lagging (1980 was an apathetic year, she kept hearing), so on the last mailing she'd started writing personal notes to anyone she even vaguely remembered. She had written one to her sister, though that hadn't produced a check yet. Steph didn't like to leave San Diego, not to come home anyway. She usually made it back once a year, a long weekend at Christmas squeezed between strategy sessions for her software company and spent smoking in their parents' garage, complaining about the Connecticut winter.

Jennie flipped through the return addresses. Most were still nearby: Connecticut, Westchester, a few in New Jersey or Long Island. There were three or four Manhattans, mostly Upper East Side, and one Brooklyn. Still single, she thought. Bankers, lawyers, people in advertising. The accountants and engineers stayed in the suburbs, even if they never married. Very few had left the East Coast, and if they had it was for California. At a ten-year reunion, those who were going to move away had usually done so; by the twentieth, most of them were back. "I know the demographics," she'd say to Chris in a mock-actuarial tone that parroted Mr. Shipley, the social studies teacher they'd both had in high school. "You got your wanderers but these New Englanders usually return to their roots to raise their kids the way they were raised."

She always noticed the ones who had moved away, curious about what path had taken them there. For that reason, the California address interested her. Stephanie finally? No. She couldn't believe it. Joel Tarn had actually replied. She had found his address within seconds by calling directory assistance in L.A., but that was months ago; it had taken a personal note on this third and final mailing to get him to respond.

She slit open the envelope and was surprised, almost disappointed to see the check. Joel was the kind who had *left home*. He seemed above these hometown dramas and reunion clichés, even more than Stephanie was. On the return form he had written a note: "OK, I fell for this. Knowing there's someone behind this (knowing it's you) made me sign my name, though it's been years since I've been back. What the hell."

It struck her as a flirty kind of note. Had hers been?

Probably. The thought of him still brought a teenager's queasy excitement.

Years, he'd said, *years* since he'd been home. Jennie herself hadn't seen him in eighteen years—not since the summer before her senior year in high school, when he had returned home after a couple of years away at college. Even that summer she'd seen him only once, at a party her sister had thrown. At that party, Joel Tarn had the distinction of being the first boy Jennie had ever slept with. The only boy ever, other than Chris.

She looked at the note again. He had addressed it *Jenny* and she thought, *Okay, so he was this major lust in my life and I'm so inconsequential in his that he can't even remember how to spell my name.*

Joel. She had practically worshiped that *l* in his name. Joe rhymed with hoe, mow, schmo, blow; but Joel was droll, Joel had a soul. That *l* said, "I'm worthy, I've earned it." He had worn black turtlenecks (in high school! in the seventies! in Connecticut!) and spoke with a slight lisp that seemed to have something to do with the sexy space between his two front teeth. He was pale with hair so dark it was almost black, and everything about him was taut and angular, not at all like Chris, whom Jennie had first loved for his plump ass in jeans, the way his shirt opened at the collar, the curly blond head of hair that even now had not begun to thin. Joel had this mind—well, they all seemed to think he did anyway. He gave that impression. He'd been Stephanie's boyfriend for a while—who hadn't?—and Jennie had always found him devastatingly sexy.

She lifted herself out of the chair after lunch, not able to bear a fold in her body after eating. She had to be vertical or horizontal, preferably horizontal, but first she had to pee. Even to get to the bathroom and back was an accomplishment these days, and when she finished she lay on the couch. It was essential that she sleep each day or she found herself so exhausted she could barely speak words to Tara when she came home from school or to Chris when he returned from work. As it was, she and Tara usually found something to "disconnect" about, as Tara called it. At times it was nearly impossible for Jennie to deal with Tara's teenage hormones and her own pregnancy ones at the same time. She felt guilty about how much she let things slide with her daughter sometimes, waiting for Chris to come home because he had always had an easier time handling her.

Joel Tarn. She enjoyed the private, foolish reverie his name conjured. A few years ago she would have already been on the phone with her best friend Elizabeth: *You'll never believe who I heard from.* But now she had no one to tell, really, no one to whom she could say *Joel Tarn* and have it mean something. Still, it was nice to have something else to obsess about besides the baby, who lately had claimed Jennie's every moment.

She was remembering that party. Their parents had been away for the weekend, as they often were, and the party was planned to last all night. By 4:00 A.M. only a select handful of Steph's friends remained, smoking pot on the patio while Jennie and Elizabeth sat with them, pretending they belonged. Jennie hadn't tried pot yet, mostly because it was one way in which she could choose not to copycat her older sister, but she and Elizabeth were drunk, trying to act as cool as the twenty-year-olds around them. It was early June, chilly enough at night to need blankets on the patio, so Jennie and Elizabeth had carried them out, and somehow Joel and Jennie had ended up side by side on the vinyl cushions of the patio couch. They shared a blue, nubby blanket, an electric blanket that no longer worked. Jennie could feel the thin loops of wire throughout, the heavy plastic plugs resting on her legs.

Almost idly, while Joel was telling his L.A. stories—dance clubs and parties, the most amazing people, the coolest places—he had taken Jennie's hand under the blanket and then, as if it happened every day, let go and began to work his hand between her thighs, edging into her underpants. Jennie looked over at him to make sure he knew who she was. Not Steph, but Jen, the younger sister. He'd given her that confident, ironic, gentle stare and said her name. "Jennie, so what do you think about coming out to the West Coast for college?"

"Well, I've looked at Stanford," she had said. "But now I'm thinking more of Northwestern or the University of Chicago." She had replied in such a schoolgirl tone—she could hear herself even now—talking as if he were a guidance counselor or someone's dad while his slim, cool fingers were parting the lobes of her labia.

"Ah, the Windy City," Joel said.

"She can go wherever she wants," her sister had said. "Double eight hundreds on the SATs."

Jennie hadn't even been able to move her head to give Stephanie a look, for as the conversation went on, Joel's fingers slid inside her. She was sure she was blushing, but it was dark and he'd smiled at her warmly and continued—both talking and touching her—and in the end, when most people had gone home and Stephanie had gone driving somewhere with those who were left, and Elizabeth, who was supposed to spend the night, had discreetly gone to the other end of the house, Jennie and Joel went inside to her room. Kissing her against the door, Joel had started to unbutton her blouse and asked, "What about birth control?"

"Wait a minute," she had said, dropping to the floor and drawing up her knees. "I need to think about this."

"You're not sure?"

"I'm a virgin," she said.

"So was everyone at one time." He smiled. "Even I." Normally she would be irritated by this arrogance, but Joel had a way of making you love it. And he took your eyes and locked them to his, as if he were going on a thrilling adventure and you, only you, could accompany him.

"Shall I leave you with your thoughts then?" he asked, and when she was silent he got on the floor with her, kissing her neck.

"No," she giggled, and they were kissing again. His hand was under her shirt, going at a breast. He was already doing things no one had done before—after the Spring Dance Carl Lindt had touched one breast, not both, and no one's fingers but her own had ever gone inside her like that. She was astonished, really, by the places of a girl's body a boy knew to touch. She wanted this to happen. It was as simple as that.

"I've got some condoms in my jacket pocket," Joel said.

He put on some music and they went into her twin bed. He readied her, spent forever with his fingers and tongue so that when he finally pressed his penis against her and then inside she'd felt only that—a pressing open, a pressing in, not much pain, very little blood.

She'd loved it. She was a good girl captivated by sex, taken in by it entirely. They did it twice that night, and after that she had said no more, that was enough for her first time. He held her for the rest of the night, one of her legs between his two thighs, his bare chest against her side. It had been the most exciting night of her life.

He left in the morning, before her sister was up, so that Steph had never known that her little sister, the smart, virtuous one, had lost her virginity at age sixteen to Joel Tarn.

Only Elizabeth had known—nothing had ever seemed real until it was told to Elizabeth.

"So," Elizabeth had asked casually, slyly, "what did you think?" and they'd both burst out laughing, hugging each other, jumping up and down until they could calm themselves enough for Jennie to tell Elizabeth everything.

So many years had passed since that night with Joel—more than half her life—that it seemed more fantasy now than memory. She found herself getting wet, felt her clitoris throbbing as she relived the course of that summer night. She wondered if she would laugh or cry if she saw that sixteen-year-old body next to this one, twice as old, maybe twice as big, with an infant ready to burst from it. Maybe that night had entered the world of fantasy from the moment it happened, for in all this time she had never seen Joel again. He'd never called afterward; she'd never spoken to him again. She'd cried about him, about *things,* assigned various meanings to him at one time or another, but later she felt like it was the perfect way for it to happen, unsuspected and completely pleasurable, with someone she'd lusted after for so long. At that age, and even later, she carried this dramatic attitude about experience, that it shouldn't be diluted, that true life moments were unique and never repeated, that it was the once-ness of each thing that gave it its power. When she began dating Chris later that fall she didn't look back. Joel was a one-night stand, her first and only; Chris she fell in love with.

Jennie had often wondered what might have happened if it had been that night with Joel that had made her pregnant and not one of those nights, more than a year later, with Chris. There would have been no question of marriage then. Could she have brought herself then to have the abortion that her mother and sister tried to persuade her to have later?

These were all things she had thought about daily, hourly, obsessively years ago. Now it was rare that she considered them, though they still brought with them an instant ache.

She got up to go to the bathroom again but didn't make it.

"Damn," she said, pulling off the wet underpants. Bladder control had been slipping, but this had never happened before. She wadded up the wet clothes and threw them into the tub, sat again on the toilet. She hadn't even left the bathroom before she had to go again, streaming onto the floor.

"What is going on?" she said aloud. She stuffed a towel between her legs, then went to the phone to beep Chris.

"I think my water's breaking," she said when he called back.

"You think?"

"I thought it would be this gush but instead it feels like I have to pee again and again but I can't hold it. It's just everywhere."

"Did you call Dr. Perrin?"

"I haven't had any contractions yet. We don't need to rush off. I just wanted to tell you."

"I'm in Southport. I can make it in a half hour. Do you want to call your mother?"

"No! No, nothing's going to happen in a half hour." Jennie paused, spoke slowly and calmly. "The pleasure of your company is requested. However, you don't need to hurry."

"I will hurry. I love you."

"And I love you."

"Jen?"

"Yeah?"

"We're having a baby today. 'Bye."

She could imagine the smile on his face when he said that. The grin. He probably had to check himself as he went out to tell the guys that he had to leave, to make sure they didn't see him beaming. Chris could do that—beam—and she smiled too as she pictured his face.

Jennie went back into the bathroom because every time she moved more fluid leaked out. *So much for Joel Tarn,* she said to herself in the mirror and then laughed.

She was glad Chris would—and could—be there soon. Now that Chris's parents lived in North Carolina it was really Chris who ran Brezione Landscaping—a small firm, two trucks, two crews. The guys might slack off without Chris working beside them, and they couldn't afford to during their busy season, but at least he had the freedom to come home.

She knew she should call the doctor but she wasn't ready for that. She was feeling invincible, confident, a little proud. "After all, you've done this before," everyone kept telling her, but that had nothing to do with it. She had been a terrified eighteen-year-old the first time and wanted this birth to be nothing like that one, when almost from the start she was moaning, "I can't do it, I can't do it," finally letting them slit her open to take Tara out because she didn't know how to push anymore. This time she and Chris had taken radical-warrior childbirth classes—that's what Chris called them—where they did role play as fetus and placenta and practiced screaming, "Stop! That's my body!" at interfering practitioners. They had driven into the Upper West Side of Manhattan each week for these classes; there was nothing like them in Connecticut. Jennie was determined to be in charge of this birth, even though she realized how ridiculous that sounded, as if anyone could be in charge of a child coming into life. But she wanted to be anything but eighteen-year-old Jennie again, overfull with the shame of having that baby, of meeting her high school friends' parents in the grocery store later and seeing the shock in their eyes as they told her of their child's internship or junior year abroad while all she had to show them was the squirming toddler in her grocery cart.

She had begun crying when Chris came home.

"Is the pain bad, Jen?" he asked. He knelt beside her, smelling of grass and sunshine and sweat, his hair all matted curls from wearing a baseball cap.

"I still haven't had any contractions," she answered. "I was just thinking about how it was last time. With Tara. I did such a shitty job."

"We were eighteen. We didn't know anything."

She ran her palms up his arms, from wrists to biceps.

"It's going to be different this time," he went on. "It already is. Look, remember your mother, practically ordering you when to have your contractions, your dad just watching TV?"

Jennie winced, then giggled. "God," she said.

"What can I do for you?" Chris asked. "A back rub? A snack? Are you hungry?"

"I want you to take a shower."

"Are you kidding?"

"No. You kind of stink. I want you to be clean on your baby's birthday."

Jennie stayed in the bathroom as Chris showered, then followed him into the bedroom to watch him get dressed. It felt odd, just the two of them home during the day. Jennie was usually alone all day until Tara came home, followed an hour or two later by Chris. Weekends, if Tara was out, she and Chris were usually doing something, catching up on projects, running errands, not simply sitting and talking, not a thing to do in the world but watch each other. She felt almost as if they were back in high school, relishing time together in each other's houses while parents and brothers and sisters were out.

Only this was *their* house, had been for eleven years. They had lived with Chris's parents after they'd married, to save money while Chris worked for his father and Jennie worked nights at the food market. When Tara was two they had moved into their own apartment, and when she was five they bought this house. They probably would have been able to buy a little house earlier if they hadn't used their savings to send Jennie to college, two courses a semester for eight years, until she got her degree. Houses in Sheldrake were so expensive and they weren't able to afford much, but they had saved up because it made sense to buy a house. Jennie had hated the house when they bought it, and still hated it when she had time to think about it, not because it was small—two bedrooms and a bath and a half, a living room, a small kitchen and a long, narrow family room at the back that doubled as her office—but because it was so final. At twenty-three years old she had been able to imagine someone cleaning out the attic when she died.

"This is who we'll always be," she had said the day they'd moved in. It seemed the relinquishment of all possibility.

"You're lucky to get even this," was what her mother had said. "On a landscaper's salary."

"This is kind of nice," Jennie said now, lying on the bed and watching Chris dress. "The two of us alone in the middle of the day."

"Want to have sex?"

"Maybe in about six weeks."

"Oh, okay. Then how about some cards?"

"On the floor. I want to lie on my left side on the floor with pillows under my knees."

"I'm going to miss this about you being pregnant," Chris said. "These eccentric demands. 'I want pink lemonade very, very cold but with no ice and two pieces of toast, one with peanut butter and one with jelly.'"

"Shut up," Jennie said, sliding to the floor, where they played gin rummy, game after game on the rug. Nothing happened for an hour. Chris made himself a sandwich; Jennie called the doctor.

"Come in and we'll take a look at you," Dr. Perrin said, sounding weary.

"I want to stay home a little longer," Jennie answered. "I just wanted to let you know what was happening."

"Don't stay too long. With second babies they can really rush you. Once they start to come they come fast."

"What are we waiting for?" Chris asked when she got off the phone.

"We can't leave until Tara comes home. I don't want her to just find a note: 'Hi, we're at the hospital. We'll bring home a baby, need anything else while we're out?'"

"Your mother could come over and wait."

"I'm sure she has some luncheon. Besides, I want Tara at the hospital with us."

"Shouldn't she be home? Isn't school, like, out at three?"

Jennie flashed him an annoyed look. She hated having to carry every little detail of Tara's schedule in her head—cheerleading practice, dance class, volleyball nights—while being the major shareholder of Tara's scorn, while Chris could ignore it all and still win the role of Beloved Daddy. "She has practice until four-thirty," Jennie told him.

"Today?"

"Every day, except for Friday." Jennie frowned. "God, it's Friday. She goes to the Y on Friday with Rachel and Erica."

"The Y? The Y? Why the Y?"

"Supposedly to swim. I think it's to see that guy."

"Which guy?"

"Remember, that guy Matt? The Christian lifeguard? They met him swimming over the winter? He doesn't go to school, he's home-schooled, they were talking about that for a while."

"He's a lifeguard?"

"He's not really a lifeguard. He just pulled an old lady out of the pool during an Aquacise class while she was experiencing shortness of breath. Tara thinks he's a hero."

"Have we met him?"

"I have. Once."

"What's he like?"

"Very nice. Polite. *Really* polite, but not in an ingratiating-little-dweeb sort of way. He's talkative, very self-possessed. Kind. His family is very . . . Christian . . . or something. With this home-schooling thing, I mean."

"Serves us right for not taking her to Sunday school all those years. Now she's going to go off and get born again."

"They're infatuated with him, that's all. Did I mention he's gorgeous? I think that's why they still go to the Y." Jennie had thought this unconventional life of Matt's was the attraction for the girls until she'd actually seen him. Drop-dead handsome was this boy. Light brown hair, dimples, blue eyes. He was tall with a swimmer's strong arms, broad chest, unusual for someone his age. To top it all off he had the kind of warm, generous smile that would transform the most ordinary face into one of beauty, and on him it dazzled.

Jennie and Chris were still playing cards when Jennie felt the first contraction, just before 4:00. It was mild, a tight, menstrual cramp feeling. She didn't tell Chris until she'd had the next one because she wasn't even sure what it was. They played more gin rummy; Jennie had a few more contractions, barely noticeable. Neither of their watches had a second hand so they pulled the kitchen clock off the wall to time them. Seven minutes apart.

When the phone rang she was on all fours on the floor, stretching out her back.

"You don't want to talk, do you?" Chris asked. "It's a reunion person."

"Did you get a name?"

"Sorry."

"Just . . . just take a message." Another contraction beginning. She tried to relax and breathe through it but she was actually thinking about her business. It suddenly seemed so overwhelming. How could she possibly attend to the hundreds of details each reunion required with a new baby at her breast?

"Let's go for a walk," Jennie said to Chris after her contraction was over. "That's supposed to make things happen."

Chris helped Jennie off the floor and they went outside to walk up and down streets they hadn't walked in ages. On almost every corner Jennie had to stop and lean against Chris as she eased through a contraction. They were getting stronger.

"That was six and a half," Chris said. He was carrying the round kitchen clock under his arm.

"I don't really need to go until they're five," Jennie said. At 5:30 they were six minutes apart. Jennie felt tired, and she and Chris walked back to their house. Tara still wasn't home, and by 6:00 the contractions had jumped to five minutes apart. Jennie was having trouble breathing and couldn't talk through the contractions anymore.

"We really should go," Chris said.

"Where is she, damn her? I still want to wait. They're not that . . ." But then she had to be silent. She felt her body taking over, telling her what to do. It was getting serious, it was really happening. There was no way of stopping it now, and Jennie had the feeling of having waited in a long line to board a terrifyingly fast amusement park ride, and now, finally being buckled in with no way of getting off.

MATT

IT WAS JUST OVER four miles from his house to the Y but there was
one hill after another, and even pedaling fast it took Matt a full fifteen minutes. Monday through Thursday, at least one of his brothers or
sisters had an activity at the Y—T-ball or soccer or ballet—and his
mother drove them all in the van. But on Friday afternoons, Mom
dropped Brian at Boy Scouts and then took Pete, Katie and Em to the
park so if Matt wanted to swim on Friday he had to cycle to the Y. He
didn't mind it, except today he was running late after helping Mom
present nature lore to the Boy Scouts. By the time he got to the pool
there were only forty minutes left on the lap swim. Spending less than
an hour in the pool was hardly worth the trouble of changing, getting
wet, showering, drying off and getting dressed again, but he was there so
he decided to do it anyway.

He spotted the girls in the water instantly—Tara, Rachel and Erica, all
using the same lane, all wearing the same neon flowered bathing cap.
That's all he could see of them—those bathing caps and their long arms
rising above the water for their strokes. Erica was the only serious swimmer. He saw she was swimming freestyle, maybe to prepare for the race
she had told him about. Matt wondered how she could stand having Tara
and Rachel in her lane. Tara moved slowly and with no particular fashion.
She had told him once she just liked being in the water. Rachel was fast,
but with big sloppy strokes. Rachel was all splash.

Matt chose a lane and dove in. He liked to swim a very organized
workout, in tight intervals. Today, since there were only thirty-five minutes left before the Aquacise class would come in, he decided just to see
how far he could get. He knew it would be between 1,000 and 2,000 meters and he was hoping it was closer to two. He began with 200 freestyle.

He loved to swim. It was a bit like sleeping and having a really useful dream. Sometimes he used the time to conjugate French verbs but most of the time he let his thoughts wander and leap from subject to subject. On Fridays, especially, he liked to go through concepts he had studied that week, books he had read, the projects he was working on, and if he did it while swimming everything seemed to be related to everything else—physics and English, philosophy, history, even math. That would make Mom happy. She didn't like segmenting learning into subject areas. "It's a whole body of knowledge out there," she would say. "A continuum, not neat little packages." She talked a lot about holistic learning and sometimes, usually when he was in the pool, he could actually feel what she meant. It would all fit together in the pool, but it was hard for him to keep it connected once he got out of the water.

Today he was thinking about Darwin, a thought running through his head about how man was one of the most helpless creatures in the world. Darwin thought man pitifully weak—he had minimal strength, he lacked huge teeth or claws to defend himself, he was unable to avoid danger by smell. Matt thought it was a good thing man was smart enough to invent all kinds of weapons or he would have been wiped out long ago. Even today, one on one, against any of hundreds of animals, man would lose. It was almost comical that he should bother swimming, that people should come day after day to the gym to build up muscles and endurance when one encounter in the jungle with a tiger would show that none of that could make any difference.

His thoughts were distracted by someone entering his lane. This pool was just too crowded. He would have preferred a team sport, like baseball or soccer or basketball. When they first moved to Connecticut, Mom had looked into having him do sports at the high school as he had done at home in Oregon, but the school district wouldn't allow home-schoolers to participate. His brothers and sisters were lucky. They were younger. They met all sorts of kids in their activities and they were good at making friends. For Matt, it was frustratingly hard to meet people. That was the other part of why he liked to swim on Fridays: Tara, Rachel and Erica.

He managed 1,700 meters by the time the 5:30 buzzer rang. The girls had already left the pool area for the locker room and he supposed it was just as well. Sometimes he could get out of the pool after a disciplined workout and just seeing the water drip down their skin from ten feet away would send his body out of control.

The pool clock said 5:27 and he stopped by the desk to tease Mike, the pool manager.

"Hey, I got gypped out of fifty meters," he told Mike.

"Sorry, Matt. Everything's booked to the minute. I tell you, we could use two pools, the kind of use this one gets."

"Sounds good to me," Matt said.

"You get a shovel and I'll get a shovel and we'll both start digging." Mike gave him a wide grin. He was tall and bald and had the kind of face that would play well as Santa Claus in a few years.

"Hey Matt, got a question for you. This pretend school of yours last all summer?"

"No, just to the first week of June." He didn't mind Mike's teasing. Most people fell into embarrassed silence when they learned about his home-schooling, assuming, perhaps, that he was from some illiterate family who didn't know the meaning of a good education.

"I was wondering how you'd like a summer job here at the Y. You sixteen?"

"Not yet. In August."

"Can you get a work permit? I could use you almost full-time, all the kiddie classes, day camp groups we have running in and out of here this summer. Need someone at the desk all the time since I've got to be running around with all these groups."

"Sure. That would be great. I could really use the work." He tried to sound casual but he felt like letting out a whoop. This was so unexpected, so easy—and yet so necessary. He'd walked around his neighborhood in March trying to line up lawn-mowing jobs for the season, but it turned out most people had services. It was tough finding work as a fifteen-year-old and here this job had practically fallen in his lap. He couldn't wait to show up at home and mention to Mom, "By the way, I found a job."

He found himself whistling as he showered and changed into a clean gray T-shirt and jeans. As he rolled his wet swim trunks into a towel he noticed the exposed white threads at one seam of his trunks. He'd had the trunks two years and they were really too small. Suddenly he didn't care. Soon he'd be making money enough to buy new ones.

Money had been in short supply since they'd moved to Connecticut. The town was helping them with the rent on their house here; that was part of the deal they'd offered Dad when they'd recruited him for the conservation director job. But Mom and Dad hadn't counted on everything else here being so expensive too. Even food. Even clothes. Even gas was more than at home. According to Dad, Sheldrake was one of the most expensive suburbs in the country.

Usually Matt made it out to the snack bar before the girls, though today they were there first. Rachel and Erica were sitting at the table facing him, but it was Tara's back he noticed first, the long thin curve of it a question mark in a blue-and-white striped shirt. Her damp dark blond hair was hanging perfectly straight to just below her shoulder blades as she leaned over the table to drink from a straw. He wanted to grab onto those sharp shoulder blades almost as much as he wanted to reach out for Erica's breasts, huge and round in her tight white T-shirt. He felt that small gurgle in his throat, and that feeling of his stomach reaching back to touch the base of his spine. He had been so glad he didn't have to talk to them while they were wearing their swimsuits but now, even seeing them fully clothed, all he could do was picture them after swimming—Erica's breasts, Rachel's long legs, the café au lait mark on Tara's underarm that you would never know was there unless you saw her in a swimsuit. Or naked.

Matt walked slowly toward them.

"I can't believe it. I just can't believe it," Tara was saying.

"Hey," Matt said. He set his backpack next to the table, took out his water bottle.

"Hi, Matt," they all said.

"What can't you believe?"

"Tara's obsessing about this art history exam she had today," Rachel said. "I'm one hundred percent sure I failed my chemistry quiz, but do you see me obsessing about that?"

"Forgetting that *Fe* is iron or whatever is just a mistake. You didn't humiliate yourself." Tara turned to Matt. "This is what happened. I was doing the essay question about the Renaissance painters and halfway through Leonardo da Vinci turned into Leonardo DiCaprio. I swear." She scrunched up her face and put her fingertips on her forehead. "The thing is, I didn't notice it during the exam, but while I was in the pool I was sort of tracing through my answer and I just saw it there on the page, clear as day. Leonardo DiCaprio. Oh God." She put her head down on the table and covered it with her arms.

"Maybe he won't be able to read your handwriting," Rachel said.

"Of course he will," Tara said, voice muffled. "My handwriting is completely easy to read."

"Maybe he'll grade it on the train on the way home from one of those gallery openings in New York he's always talking about. Maybe he'll be drunk from too much wine and cheese and he won't notice."

"I'm sure he wouldn't grade you down for it," Matt said. "How could he?"

Tara lifted her head up and looked imploringly at him.

"Grading down I could take. He won't grade down but he'll write something insulting in the margin: 'Perhaps next semester you might consider enrolling in Teen Heartthrobs 101, Miss Breeze.'"

"Maybe you can head him off," Matt said. "Go and see him first thing on Monday and say, 'Excuse me, Mr. . . . .'?"

"Tremain."

"'Excuse me, Mr. Tremain,'" Matt said, putting on a bit of the English accent he had used once to play Professor Higgins in a community theater production back home, "'but I was reflecting on my response to the essay question on Friday's exam and I realized I must have had a synaptic lapse that you may find somewhat amusing.'"

"What's a synaptic lapse?" Rachel asked.

"Well," Matt said, trying to explain it so they would understand, "a synapse is when a signal passes from one neuron to another. It's just part of our normal way of thinking. But if something happens to prevent this normal passage, it's a lapse and it can make a person do something wrong or forget something momentarily."

"Does anybody have any gum?" Erica asked.

"Don't interrupt, Air. Matt's helping me construct my defense. What happens to cause a lapse?"

"It can be anything. They're doing lots of research about it now. The main point is that you can briefly forget something you usually know very, very well."

"It sounds like a more scientific way of saying 'spaced out,'" Tara said.

Matt felt his face go red. She was clever, she could sense hot air. "I guess that's true," he said. "But if you present it the right way, that is, better than I have, perhaps Mr. Tremain won't make the connection."

"It just might save me. I can't have Mr. Tremain thinking I'm the planet's shallowest soul."

"She has the hots for him," Erica announced, nudging Rachel and pointing at Tara.

"I do not have the hots for Mr. Tremain," Tara said. "God. He's a good teacher, but he always has to make these snide comments. 'Perhaps if Miss Breeze is not too hoarse from yelling *ra-ra-sis-boom-ba,* she can tell us why . . .'"

"That's just harassment," Erica said.

"But it's good-natured. I mean, he's not vindictive. He's just . . ."

"Maybe he's jealous," Rachel said.

"Because he wanted to be a cheerleader too?" Erica asked.

"He's not any of those things," Tara said. "He just wants to make it clear that he can't take my work seriously because I'm a cheerleader. He's like my mom. Why can't anybody understand that I just do it because I think it's fun? I like gymnastics, I like dance, I like running around yelling and I like watching the games. That's it. Period. I'm not in it so I can blow the entire football team. Oh my God." She put her hands over her eyes and hunched her shoulders forward.

"Sometimes she really comes out with one, doesn't she?" Erica said to Matt, who struggled to find something to say.

"How did we get to that from Leonardo da Vinci anyway?" Rachel asked.

"I guess some of us are in the stars looking down at the gutter," Matt said, wondering if his inverted Oscar Wilde–ism worked. Blank stares. Didn't work.

"Let's move on from that one," Erica said. "So, Matt, we're going roller-skating tonight. Want to come with us?"

Tara uncovered her eyes and said, "There's this great indoor rink. Galaxy?"

"Where is it? Can you give me directions?"

"We can take you. We can pick you up," Tara said. "Right, Air?"

"Sure. Just tell us where you live. If you want to come."

"I'd like to come," Matt said. He took out a pen and wrote his address and phone number on a piece of notebook paper, pleased. They had never invited him out before. He had never seen them away from the Y.

Erica was fishing around in her backpack for something so he handed the slip of paper to Tara.

"Oh my God," Erica said. "I really need gum. Does anyone have gum?"

"Air, Air, Air, I'll get you your gum." Tara jumped up. "I'm going for a Coke anyway."

"I'll go with you," Matt said. "I need some more water."

Tara left the table with him and they walked through double doors to the vending area. Matt filled up his water bottle from the drinking fountain while Tara put in money for two Diet Cokes and a gum. "It's funny that swimming makes you so thirsty," he said.

"Ironic, isn't it?" Tara asked, smiling.

Matt loved Tara's voice. It was deep, husky, attractively mismatched with the way she looked. Matt said "Yes," and grinned too. He had the feeling that neither of them knew why they were smiling.

Tara leaned against the candy machine, holding the Cokes and gum in front of her. She was so pretty. Beautiful was more like it, with small, perfect features, lovely clear skin. Long, lean torso, barely any breasts or hips. He thought *feline* when he saw her shape.

"I forgot to ask what time," Matt said. "Tonight."

"Seven-thirty, I think," Tara said.

"Thanks for inviting me to come along," he said

"Thanks for giving me the synaptic lapse angle. You really saved me."

"Hope it works," Matt said.

"And by the way," Tara said, "I do not have the hots for Mr. Tremain." As if to prove it, she stepped forward and kissed him on the lips. He felt the heat of her mouth on his while the cold cans of Coke pressed against his chest.

"'Bye," she said and turned quickly to walk away.

"'Bye," he called after her, astonished at the kiss, which seemed over before it began. She was like a tiny bird, a hummingbird flitting in so quickly and lightly that he'd felt only the weight of the kiss, none of her body at all. It was his first kiss from a girl in his life and he was left wanting to know not so much what he had done to make her kiss him, but what he could do to make her do it again.

JENNIE

"THERE SHE IS," Chris said, looking out the window. Jennie watched with him as Tara came up the driveway. She wore her backpack but was also bent to one side by the heavy art portfolio she insisted on bringing home each night in case the school burned down.

"She's such an artist," Chris always said in Tara's defense when Jennie complained that she'd expected her daughter to be an intellectual but instead had gotten a cheerleader.

"How serious can that be?" Jennie would joke. "Have you ever heard of any famous artist who was a cheerleader? Do you suppose Georgia O'Keeffe's memoirs talk of the tough moral choices she faced when doing the splits?"

"You're so mean," Chris would say. It was a sort of riff.

Jennie had been a nerdy, brainy sort of high school student and she and her friends had always believed the stereotype about cheerleaders. Only now that her own daughter was one, she realized why cheerleaders were so popular. Tara was not only beautiful, but probably one of the kindest, most friendly teenagers you could ever meet. And this gift for painting and drawing—who knew where that came from? Neither Jennie nor Chris had an ounce of artistic talent. They found themselves constantly baffled, immensely proud.

Tara walked quickly, looking slightly off to the left, not focused on anything in front of her. She looked as if she might end up inside the house or just as easily somewhere else. Chris said, "Doesn't she have a way of walking as if the wind's blowing her?"

He hurried to open the door for her. "I'm glad you're home. We have to go to the hospital right now."

"She's having the baby? Mom, you're having the baby?"

"It looks that way."

"How long do you think it will take?"

"How long? Do you have some pressing engagement?" said Chris.

"Well, yeah, I'm supposed to go roller-skating."

"Not tonight. Not when your mom's in labor."

"That's labor? She's just sitting there." In fact, Jennie was feeling the need to squat and she did just that, next to the kitchen table. Another contraction. She focused on her muscles, but also let her mind consider poor Tara, at an age when no doubt she would like to forget that her mother even had a body, and here Jennie was, as physical as you could get without emitting bodily fluids. Tara was watching her almost in revulsion and Jennie suddenly remembered a two-year-old Tara, waiting for her to come out of the shower, holding a clean pair of underpants and a panty shield, proudly saying, "Mom, need one?" or, at four, seeing Jennie scrub the calluses from her feet with a pumice stone and kneeling down, wanting to help. Tara would absolutely die if Jennie told her those things now. That devotion, Tara's love of her mother's body had deeply humbled Jennie in the past and now it touched her. Against all bidding, tears came.

"Look," Chris was saying, "if it was some dance or something, some special occasion, of course we'd let you go. But it's just roller-skating."

"I'm so glad you know exactly what events I can and can't miss," Tara said. "I'm so glad you're the judge of what's important to me."

"We don't want to worry about you. I don't want your mom in the hospital worrying about you."

"Then don't worry. Nobody's asking you to." Tara was being uncharacteristically bratty, Jennie thought, and she actually enjoyed it that Chris had to deal with her. Usually he was the adored daddy, always on appeal.

"Your mom is having a baby," Chris was saying in a patient voice. "I don't know what else to say to you, Tara. You're part of the family and we want you there. What are you thinking, roller-skating? Maybe I should go bowling." He began to laugh, not a derisive laughter, but an authentic one to point out the absurdity of what Tara was saying. It was a technique he'd used when she was a child, crying or pouting for something ridiculous. He had always been able to joke her out of it.

She was quiet a minute and then a tiny giggle erupted. "Okay. God, sorry." She gave him a smile, even let it rest on Jennie a moment. "Just let me call Erica and tell her. But if the baby's born by seven-thirty, can I have Erica pick me up at the hospital?"

"Yes," Jennie said from her position on the floor, certain beyond wagering that it would be more than an hour and a half before the baby came.

Chris helped Jennie pack a bag for the hospital and from their room they could hear Tara on the phone to Erica. "My mom's having the baby. Yeah, I'm going to the hospital with them, they really want me to. They really, like, think they need me or something." When Tara hung up she dialed again, this time asking for Matt, and Jennie immediately understood the allure of the evening, the reason why it was so hard for Tara to let it go. Matt was coming, and whatever group activity this was supposed to be, no doubt Tara had seen it as their first date.

"Looks like roller-skating is off," Jennie heard her telling Matt. "Yeah, my mom's going to the hospital to have the baby. I kind of have to be there. Maybe we can go another time, maybe tomorrow?" She was so smooth, Jennie was thinking, rather impressed until that last *maybe tomorrow* came out as an almost desperate question, a childish break in her voice.

"The truth comes out," Jennie whispered to Chris. "It's the Christian lifeguard."

"Who?"

"That guy I was telling you about before, from the Y, rescued the Aquacise lady . . ."

"Right, sorry. Home-schooling."

"Why do you have to remember nothing and I have to remember everything?" Jennie asked, irritated again.

"'Cause I have other important things to do. I just can't remember what they are right now."

"Tara's a pro," Jennie said. "These other girls don't have a chance. Jesus, we've really got to go." That was the last thing she was able to say before the clamp came again to her abdomen, gripping her uterus and squeezing until she felt there was nothing left.

"I'll call Dr. Perrin and tell her we're coming," Chris said. Jennie groaned through the contraction, then tore out to the car and threw herself in the back, writhing and bellowing, worried that they really might have waited too long. She'd always thought the idea of women giving birth in taxis was preposterous—she had used all her strength to push a baby out the first time and still she hadn't been able to do it. But now she felt the baby could erupt at any moment.

"Help me, help me," she was whispering as another contraction came. "Oh God, oh God."

"Mommy, are you all right?" Tara asked.

"Hold on, Jen, we're going."

"At least turn on the radio or something," Jennie yelled when the contraction had passed. Some hip-hop thing came on and she said, "I hate that. Turn on something else."

"It's WNEW," Chris said.

"I don't care. It's so annoying."

"Okay, okay," Chris said. "Tara, see if you can find something."

Tara flipped the dial—talk, jingles, static—and Jennie snapped, "Oh, just turn it off."

She had three contractions on the way to the hospital, and once they pulled up to the emergency entrance Jennie all but ran in, single-minded and alone, paying no attention to Chris and Tara; she was in her own place now. She could feel everything else in the world slipping away, making a bubble only big enough for herself and the baby.

Dr. Perrin hadn't made it to the hospital yet so a resident examined Jennie.

"Is this her first baby?" the resident asked.

"I can talk for myself," Jennie said. "Oh God, here comes another one. That was no three minutes." Jennie turned in the bed they'd placed her in, concentrating on the tiny red call button on the bed railing until she made it through. When she turned from the bed, moaning softly, "Oh God, oh God, oh God," her eyes took in Chris, the resident, the delivery room nurse in pink scrubs and finally Tara. She stood with Jennie's overnight bag slung over her shoulder, looking so small and bewildered that it brought Jennie back for a moment.

"Mom," Tara asked. "Where am I supposed to be?"

"Oh Tara, sweetie." Jennie's eyes swept the room. Why had she thought Tara needed to come? "Is there a place in the hallway?" she asked the nurse. "Some chairs?"

"I'll take her," the nurse said.

"Is it okay if I call Erica?" Tara asked. "Just while I'm waiting?"

My God, Jennie almost exploded, *can't you think of anyone but yourself for one moment?* But Tara looked so lost, so out of place and overwhelmed by all this, that from some motherly place a tenderness welled up in Jennie, tenderness for which she was to be speechlessly grateful later, whatever its mysterious source.

"Yes," was what she said. "Call your friend."

MATT

MATT WAS ON his bed after dinner, trying to decide whether to read more Darwin or listen to his Walkman. What he finally did was get out the book because the Walkman sometimes worked, sometimes didn't, and he didn't need more aggravation tonight. Any minute now one of his brothers or sisters would come up to tell him they were starting the video. Friday was family video night—time for *Flipper* or *Toy Story* or one of the *Homeward Bounds*. Up until dinnertime, Matt had thought he would miss it, but then Tara had called and told him roller-skating was off. Her mom was having the baby. It was a valid reason, but he had expected this Friday night to be different and now it wasn't going to be. It was going to be the same as every other Friday night he could remember from his whole life. Even moving to Connecticut hadn't changed that.

On the small list of wishes Matt had for his life was wanting one night of it to be different from all those that had come before. It was a list so personal and specific that it sometimes embarrassed him and he felt he should add *peace on earth* or *stop the famine in Africa* so as not to appear so selfish. But those other things, they were what he prayed about. He would never pray for the things on his list, which were:

1. His driver's license
2. A new pair of swimming trunks
3. A new Walkman
4. Something different to happen in his life

The first, he knew, was out of his control. It could only happen at a certain time—he didn't turn sixteen until August—but he wanted to be ready. He had gotten his learner's permit so he could go driving with Dad, but Dad had only been able to take him out a couple of times. He always promised "this weekend" but Matt knew how weekends went. Dad would say, *Let me just change this lightbulb first,* only on the way to the garage he'd find a loose doorknob and on the way to the toolbox there was a bush that needed replanting and then back to the doorknob but there was a bolt missing and he'd have to go to the hardware store and then it would be Sunday night, and the chance for a driving lesson would be gone.

Wishes two and three on his list had been put off for the sake of wish one; he was saving all of his money for a driver's ed course. But now if he were to work at the Y all summer he would be able to take care of wishes two and three too, and not even have to wait for his birthday. Suddenly it seemed as if it was going to be the easiest thing in the world to cross all these wishes off his list.

Except wish four: that was supposed to have been taken care of tonight, but with Tara's call, it wouldn't be. He had been so sure it would start tonight—his social life. His life. Hadn't it started that afternoon, with Tara's kiss?

It was all he could think about, that kiss. His first. It set his life in motion; that's what it felt like.

That kiss, juxtaposed with her comment that she wasn't going to blow the whole football team, had sent him racing up to his room as soon as he got home from swimming.

Her kiss, her comment: together they equaled her mouth on his cock and that's what he beat off to.

And only moments afterward Tara called.

"Roller-skating is off," she said.

It's all off, is what he heard. She knew. Somehow she understood what he had done in his room by himself and never wanted to see him again. That kiss: his first and last.

Matt hadn't told his parents he wasn't going yet. He just did his part of dinner cleanup and went up to his room, wanting to be away from his family for a while. Sometimes he felt they were all in a certain boat and he was swimming along beside them. He was a good swimmer, he could keep up, but he wanted sometimes to be able to turn and swim in another direction.

It was just before eight when Mom knocked on the door.

"They're here," she said.

"Who?"

"What do you mean 'who'? The girls. Didn't you say you were going out with your friends?" She asked it as if he did it all the time, go out with his friends. "Rachel and Erica."

Matt got up off the bed.

"I thought . . ." he said.

He hadn't combed his hair and he wasn't about to do it in front of Mom. He tucked in the shirt he would have changed if he'd known they were coming and went downstairs.

Rachel and Erica were squeezed onto the couch between Brian and Katie.

"Hey," he said.

"How's it going?" Rachel asked.

It seemed too weird to ask them anything in front of his mom. It was like those two things should just be separate, the way you are with your family and the way you are with girls and people your age. There should be some law that you should never have to talk to them both at the same time. The ways of talking were just too different.

He waited until they were all outside, in the car, to ask, "Did Tara's mother have her baby already?"

"No, she's at the hospital. But the rest of us can still go out. There's this party at Paul Rama's?"

"I don't know him."

"He's Jeff's best friend."

"Jeff?"

"My boyfriend," Erica said.

"Oh." He hadn't known she had a boyfriend. Sitting in the backseat of the car as they drove away, he realized he didn't know much about Rachel and Erica, or even Tara. What if Tara had a boyfriend?

"This is a nice car," Matt said. An understatement. You rarely saw a BMW in Eugene, but out here they were all over the road. This one was an old one. Classic. Erica looked quickly over her shoulder. "Yeah, well, my dad got it for me when I turned sixteen."

"Nice dad."

"Yeah, nice." Erica dug into her pocket and pulled out a fifty-dollar bill. "Tonight he was supposed to come over and take me out for dinner on his way home from work and it ended up he couldn't so he dropped this off." She let the fifty-dollar bill fall onto the seat.

"Your parents are divorced?" Matt asked.

"Yeah."

"I'm sorry."

"It only happened like seven years ago or something. You'd think I'd be over it by now." Once again her eyes were on the road. "We could get pizza," she said. "My treat."

"I've already eaten," Matt said, then felt rude. "But I'm always hungry for pizza."

"I could eat a piece," Rachel said.

"Forget it," Erica said. "I'm not going to sit there while you two watch me snarf a whole pie by myself." She turned from the wheel with a screwed-up mouth when she said this. Matt had always thought she was a sarcastic person, but now it seemed like a kind of sadness that just looked like sarcasm.

"Where's the party?" Matt asked.

"It's too early," Erica said. "We can't go there yet."

"When do you think Jeff will get there?" Rachel asked Erica.

"I don't know. I'm not sure I care. He just had to do this guy thing and of course I wasn't invited. I don't want to get there until after he does, that's for sure."

"Maybe he just forgot to ask you," Rachel said.

"So we're not going roller-skating?" Matt asked.

"That's really Tara's thing," Erica said. "Well, what do you want to do?"

"Let's go to Lou's," Rachel said. "I guess I am pretty hungry."

Erica had seemed so much in charge in the car but once they were in the pizza place it felt more equal. Erica and Rachel sat on one side of the booth and Matt sat across from them. They let Erica choose the toppings and she made a big deal about what to get, even went over to a table across the room to see what this group of guys had on their pizza. When she came back to the table she kept looking over at them, smiling and gesturing in a cute sign language. One of them came over, but as soon as he sat down at the booth with them Erica got up and went to the bathroom.

"Well, pizza's getting cold," the guy said, and went back to his own table.

"She's always doing that," Rachel told Matt. "Getting guys' attention and then making us get rid of them. Don't get me wrong. I love her. She just has to get all the attention. I know why she's doing it and then again I hate it. Do you know what I mean? She's so . . ." Rachel either couldn't find the word she was looking for or didn't want to tell Matt.

When Erica returned to the table she didn't even glance over at the guys at the other table, but instead looked at Matt and Rachel with an expression of intense concern.

"Someone's smoking," she said. "I can smell it on my hair."

"We asked for no smoking," Rachel said.

"It doesn't matter how far away. My hair's so porous. It just absorbs it."

"How do you know your hair's porous?" Matt asked.

Erica bent her head toward Matt across the table, all but inviting him to put his nose to her hair. "Can't you just smell it?" she asked. "It must be porous." Rachel too was looking at Erica's hair and Matt was sure if that guy from across the room was there he would have too. She was the kind of girl who could transfix a roomful of people with her porous hair.

She had beautiful hair—shoulder length, blond, swooped in a glamorous way. It reminded Matt of a hairdo a woman might have. Not that she looked old, but from across the room, from the way she walked and carried herself, she might have been twenty-five or thirty, not sixteen.

When Matt had been with Rachel and Erica and Tara before he had always wanted to know more about them but it always felt like a lineup, asking each of them what music she liked, what were her favorite sports, what books she had read more than once. Now that there were only two of them, the natural thing seemed to be to inquire about the one who was missing.

"So does Tara have other brothers and sisters?" he asked after the waiter had brought the pizza to the table.

"No, she's an only child." Erica corrected herself. "Until tonight, anyway. Like me. That's why we became friends I think. We met when she was five and she moved around the corner from me."

"So you live close to her?"

"Lived. Past tense. Until my parents decided they needed a big house in the backcountry. We moved away a year later. Tara and I still saw each other sometimes for sleepovers and stuff, but we went to different schools so it was hard."

"Tara was all heartbroken when Erica left," Rachel said, "but then I moved in—same street, I mean, not the same house—and we became best friends."

Erica took up the story. "Tara and I didn't see each other for a few years and then last year when we started high school we were in the same homeroom and we were both like, wow, you used to be my best friend when I was five. It was spooky. Good-spooky."

"So now it's the three of us," Rachel said.

Matt wondered if there were any jealousy or if they were all best friends. He sensed more friction between Erica and Rachel than he'd ever noted when Tara was there. Maybe she was the one who unified the two. Rachel and Erica seemed different tonight. Or maybe not. Maybe he wasn't intuiting things correctly. Sometimes he felt he got human relationships all wrong; he understood how his own family worked but could be unbelievably off the mark with others. Perhaps he was wrong and they were the Three Musketeers.

He said it aloud—"the Three Musketeers"—and immediately cringed. Cheesy.

But Erica and Rachel didn't seem to mind the cliché. Erica gave her porous hair another sniff and then tossed it aside.

"Just two tonight," she said. And smiled.

JENNIE

PUSHING THE BABY OUT took hours, almost three of them. The contractions came one on top of the other, with barely seconds to rest in between. Chris put ice chips in Jennie's mouth when she asked for them, but beyond that he could do nothing to help her. No one could. She and the baby were alone in this now, and she wanted nothing more than to shake the baby from her body, free it into the world.

"Push where it counts," the nurse was saying. She was a kindhearted Filipina in pink scrubs. "Stop scrunching up your face. You can't push baby out your face."

"She's right, Jen," Chris said. "You're creating too much tension in your face, you're just tiring yourself out."

"Don't you think I know that?" Jennie yelled at all of them. "*You* push harder! *You* try!"

Jennie could feel herself pushing through her face, through her eyes in a way that was to pop so many blood vessels that both of her eyes would be bright red for weeks after the birth. She knew what she needed to do but could not summon the strength. In her brief moments of rest she moaned "I can't do it, I can't do it" over and over again.

"Yes you can," Chris said.

"No, you don't understand. It's not humanly possible," and then she was off again, screaming, clenching her thighs, bearing down with every muscle. She was glad Tara waited down the hall. She couldn't let her daughter see her this way, at the glorious animal level, her body doing the hardest work of its life. What happened to a woman in childbirth wasn't for your children to see, she thought, only for husbands and strangers.

"Just push a little harder and you'll see your brand-new baby," Dr. Perrin said.

"I don't want to see the baby," Jennie yelled. "I want to go to sleep." What if they told her instead, *Just a few more pushes and nobody will make you do anything for the rest of your life.* That might have worked.

Finally, it was time. The rip and the baby's head, then each limb sliding through, slithery as a knot of snakes.

"A little girl!" Dr. Perrin said, seeming to throw the baby on Jennie's chest. Jennie could barely raise her head to look at the tiny face, eyes wide open. The baby was covered with blood and peeing.

"Look at her, look at her," Chris was saying.

Two ultrasounds had told them it would be a girl and they hadn't even been able to agree on a boy's name, but somehow the only words Jennie could manage to utter were "A girl." She held the baby only a moment, before they took her to be cleaned, suctioned, weighed, the steps toward civilization. The time of the body, of being mother and baby animals together, was already slipping away.

"That was the most amazing thing," Chris said, bending down to rest his moist cheek against hers. He had sweated through this too.

Jennie was finding it impossible to move. Her legs were still folded up and she wanted to ask for help in getting them down, but even speaking was too much work. She just sat there, did what she was told, barely registering when Dr. Perrin began to stitch her up, when the nurse brought in a basin to clean her. Chris stayed with her until they moved her to the recovery room and then he went off to tell Tara.

Jennie asked for a blanket and the thin weave clung to her form, mummylike. Her stomach was a huge mound. She still looked pregnant, still felt so, and every time she drifted off even for a second she was sure she felt another agonizing contraction beginning.

When Chris returned he said, "We've been making calls. The grandparents are thrilled, both sets. A lot of people aren't home though. Frank and Janet, Paul and Kristy. It's a Friday night, after all."

"How dare people have plans when we had a baby?"

"I left cryptic messages. We'll have lots of return calls."

"My mom and dad aren't coming over, are they?"

"I told them the morning. I told them you were exhausted."

"Thank you."

"Where's the baby?"

"They haven't brought her back yet."

"I'll go find her."

Jennie caught his arm and pulled him back. "Wait, are we agreed? Alison Grace?"

"Alison Grace," Chris said.

Jennie closed her eyes when Chris left and tried to rest. She knew she had a day or two of healing before it would begin, this responsibility of caring for a baby every possible moment of her life. She dreaded it in a way, panicked at the memory of all the things she'd done wrong the first time, but she felt optimistic. Tara's birth had been one way, Alison's another.

After Jennie was moved to her own room, a nurse wheeled Alison in in a plastic bassinet, closely followed by Chris and Tara.

"She's yours now," the nurse said and left.

Chris bent over the bassinet and picked up the baby, holding his face close to hers so he could study her. He smiled at her so tenderly and Jennie saw one small tear drop the few inches from his face to hers.

Alison barely stirred when he handed her to Jennie. She was a loaf of bread, an armful of flowers. With a blanket and cap, only her tiny face peeked out, eyes tightly closed.

"I'm going to go finish the phone calls," Chris said, and as he left Jennie's bedside, Tara approached it.

"Is she Alison?" Tara asked.

"Yes. Alison Grace. You want to hold her?"

"Not yet. Maybe later." Tara sat on the bed next to Jennie. "You were a maniac, Mom. I could hear you screaming."

"It was pretty intense."

"Was it the worst imaginable pain in the universe?"

"Not pain. No, it didn't hurt. It was intense. It takes you over, like aliens."

Jennie knew she should try to nurse Alison now, but the baby seemed too soundly asleep. Jennie touched her little mouth and Alison stuck out her bottom lip. Jennie laughed and so did Tara. Her daughter's laughter suddenly seemed the most beautiful sound in the world.

"Her face," Tara said, "it's smaller than the palm of my hand."

"Small? She was eight pounds six ounces."

"What was I when I was born?"

"Smaller. Seven pounds nine."

"Can I see something besides her face?"

Jennie loosened the tightly rolled blanket to show Tara a hand.

Tara picked up the baby's curled red hand. "Look! She has a hangnail already."

"She was born with it."

"That is so bizarre. I don't know why it seems so odd that she has fingernails and hair and stuff when it seems totally normal that she has arms and legs."

Jennie carefully tucked Alison's hand back into the blanket. The baby opened her eyes for a minute and looked at Jennie, then closed them again. Jennie smiled at Tara, savoring this moment. The tender peace between herself and her teenage daughter as they both looked at the baby.

"Did you call Rachel and Erica and tell them?" Jennie asked.

Tara shook her head. "No. I mean, yes I called Erica but she wasn't there."

"Oh."

Tara looked away, then back with tears in her eyes. "Oh Mom, they went out anyway. Without me."

"Oh. They're allowed, aren't they?"

"With *him*. They went with *him*."

"With . . . ?" Jennie asked because she knew she wasn't supposed to know.

"With Matt Fallon. No one was home at Erica's so I called Rachel's house and her mom told me."

"I'm sorry, sweetheart. I—"

"They weren't supposed to go. It was my idea. How could they do this? They know I met him first."

"Give them a chance, Tara. You don't know what they were thinking." Jennie instantly regretted these words. Tara was always accusing her of taking everyone else's side, and at this moment, while she was cradling her second baby, she didn't want to do anything to let down her first.

"I feel so tricked," Tara said. "How come they're doing this to me?" Jennie heard real pain in Tara's voice and felt the way she did when Tara was younger and came home to say someone was mean to her, someone made fun of her, someone called her stupid. That surge of *Let me at 'em, I'll kill the kid*, followed by a more sophisticated, equally complicit anger.

"I'm sorry, sweetie," she said, feeling a sense of pride that Tara was confiding in her. This kind of intimacy had been rarer and rarer the last couple of years. She needed to be up for this, she needed to get it right.

"I hate them," Tara said.

It all rushed into Jennie's head suddenly, what happened in a life, what even an easy life had in store. Jennie could remember Tara's face, aged precisely four years and three months, when her best friend in preschool told her, "You're not my friend anymore." She could remember the day Tara first understood that her parents would die. The day she came home from fifth grade sobbing because she had first learned about the Holocaust. All these hurts were still in front of Alison—these and more. The world was becoming fuller and fuller of heartbreak. Jennie didn't know how she could possibly be expected to see another child through, especially when the first one wasn't even raised yet.

Tara sat down on the other bed in the hospital room and began to cry softly. Jennie wished she could sit next to her and stroke her hair, she wished Chris would come back and hold the baby, but when none of these things happened she was reduced to murmuring, "I'm sorry, sweetheart," which only seemed to make Tara cry harder.

Her pride at being taken into Tara's confidence was being washed away by her utter helplessness. She knew how Tara felt. She could think of a dozen betrayals from high school, from that time when you were absolutely unable to suspend judgment, to wait for the truth. Tara was hurt, but what good did it do to say, *I know how you feel.* She had said it many times, always greeted with that same scornful stare that said, *You? How could you possibly know?*

"It will be all right, sweetheart," she said aloud. "See what happens tomorrow. You can talk to them—"

"I hate them," she said with venom, turning her head toward Jennie. "I'm never talking to them again."

Tara's crying increased and she lay down on the bed, turning from side to side and fidgeting, unable to make herself comfortable. Jennie slowly pulled herself up, every movement inch by inch, each part of her body sore. Even her lungs ached. She wanted to sit next to Tara so she continued on, keeping hold of Alison with one arm, pushing herself up with the other, but as she did so, Tara began to quiet down, still fidgeting, but with easier breathing, closed eyes. It was the way she had always fallen asleep. She would twist and turn and hum and sigh and sing and Jennie would believe nothing could make the child sleep until suddenly, miraculously, she would be out. And it happened just that way now. As soon as Jennie was able to lay Alison on the bed and pull herself upright, Tara was asleep. Jennie hobbled over to the bed.

"You're not supposed to be up yet," Jennie heard. A nurse named Carole had come into the room. "I'll get you a bed pan."

"No, I don't . . . I just . . . could you throw a blanket over her?" She gestured toward Tara.

"She's not allowed to sleep here," Carole said. "We may need that bed."

"Please," Jennie said.

"Husbands can stay, but . . ." Jennie gave her an imploring look and suddenly she softened. "All right, it's a slow night."

The nurse placed Alison in the bassinet and helped Jennie into bed before dimming the lights and leaving. Jennie watched her two girls sleep. Though she was bone-tired, she couldn't possibly sleep herself—she didn't want to lose a moment of this.

When Chris came in, he took in the scene and instantly became part of it. Tiptoeing over to Jennie, he kissed her and then each of the girls. He sat down on the yellow vinyl hospital chair.

"I love you," he mouthed, and she back.

He tipped his head back and fell asleep almost instantly, arms folded across his chest. She had always been appalled at how easily he could fall asleep, his breaths becoming deep and steady each night before she had even begun to unpack her mind of a day's events. But it was sweet to watch him now. She wanted to watch all night, for when would this happen again, her whole family sleeping in one room, the hardest work done, just waiting now to go home together?

Alison would learn to squeal with glee at a song she loved, to crawl across a room toward a bunny or bear, to beam because a friend invited her to a birthday party. And though she was hurting now, Tara had wondrous things in front of her: finishing high school; finding the college where her artwork would flourish; saying her first *I love you* to a boy. It was all ahead, it would all begin when they left this room, but for now she had them all here, life in the world suspended for a moment, everyone reduced to a life within her gaze. Here. Safe. Loved.

MATT

AFTER PIZZA, Erica drove them around town until she decided it was time to go to the party. They traveled out through dark back roads to where the houses were bigger, with a lot more land, many of them set far back from the road behind trees or ponds or long stone walls. Matt had been back here once before, to the nature conservancy with his family, to learn about birds of prey. He still had trouble believing it was the same town.

The party house was easy to spot—lights on in every room, front door wide open, cars clustered up the long driveway and all along the road. Erica and Rachel wanted to drive around for a few minutes, looking at cars. Looking for Jeff's car.

"You probably think we're crazy," Rachel said. "Don't tell anyone we're doing this."

"There's the Honda," Erica said. "Let's go in."

Once inside, Erica said, "We've got to check on something," and she and Rachel disappeared. Matt stood alone in the huge entry hall. He could hear music and laughter but couldn't immediately tell where the people were. The room across from him—grand and formal with some serious-looking drapes—was empty except for five brown-haired girls on the floor who glanced up at him then back at each other, tightening their hushed cluster around the glass coffee table.

He didn't want to chase after Erica and Rachel so he walked the other way down the marble hallway past some closets, a stairway, a wall of cabinets, an empty den. He was amazed, not only by how big the house was but how decorated or something it was. Each room looked like a hotel room, or a hotel lobby, or one of those living rooms in a TV movie, with dark polished wood and everything just so. No stacks of books or magazines or artwork like at his house, no bins of Legos or half-finished projects carefully blocked off in some corner. Although the house was apparently full of people, nobody appeared to live here.

Eventually he found his way into an empty study and then a very large room, also empty, very dark. The ceiling must have been two or three stories high and there was a massive stone fireplace on the far wall. Then he saw the bed, so high off the floor it had a stepladder next to it.

The room was as big as a church. As his eyes grew accustomed to the dark he walked farther into the room.

"Jesus," a boy's voice suddenly said, and from the voice Matt located the boy, with a girl, just a few feet away from him on a chaise lounge. The girl sat up, blouse unbuttoned, but the boy pushed her back down.

"Sorry," Matt muttered, hurrying out of the room, back into the hallway that led to the front door. He passed through the empty dining room, then went into a kitchen which adjoined a family room. This was where everyone was.

Rachel sat on the kitchen counter, talking to a guy and two blond girls. He didn't want her to think he was following her but she smiled at him and waved him over.

"You haven't seen Erica, have you?" she asked.

"No."

"She still can't find Jeff. It's weird. His car's here. Have you seen him?"

"I don't know who he is."

"Oh, right." She swept her hair back into the scrunchy red thing that had been on her wrist, put it in a ponytail. She was one of those girls who could change her hairstyle ten times during a conversation, the long crinkly strands being drawn from side to side, all up or all down with one smooth move.

"Matt, this is Julie, Patrice and Sean. This is Matt."

"Hi," Matt said.

"So you don't go to school at all?" the girl called Patrice asked.

"Patrice, God," Rachel said.

"Not even a little bit," Matt said. "I'm home-schooled."

"So your mom is like your teacher?"

"Sort of. She oversees. We have these videos and we do independent study. Lots of papers, lots of projects."

"But what if you don't like your teacher?" Patrice said and they all laughed. Matt had heard that question a hundred times. A thousand times.

"Let's have a beer," Rachel said. She pulled a six-pack out of the refrigerator and handed one to everybody. When she got to Matt, she said, "Oh God, do you drink, or does it go against something you believe in, like . . ."

"The law?" Matt asked, accepting the beer. Rachel laughed, a giggly but clear laugh. He really liked the feeling of being handed a beer at a party by a pretty girl. Things were going well. Usually when people found out he was home-schooled he might as well have been from Mars.

Erica came into the kitchen then, looking straight at Rachel.

"In the car," she said. "Now."

Matt set down his beer and followed Erica and Rachel to the foyer, but at the front door a guy came up to Erica almost out of the shadows and touched her arm.

"Hey girl," he said.

"Come here," Rachel said, pulling Matt into the hallway.

"Is that . . . ?"

"Jeff. Yeah."

"I've been looking everywhere for you," Matt heard him say to Erica. *Guess she wasn't on that chaise lounge,* Matt wanted to say.

Matt followed Rachel to the big empty room, where they waited until Erica and Jeff had left the foyer.

"That was a close one," Rachel said. "I'm glad we don't have to leave. Outstanding party, isn't it?"

Matt nodded, a bit surprised at the question and how he should answer it. Should he tell Rachel about Jeff and the other girl? Should he tell Erica?

He followed Rachel back into the kitchen. He thought he would reclaim his beer but there were about six on the counter. He held them up one by one.

"Don't do it," Sean said. "You want to do it but you'll be sorry. I got a mouthful of ashes that way once." He handed Matt a new beer.

It turned out Sean was on the swim team at the high school and he was going to introduce Matt to some more swimmers who were there, but then his girlfriend Heather showed up and he went off with her. Rachel announced she had to go check on Erica, so Matt was alone again, drinking his beer. He went back to walking from room to room. Up a back staircase was a sort of mezzanine with some exercise equipment and a big-screen TV. People were watching the TV; no one was really talking too much so it didn't feel odd not to know anyone. When a space opened up on the couch he went over to sit down. The girl beside him turned to him and said, "What year are you?"

"I'm in tenth grade," he said.

"A sophomore? Me too. What's your name?"

"Matt Fallon."

"How come I don't know you?"

"I don't go to Sheldrake."

"St. Bernie's?"

"No. I'm home-schooled."

"What's that?"

"It means I do all my work at home instead of going to school."

"Really?" The girl made owl eyes of surprise.

"Really." Matt took a long sip of his beer and set it down.

"Why do you have to do that?" the girl asked.

"I want to," he said. "And my parents want me to."

"It must be boring. God."

"No, it's not, it's . . . I learn a lot."

Matt looked at the TV. Why did it always have to start out this way, he thought. Why did he always have to explain himself and have people think he was weird before he even had a chance to get to know somebody?

The girl whose place he had taken came back into the room and he got up to give her his seat.

"See, I told you," the girl he had been talking to told the girl who returned. "He doesn't go to Sheldrake. He doesn't even go to school."

"What?"

Matt decided to go wandering again. He excused himself and went back down the stairs into the family room, where a very tall, very drunk guy stopped him.

"Have you seen Megan?" he asked.

"I don't know her."

"My *girl*friend," the guy said.

"I think she went thataway," Matt said, pointing randomly up the stairs.

"Cool," the guy said. He ran his hands through his hair in slow motion and climbed the stairs, clinging to the banister as if it were a tow rope.

Rachel came up from behind him and grabbed Matt's arm.

"We're leaving again," she said and led him back into the kitchen. "Now where did they go?" she asked Sean and his girlfriend, who were mixing something pastel and frothy in the blender.

Sean shrugged.

"Oh Jesus," Rachel said. "This probably seems like the weirdest thing to you. I can tell you, something big's going down with those two tonight."

"The Jeff and Erica show," Sean's girlfriend said.

"I've never seen it this bad," Sean said. He poured what was in the blender into coffee mugs and handed them to Rachel and Matt.

"Is this your house?" Matt asked Sean.

"No. I don't know where the Rama man is. Rachel?"

"I haven't seen him."

"Maybe we should go look for him," Matt said, giggling, getting into the spirit of things. It seemed to him that all people did at this party was look for other people and then when they found them, lose them again so they would have someone to go look for.

"Those two," Rachel said. "It's always something. Tara could probably explain it better. Everything's so difficult for her. Erica, I mean. It's like every breath she takes is the hardest thing anyone could ever do. I don't know why people just can't be happy."

"Sometimes they can," Matt said.

"Okay, it's not really fair." Rachel was shaking her hair free again from its ponytail and it fanned across her shoulders, massive amounts of hair, dark, stringy curls. She took one strand of hair to twist. "I mean, my parents aren't divorced so I don't know what it's like, but still. I know it sounds really shallow to say, Why can't people just be happy? Do you think I'm shallow? I just want her to . . ."

Here Rachel surprised Matt by beginning to cry.

"You're a drunken sop," Sean said, leaning over.

"I've had like half a beer," Rachel said.

Sean hooted. "Half a beer? Rachel Cleary? Never."

"I don't think you're shallow," Matt said. "I don't know you that well, though." Everyone laughed at that, even Rachel.

"Let's get out of the kitchen," she said to Matt. She pulled him into the dining room. On the table sat a single metal bowl, tiny potato chip bits making greasy rings on the napkin inside of it. Rachel scooped up what was left and began to eat.

"You know," she said, "Erica's so pretty and popular and everyone thinks Tara's so creative and artistic and everything and me, I'm just sweet and innocent Rachel."

"It doesn't matter what everyone thinks," Matt said. "Everyone is usually wrong. It's just what *you* think. Really. You and maybe one or two other people who you really love and whose opinions you value. I know that for sure."

Rachel looked at him with wet eyes. Part of her hair was now in a loop shooting off to the side of her head and to Matt that somehow made her appear cheerier. She threw her arms around his neck. "You're pretty fun to hug," she said. And then, tasting like potato chips, she kissed him on the lips. Matt could even feel the little crisp bits pass from her lips to his, the salt and oil coating them. Then she was gone again, and Matt stood alone, the breeze of Rachel still with him. He didn't know whether to go after her. These girls seemed to have some mystery to them he didn't know how to solve. Rachel *was* sweet. That wasn't a bad thing. He wanted to say that to her, and to say something else, but he didn't know what. He went to look for her in the kitchen, tried to locate his drink.

"Alcohol loss," Sean said. "It's a terrible thing." He had a new beer for Matt.

"Thanks," Matt said, feeling guilty that all these beers had been opened for him and he'd probably had twelve sips. He started walking through to the hallway, where he ran into Erica.

"Hey," he said.

"I need this," she said. She took his beer from his hand and drank the rest of it down. "We've got to go. Where's Rachel?"

"Just stay here and I'll find her," Matt said. "Don't move. If you're really ready to go, I mean."

Erica shrugged. "Come with me," she said. She took him by the hand and led him to the foyer and then out the door. She sat down on the front stoop and he decided to sit down beside her.

"Everything's not all right?" he asked.

"I hate men. I mean all men. Guys. Boys. Males."

"I get the idea."

"I have this two-year-old cousin—Anthony? I even hate him."

"Poor little Anthony."

"Why do they, why do *you*," she said, pounding Matt on the arm a little, "always have to say you're going to do a certain thing or be a certain way and then do the opposite?"

"What do you mean, *me?*"

"I mean all guys."

"I think it's dangerous to generalize."

"If you'd had my life, that's all you'd do. Generalize."

"I'm sorry for that," Matt said. She must have found out about Jeff.

"Let me just ask you something. Don't you think I deserve better than him? Don't you think I do?"

Matt was searching for something light, a little joke, but then he sensed she just really needed someone to back her up.

"Yes," he said. "You deserve impressive and valuable things."

"Thank you." She sparkled. That was the only word for it. Sparkled, and he'd made it happen. She laid her head on his shoulder for a moment and all he wanted to do was kiss her. It did seem that almost anything was possible now.

"I'm cold," Erica said. "Let's go in. No, let's just go. I don't want to see anybody and I don't want anybody to see me."

"We have to find Rachel. Just wait here. I'll get her." Matt turned back to look at Erica. "Now don't move," he said. He started to walk into the house but turned around again. "I mean it." This time Erica giggled. Not giggled but laughed, threw her head back and laughed. Matt walked inside, smiling himself. He had made the pretty girl with wet eyes laugh.

The party was more crowded now. While he and Erica had sat outside, new groups of people had been arriving and he searched the crowd in the living room for Rachel.

"Looking for Rachel?" somebody he'd never seen before asked.

"Yes."

"She might be downstairs."

"Downstairs?"

"The basement."

Matt hadn't even realized people were downstairs but this girl pointed him to a door that led down the stairs to a huge room with a pool table and, beyond that, Ping-Pong. There looked to be another thirty or forty people down there and it occurred to Matt that he could just pick anyone to start talking to and possibly make a new friend. He had met so few kids his age and here were dozens.

And this was just one party. Maybe if Erica and Rachel—and Tara, of course, though so much had happened since Tara's kiss had set this all in motion—invited him, he could go to other Friday night parties and get to know people, the kids he might have known if he went to school. *Like everybody else,* he added, echoing the words his mother and father had to hear so many times from his grandmother, who still didn't approve of home-schooling, though his parents had been doing it forever.

When they had first moved to Connecticut, Mom and Dad had given him the choice: he could continue being home-schooled or he could go to the high school. He had sat in on a few classes at Sheldrake but he hadn't been very impressed. A lot of the kids hadn't seemed to pay much attention to what was going on in class, and there were three or four rumbly conversations scattered around the room. So much wasted time. He felt he could accomplish more at home. He had been reading Emerson at the time and he liked to think of himself as self-reliant. He hadn't thought about how hard it would be to make friends and how much their absence would mean to him.

But now, he could have a social life, have a job for the summer, even, it seemed, have a girlfriend once he knew which one he wanted.

He found Rachel watching some guys play pool.

"Erica really wants to go now," he told her.

"Okay, just let me . . ." Rachel picked up a beer and drank it down. She handed the empty can to one of the pool players and said, "Thanks, James." She giggled and grabbed Matt's hand. He felt resistance as he pulled her upstairs. "Wait," she kept saying, "wait," for no reason, and once they were outside she said, "Let me just . . ." and took one step off the stoop and fell flat on her face.

"Fall in the mud!" she yelled, laughing. "Let me just fall in the mud!"

"Oh God," Erica said, coming toward Matt. "There's no way I can get her to drive home."

"I fell in the mud," Rachel was saying, still on the ground. "I fell in the mud."

"I'm so out of it," Erica said. "I've had too much to drink. Here, Matt." She tossed the car keys toward Matt. Rachel, almost up, staggered and tried to catch them, then fell on the ground laughing again.

Matt slowly picked up the keys.

"I don't know," he said.

"You're not drunk," Erica said.

"That's not it. It's just that I don't have my license yet."

"Look at her," Erica said. "Look at me. You've got to drive. It's not far."

They were walking toward the car, even Rachel, who all but fell into the backseat and just lay there without closing the door. Matt tucked her legs in and closed the door for her. He felt uneasy about doing it, but he got in on the driver's side. Afraid he would do something stupid like turn on the windshield wipers or honk the horn, he took his time, was very slow and deliberate in his movements, buckling his seat belt carefully, adjusting the seat and mirrors, turning the key in the ignition. He turned to look at Erica's face but she wasn't even watching him. She was slumped way down in her seat, almost on her back, her knees pressed tightly against the glove compartment. She looked out the window at the party house. Just as he started to look away from her she turned toward him.

"That's the problem, meeting a nice guy like you," she said. "You start to think there's hope."

"You sound like somebody old and full of despair," Matt told Erica. "I don't know, like you're thirty-five years old or something with no hope of finding the right person."

"That's how I feel sometimes."

"Where are the lights?" Matt asked. "I can't find the headlights."

Erica reached across him with almost her whole body to turn them on. Matt shifted into drive and headed slowly to the end of the cul-de-sac, circling it to get back out to the main road.

"Make a left," Erica said and sighed deeply. Matt looked over at her. He wanted her touch again.

"There's this other party I know of," Erica said.

"No," Rachel said. "Oh my God."

"I think I should get home," Matt said.

"It's still early," Erica said.

Matt felt he was pushing his luck already. If he got caught driving without a license, who knew what might happen.

"It's just at my neighbors," Erica said. "Let's just drive by." She popped in a CD and turned up the volume.

He followed Erica's directions, which involved a lot of quick turns because she didn't say anything until it was time to take a turn.

"You'd think I'd know where my own house is," Erica said. "Maybe I just want to forget. Oh, turn up here. Left—right—left I mean. How're you doing back there, Rache?"

"Oh my God," was Rachel's reply, a muted monotone.

"'If it makes you happy,'" Erica sang out loudly with the CD, "'then why the hell are you so sad?' Oh, there it is," Erica said and Matt quickly applied the brake, careening to a stop just past a driveway.

"Sorry, I just meant that's my house, not the party." Matt peered into the blackness. The house was far down the driveway, not very well-lit, except for floodlights that made the surrounding trees look blue and ghostly, part of a horror movie set.

"We moved up here because my parents wanted a *big house*," Erica said. "We lived here a total of one whole year before Dad moved out."

"Oh," Matt said, really not knowing what to say, still trying to concentrate on the road.

"I think sometimes, if only we hadn't moved . . . maybe my dad would have stayed with us. We were happy in that little house. One of those ranch dealies like Tara has. I had a lavender room. Hey, that was a stop sign."

"Oh, I'm sorry," Matt said nervously. He quickly stopped, put the car in reverse and backed up. Going forward again, he made a full stop at the stop sign and then went on.

"That was so cute," Erica said. She touched Matt's knee. "You're funny." Her body turned toward him. Matt could see it peripherally, but more than that, feel it. Opening up to him.

The roads were narrow and curvy up here and there were so many trees. It was like being in the forest.

"Keep going to the next road," Erica said. "Ina's house, there it is." A few cars lined the road, pressed into gullies. "Just drive up," Erica said. "They have . . ."

"Ample parking!" Rachel squealed from the backseat, as if it were some inside joke, and then she couldn't stop laughing again and neither could Erica.

Matt turned down the driveway but there were only a few cars there.

They circled, naming cars, until Erica finally said, "Forget it. It's too depressing."

"What do you want to do?" Matt asked. Erica was silent. She was edging closer to him. He could feel the warmth of her body. In the backseat, Rachel was silent.

"Let's take her home. She's passed out. Turn on this one."

Matt was happy to see that *this one,* finally, was a bigger road with the occasional streetlight. More confident, he picked up speed. Here the homes were still large but closer to the road, some lit up grandly, like luxury ocean liners. He knew it must be his imagination, but it seemed that there was a party in each of them.

"What's the speed limit back here?" he asked.

"There is no speed limit," Erica said. "I mean there is, but I don't know what it is. They don't want to put up signs here because it like ruins the landscape or something."

Erica leaned her head against Matt's shoulder again, just as she had on the stoop outside the party house, but this time there was more. He could smell her perfume, the distinct scent of her skin, even the faint smokiness she had complained about so long ago at the pizza restaurant. She turned her face toward him. "What do I want to do?" Erica said, returning to Matt's question. "That's always the question, isn't it? What is Erica going to do?"

Matt looked at her—her face was so close to his that he couldn't see more than a bit of a profile, a few strands of hair—but she looked so hurt and beautiful and determined that his only thought was to be able to take the hurt away, to somehow lift her out of this. And the moment it took him to think these thoughts, to really want to help her and then to feel he could, was a moment with no room for anything but itself. He couldn't think of Rachel or of Tara or how it would seem to other people, kissing these girls one, two, three, all in a day, how careless, cruel and careless it made him appear. He was dazzled, and by the time he remembered other things—this car he was driving, the speed, the turn—it was too late. He didn't slow down, didn't see the road split, didn't swerve or brake or turn the wheel, didn't do anything at all, until the motion had ended and he saw that he must run for help.

JENNIE

AFTERWARD JENNIE would have sworn she hadn't taken her eyes off her family all night. She was sure she hadn't slept. She never felt a moment where her alertness slipped or where it returned, except that somewhere past dawn there were just two of them left in the room—Alison, sleeping soundly in her bassinet, and Jennie, there to watch her. Chris and Tara had gone.

The nurse, Carole, came in and asked how the breastfeeding was going.

"Not too well," Jennie answered. "I haven't tried in a while."

"Try now. She's a little more alert." Carole handed the baby to Jennie and fluffed pillows under her.

"Rub her cheek. Try to get her to turn toward you."

"Have you seen my husband and daughter?" Jennie asked. *My elder daughter,* she must say now. So hard to get used to after all these years of Tara being an only child.

"No," Carole said. She was concentrating on Alison, who was crying and turning her head. "Maybe she's not hungry," Carole said. "Wait another hour. But keep trying. They get it eventually."

Jennie so wanted this to work. She hadn't nursed Tara—at eighteen she had thought of her breasts only as sexual ornaments and the thought of a baby sucking on them had seemed barbaric. This time it was different. She'd read all the literature, knew mother's milk was supposed to be the best thing to keep babies healthy, and she was determined to do it. She brought Alison in close again, just to try, but the baby, face red, began screaming again.

"Oh baby," Jennie murmured. "This isn't going to be easy."

She kissed Alison's cheek, which was the only exposed part of her body big enough to accept the press of two adult lips. With Alison this mother love was so instant. She remembered feeling nothing for Tara for weeks after her birth, but with Alison it was there, right from the start. Perhaps that was one of the things a first child did, Jennie thought: changed you into a person who knew how to love a child, taught you how to be someone's mother.

Jennie took Alison from her breast and just held her, waiting for Chris to come, and when he did come, Jennie looked up at him with a smile that withered when she saw the look on his face.

In the sixteen years Jennie and Chris had been married, neither had ever had to deliver terrible news. There had been low points in their lives, times of huge disappointment, times when they didn't know how they would pay the bills, times when Chris smoked too much pot and Jennie couldn't talk to him, times when Jennie's regrets had driven Chris to utter silence, when they would look at each other and not see tomorrow, but by most accounts they had been extraordinarily lucky: they had been healthy and so had Tara; their parents were all alive, no sudden trauma or chronic illness. Their marriage had survived its immature beginning. There had not been infidelities. Yet Jennie supposed in her darker moments that she could imagine the look on Chris's face when he told her the worst, because now, as he came toward her in the hospital room, walking so slowly it looked as if his body hurt too, she recognized instantly this look she had never seen before.

"What happened?" she asked.

"Erica and Rachel were in an accident," he said slowly.

"A car accident?"

"Yeah, and that guy Matt. He was driving." Chris looked confused, as if he weren't sure the words he was saying were true. "They were killed."

"No. Oh no. All of them? Dear God." Jennie's hand went to her throat and she could feel herself begin to tremble.

"Erica died right away," Chris said. "Rachel died during the night. At the hospital."

"This hospital?"

Chris nodded, his expression becoming even more pained. He had gone so pale.

"Oh my God. And Matt?"

"He walked away."

Walked away. Jennie seized on that phrase. She had heard it before.

Such harsh language. As if the driver would turn his back on the wreckage and actually, physically, leave it behind. Walk somewhere: away.

"Where's Tara?" Jennie asked. "You've left her alone? Where is she?"

"She doesn't know yet. She's on her way up." Chris sat on the bed next to her and took her hand. "Oh Jen, how can we tell her this?" He squeezed his eyes shut and shook his head almost violently.

"We can't," Jennie said automatically, irrationally. "How can we?"

They were both silent for a moment and then Chris leaned down to put his face next to hers. He began to shake, but there were no tears.

"What happened?" Jennie whispered. "What happened? Did someone hit them?"

"They hit a tree. The boy was driving. The car flipped over. That's all they know. There was a message on the machine from Rachel's father saying call immediately, emergency. I just talked to him. He wanted Tara to know before she saw it on the news or something."

"Oh Chris." The generosity of Rachel's father moved her unspeakably. The valor of a man whose daughter had died to think of the pain of someone else's.

"I keep thinking," Chris said, lifting his head slightly, "where can we take her, how can we take her somewhere so she can live out her life without ever having to know this."

"Chris, do you realize if I hadn't been here, if the baby hadn't . . ."

"I've already had a few minutes to think about that," he said. Jennie knew neither of them at that moment was above saying, *Thank you, God, for killing someone else's child and not mine.*

Alison began to stir, then cry softly. "Oh my poor baby," Jennie said, holding Alison, meaning Tara.

Tara came in, carrying flowers for Jennie. She offered them shyly, a mixture of yellows, purples and pinks. "They didn't have a vase," she said.

"We can ask the nurses," Jennie said, reaching for them.

"What's wrong, Mom? Are you being all hormonal?" While Jennie tried to pull herself together, Tara went on. "It's so weird that she's my sister. I don't know why, it's just so weird to have a sister all of a sudden."

"Tara," Jennie closed her eyes and said. How could she prepare her for this? "We have to tell you something."

"What?"

"We've just heard something horrible. A terrible, terrible thing happened," Jennie said.

"What? Is something wrong with Alison?"

"No, the baby's fine. She's fine. It's your friends. You see, last night, Erica and Rachel and Matt were in a car accident."

A confused frown. Puzzlement, not panic.

"It was a very bad one," Jennie said.

"Are they all right?"

Jennie fought the urge to look away. She didn't want to have to see the next look on Tara's face, the look that would stay with her forever.

"Matt's okay, but . . . oh Tara, Erica and Rachel were both killed."

"No!" Tara screamed, falling against Chris like a marionette whose strings had been clipped. Jennie saw Chris would have given anything to be able to pick her up and hold her the way Jennie held Alison, hold her and comfort her like a baby again.

"Tara, come here, honey," Jennie said. "I'm so sorry I can't come to you." Chris almost carried Tara over to the bed, where Jennie could get her arms around her, could try to reach her arms out to help contain her daughter's roaring, screeching cries.

MATT

THE WHOLE TIME he was at the police station, it never occurred to Matt that he was in trouble. Something terrible had happened and they needed to find out what had gone wrong. That's why he was there: he was helping them get to the bottom of things.

He couldn't remember much. Something had happened to make the car crash and now he was here. But where were Erica and Rachel?

They had brought him to the station right from the hospital, after he'd been examined and released. He had no serious injuries, just some tender places on his knees and forearms that the doctor told him would turn to enormous bruises over the next day or so. His chest ached in the place where the seat belt had strained to hold him.

He must have given them his phone number because Dad was there waiting for him at the police station. He held Matt in his arms for what seemed like full minutes. The officers gave Matt a chair, and one sat at the desk facing him while another leaned against the wall behind. Matt told the story over and over again, each time ending with, "And then I don't remember."

A lot of the questions were about alcohol. He told them there had been beer and some cocktail in a blender but that he'd had only sips. He didn't think of telling them anything but the truth.

"We'll see what the blood test shows," said the officer leaning against the wall.

Whenever Matt asked about Rachel and Erica, the officer at the desk said he was still waiting to hear. Toward morning, he got a phone call and he swiveled his chair away from Matt to speak softly into the receiver. When he turned back, he said, "It's very serious, son. The second girl just died."

"Second?" Matt asked.

64

He looked down at his notebook. "Cleary, Cleary girl. Rachel Cleary."

"Dear Lord," Dad said.

"What about Erica?" Matt whispered.

"Erica Linders was dead at the scene."

Matt felt the blood drain from his entire body. He felt his spine wobble and droop. It wasn't possible. It couldn't be. He lifted his head slightly toward the officer across the desk. "What," he asked, "what could have happened?"

"Officer," Dad said, "you could have told the boy earlier."

"We wanted to get his story first," the officer said.

"This is no *story*. My son is telling you the truth."

The room was pounding, beating close around him. He held onto the arms of the chair in order not to be thrown from it. "What happened?" he choked out. He felt himself fall sideways, backward, forward.

"That's what we're trying to find out," the leaning officer said. "And you're really the only one who can tell us. It's a miracle you walked away like you did. 'Course it's a real testimony to seat belts. Those girls flew around like popcorn in that car."

"We're not charging you, son," the other officer said. "We'll begin an investigation, wait for the blood tests. We can send you home but ask that you stay there."

Matt could take nothing in. Erica and Rachel. Dead. Killed. It couldn't have happened. He had been right there in the car with them. Why was he here and they . . . dead?

When they told him to go he was afraid to get up. Surely he would plummet into space. Surely there was no floor to stand on.

He'd been at the police station for hours. By now he had memorized the chairs and desks and partitions, knew that the phone beeped lightly before it rang, that the strange scraping noise was the stubborn bottom drawer of an old brown filing cabinet, knew that the soft whirring sound from behind the partition was the copy machine, that the door that swung so loudly led to the room with the coffee pot. This had been his world for several hours and he came to see that nothing bad was going to happen to him there. But now they were asking him to leave.

Dad helped him out of the chair and led him outside to a sun just beginning to rise. He felt completely exposed, stripped of his safety. On the way home, every familiar turn his father took was menacing. He had to close his eyes to keep himself from yelling something at each signpost or building they passed.

"Matt," Dad said, "I don't think this is the right time, I want you to try to get some rest first, but after you do I want you to tell your mother and me the whole of what happened."

"I did, Dad," Matt said, eyes still closed. "I told them everything."

"I know, Matt. I want to hear it in your own words, not in answer to a lot of stock questions. But not yet, son. I want you to get some sleep first. Maybe you'll be able to recall things more clearly then."

Matt opened his eyes to look at his watch, which had shattered in the crash, and then to the dashboard clock. It was almost 6:00 A.M., they were driving in the bright pinks and oranges of a sunrise, witnessing the steady removal of darkness from the sky.

"How, Dad?" Matt asked. "How am I supposed to get some sleep?"

Mom waited in the kitchen, her eyes, her whole face red from crying.

"Oh my baby," was all she said. She held him for a long time and then together, Mom and Dad walked him up to his room. It was morning, but Matt didn't want it ever to be morning again. As they creaked up the stairs he could hear his youngest sister bellow "Momma," the way she did every day when she woke.

He wanted to ask his parents to stay with him. How could he sleep? His father sat on the edge of his bed and said, "It's too late for this cup to pass, Matt. But you have to remember that you're not alone. Your mother and I are with you. The Lord is with you. You know that, don't you?"

"Yes, Daddy," Matt said, but he was sure that no one in the world was with him. His father, though inches away, could not even touch him.

Sleep, they wanted him to sleep, but how could he sleep? When they left he could barely lay down, and once down his limbs were so stiff he felt that he didn't have a bend in his body. He wasn't able to sleep, not for hours, and as he lay there, as he heard the family waking, the children's loud voices, his parents tending to his brothers and sisters though they themselves had been awake all night, Matt couldn't close his eyes, could barely blink. All he could see when he closed his eyes were Erica and Rachel: Erica's face as he reached for her, Rachel lying quietly in the backseat.

When he did finally sleep he felt his body loosen not into relaxation but to a numbness, and when that happened he did not want to wake up.

If he felt himself waking he would allow himself to get just conscious enough to wonder, *How long can I stay up here, how long before they come to check on me or offer me food?*, before he willed himself back to sleep again.

EVEN AFTER Matt could no longer make himself sleep, he didn't get out of bed. He listened to his brothers playing basketball on the driveway and seethed with anger toward them. How could they play, *play*, after what had happened?

The car that pulled into the driveway wasn't one of their vans; he could tell by the sound of the motor. He looked out the window and saw a green Mercedes. A man he didn't recognize climbed out of it. Matt thought he must be a detective, someone starting the investigation the police had told him about. He saw Brian run in to get Dad and half-expected to hear his own name called out. When that didn't happen, Matt cracked his bedroom door and listened to Dad talking to the man in the foyer downstairs.

"You can't just come over here to punish my son," Dad was saying. "The police are investigating the accident."

"He needs to pay for what he's done," the man said, voice raspy and cold.

"It's not clear yet what exactly happened."

"The hell it's not. He'll pay. He'll pay for what he did to my daughter." The voice got louder, angrier, as threatening as the words being said.

Dad continued speaking in the firm, even tone he almost always used. "Sir, my family and I can't imagine the pain you're feeling. I just ask that you please leave my son alone. It's not your responsibility to—"

"Alone? What the hell right does he have to be alone?"

"He needs to understand what's happened. He's in shock. It's been less than twenty-four hours since the accident."

"Accident? Was it an accident that he took those drinks, that he was driving my car too fast?"

Matt knew he should go down and speak to Erica's father himself. It was his battle to fight. But he couldn't make his body move.

"Believe me," Dad was saying, "my son is in a tremendous amount of pain over this."

"The hell with his pain. What about my daughter? She can't feel pain. She'll never feel anything again."

Dad was quiet and then his words came out choked. "I know that, I know. My wife and I have been praying for you."

"Is that going to bring my daughter back? I don't want your prayers. I want to break his neck. I want to kill that kid."

"I've got to ask you to leave. Matt needs his family right now, and your family needs you. I think you need to be with them."

"What family? I had a daughter yesterday. I had all kinds of dreams for her. Your kid killed every single one of them."

Matt was careening through the air again, nothing to hold onto, not even knowing which way he was going. He pitched himself onto the bed to break his fall and when he hit the mattress his belly let loose brutal, convulsive sobs that shook apart his guts. They went on, they got worse, and he stuffed the corner of the pillow in his mouth to try to make them stop. He longed for the crying to knock him out, to deliver him into a sleep, anything that would make what throttled inside him go away.

When he couldn't cry anymore he lay there aching and trying to breathe. He pulled himself out of bed and went downstairs. He heard his family outside, in the backyard, but he didn't go to them. In the kitchen, lunch fixings were still out though it was past 4:00. He squirted mustard on a piece of bread and laid a slice of ham on top. The Saturday newspaper, unread and still in one piece, lay on the table and for the next ten minutes or so—until his mother came into the house, calling tentatively, "Matt, is that you?"—he sat alone with the paper.

It was the last day he would be able to read the newspaper without being afraid of what was in it, for the accident had happened too late on Friday night to make it into the Saturday paper.

The next day, front page, would be Erica and Rachel's yearbook pictures, along with a picture of the ruined BMW. There would be no picture of Matt because he was a minor, and he hadn't been charged. The media couldn't identify him. He was "the unnamed youth."

There would also be a map of the accident scene, giving a description of how the car jumped the curb, rolled over a boulder and hit a tree. As if the car alone had done the damage and the unnamed youth was blameless.

JENNIE

BEFORE ANY OF THEM had time to move beyond the news, before Chris could do more than find Tara Kleenex, before Jennie could do anything to help, Jennie's parents arrived. Fay and Leo Northrop walked into the hospital room with an *It's a Girl* balloon, a bakery box tied with red-and-white string and an elaborately wrapped package that looked to be a stuffed animal, most probably a giraffe.

"We would have been here sooner," Leo said, "but there's no parking."

"The construction," Fay said.

"We had to leave it with an attendant. Valet parking at a hospital, for Christ's sake."

"It's just during the construction," Fay said.

"And your mother had to stop in the gift shop. Couldn't come up without a balloon." Leo let go and the balloon floated up to the ceiling.

"Don't do that, Leo. There might be something sharp up there to pop it."

"You can't pop Mylar," Leo said. "That's the beauty of the material."

"Give it to Tara. Maybe she'd like to hold it." Fay glanced briefly at Tara, sitting on her father's lap in the one chair in the room. "But where's the little one?" she asked. "We looked for her in the nursery."

"She's right here with us," Jennie said, breaking her family's silence.

"My goodness, I didn't even see her. Well, congratulations, new parents," Fay said, giving Jennie a kiss and then turning to Chris. "And a hug for the father," she said. Fay was not the affectionate type, not toward her own children, and especially not toward Chris. Hugs were reserved for big events—Christmas, birthdays, major congratulations—and were always announced beforehand.

"I'm sorry we had to come so early," Fay said, "but we wanted to see the baby before we leave for Africa. We go on Wednesday but we're highly scheduled until then."

"Fay, Leo, I need to talk to you," Chris said. He gently nudged Tara off his lap until she sat alone on the chair, then bent over to say, "Tara, I'm going to go out in the hall to tell your grandparents what happened. Then I'll be right back."

Tara looked up into Chris's face and nodded, her round eyes liquid, lids swollen. Jennie recognized Chris's tone of voice as he spoke to Tara— the even, measured, comforting way he described each step he was going to take. It was the same way he had spoken to her when she was a tiny girl, so attached to him she would scream if he left the room without telling her. At three years old, she would cry for an hour in the middle of the day if she wanted him and Jennie could not get him on the phone.

"How are you doing, sweetheart?" Jennie asked Tara quietly after Chris left the room with her parents.

Tara didn't answer and Jennie could see it was because she couldn't figure a way to get words out without sobs. Jennie began to slowly shift her body, trying to calculate how long it would take to get herself upright, place Alison back in the bassinet and reach Tara—to what? She could barely walk; how could she crouch and embrace her?

At that moment Dr. Perrin came in. She addressed the baby first, saying, "Hi, little sweet pea. I'm just going to put you in the bassinet so I can examine your mommy." She gently moved Alison, smiled briefly at Tara and turned back to Jennie, abruptly placing her hand flat on Jennie's abdomen and pushing firmly. Jennie felt pressure, pain, a flow of blood.

"Your uterus is shrinking nicely," Dr. Perrin said.

"When do you think I can go home?"

"Feeling that good?" Dr. Perrin smiled.

"When's the earliest, I mean? We've had a family emergency"—Jennie's eyes shifted toward Tara—"I need to get home as soon as possible."

"Oh, I'm sorry. Anything I can do?" Dr. Perrin's eyes roamed toward Tara too.

"No," Jennie said.

"Well, it's usually forty-eight hours. But maybe tomorrow morning if you're feeling all right."

"What about tonight?"

"I don't think we can discharge you tonight. I'd really like to see you spend the night."

"I'd like to try to leave tonight."

Jennie could see that Dr. Perrin, usually a fairly resolute type, was weighing her options, trying to decide how flexible she could be. "Tell you what," she said as Chris, Fay and Leo came back into the room. "I'll check back with you around dinnertime, see how you're doing."

"Okay," Jennie said, and Dr. Perrin patted her arm and left.

Fay went over to Tara and said, "I'm so sorry about your girlfriends. Listen, Tara, would you like to go downstairs and find some juice with me? We've brought a lovely coffee cake from Delano's for us all to share."

Tara was able to say "no thanks," and everyone in the room stared at her as she said it.

"Of course you want to stay with your mom and dad," Fay said.

"Chris," Jennie said. "Why don't you take Tara home? There's no reason for you to stay here."

"What about you?" Chris asked.

"I'm fine. I'll probably be able to come home tonight anyway."

A nurse came in the room and Tara shifted her face toward the wall. Jennie couldn't stand it that Tara's grief had to be so public.

"Take her home," Jennie said, shooting him a look that meant it had to be now.

"Or we could take Tara with us," Fay said. "If Chris wants to stay with you."

"No," Tara said.

"Thanks," Chris said, "but I'll take her."

"Then we'll stay," Fay said. "Your father has an eleven-fifteen tee-off, but I can stay."

"It's only nine holes," Leo said. "I'll be done by one-thirty, two and I can swing back to get you." Leo paused. "Of course I could cancel it."

"No," Fay said, "go. I'll stay with Jennifer."

"Whatever," Jennie said, trying to stay calm. All she wanted was for Tara to get away from all these eyes, all these voices, to get somewhere where Chris could tend to her in privacy until Jennie could be there too.

"Come on, Tara," Chris said, "come with me now. We're going to go home so you can get some rest."

Without saying a word, Tara let Chris pull her up and lead her out of the room.

"'Bye, honey," Jennie called.

"'Bye, Mom," Tara said. A small girl voice, and Jennie's heart cramped with panic, with a mother feeling that somehow she was the only one who could protect Tara, that if she let Tara leave the room, even with her father, she might never see her again. Jennie almost called after them for Tara to come back.

"Such a tragedy," Fay said.

"Yes," Jennie said, eyes on the door Tara had just walked through. She wanted to run down the hall after them, clutch Tara in her arms.

"Who was the boy?" Fay was asking. "Did Tara know him too?"

"A little, yes."

"A shame. This will be hard on her. She's so sensitive. Just like you were."

"She seems to be in quite a state," Leo said. "Poor kid. Here, Fay, sit down."

"Isn't there another chair in here?" Fay asked. "Why do they always have only one chair? Visitors usually come in twos, don't they?"

"There is nowhere to put a second chair," Leo said. "Look at the square footage in this room."

"Do they think the boy was drinking?" Fay asked.

"I don't know. I don't know any of the details." And what she did know, she wanted to keep from Fay. Jennie didn't want her mother to know that if it hadn't been for Alison's birth, Tara would have been in that car too. She didn't want Fay to turn that into a fascinating near-tragic tale to tell over and over again at the club after tennis or during her bridge game. Jennie had begun long ago to protect Tara's life from her mother's scrutiny, just as she had learned to do with her own.

"Chris said the boy didn't even go to school," Fay said.

"He's home-schooled."

"I've read about that. These ultra-ultra religious types who don't want to send their children to school so they can fill their heads with all this fundamentalism."

"I don't know, Mom. Not always. Maybe they just don't think the school is good enough or—"

"Good enough? We have one of the best public school systems in the country, if not in the world."

"I really couldn't say. I've never met his parents, but he seems like a smart kid."

"If you don't know the family, you don't know the boy. And you let Tara go out with the boy?"

"She never went out with him. They just knew each other." She was being lured into an argument, one of those unwanted arguments that seemed to make up most of her interaction with her mother. To divert her attention, Jennie jostled Alison and said, "Hey look, the baby's waking up. Who wants to hold her?"

"I will. I'm out of practice, with sixteen years between grandchildren. Though I'm certainly more prepared to play grandmother at sixty than I was at forty-four." Fay reached down and carefully lifted Alison into her arms. "Light as a feather. Look at those eyes. Will they be brown or blue?"

"It's too early to tell, Fay," Leo said. "At this point they could be either."

"Yes," Fay was saying to Alison, "yes, yes, yes, such a sweet little baby." As Fay held the baby, Jennie felt some sort of surge—of love, exhaustion, and hormones—replace her irritation. She had to frown and tighten her lips to keep herself from crying.

When Fay was tender the past could disappear and Jennie could suppose her a vastly different mother, the kind for whom an entire world lived in a baby's face. But when Fay looked up at her again, the real Fay was back and all Jennie wanted was to be alone with her baby.

JENNIE WAITED UNTIL her parents left to call home. The first time she got the machine, but the second time Chris answered.

"I'll call you back as soon as I can," he said, but it was a full hour until he called—around 5:00, when Jennie sat alone with her supper tray.

"How is she?" Jennie asked.

"Sleeping, finally. Cried herself to sleep. I almost felt like giving her something. Something to knock her out."

"Wait, what did you give her?"

"I didn't. I just said I felt like it."

"How long has she been sleeping?"

"It's been a half hour since I've heard a sound from her room. I've been standing outside the door."

"Well, stay there in case she wakes up. You need to be there the minute she does." Jennie heard the sharpness in her own voice. To her it sounded like near-hysteria but she knew to Chris she must sound like a shrew.

"I'm not going anywhere, Jen," he said.

"I know, but you head out to the garage and then—"

"I'm not going to do that."

"Sorry. I know I sound . . . I just want to be there. I want to be stronger and not fall apart."

"You're doing great, Jen. You just had a baby."

"How does Tara seem?"

"Miserable. All she wanted was to go see where the accident was."

"Where was it?"

"Up on Connaught Road. Just past the turn onto Becker."

"Are you going to take her there?" she asked Chris.

"I already did. It was the only way she would believe it, I think. She had to see it."

"You saw the car? Is the car still there?"

"No, they hauled it away. There's broken glass everywhere. Kids have been coming by and leaving things."

"What things?"

"Flowers, balloons, notes. Tara felt awful that she hadn't brought anything. I think she wants to go back."

"I wonder how these kids knew to bring things. So soon, I mean." Jennie closed her eyes, tried to imagine the scene. She knew what she would bring. A dozen irises for Erica because purple was her favorite color. And for Rachel, armfuls of the baby's breath she loved to wear in her hair on special occasions. Jennie remembered finding dried heads of baby's breath all over the backseat of her car one night after she and Chris gave Rachel a ride home from a dance.

"I wish I were there with you," Jennie told Chris. "Standing outside Tara's door."

"Me too."

They hung up and Jennie cradled the soft, living bundle that was Alison against her chest. She was holding her baby; Chris was holding his.

Chris had always been able to comfort Tara best. It had been a pattern during the most difficult periods of Tara's life. Jennie was the one to do all the research, make phone calls, ask other parents for advice, find the right books and read them, but Chris knew how to put theory into practice. He had always been able to pull Tara out of whatever crisis she fell into, but it would be a long time before Tara could make her way out of this one.

This was it. Tara's life would be changed forever because she had lost her two best friends at age sixteen.

Jennie could picture the three of them so easily. Tara, Rachel and Erica—it had become almost impossible to see them separately anymore. The image that most stayed with her was an old one, a day from more than a year ago when the three of them were sitting at her kitchen table eating brownies. Jennie remembered thinking, *Thank God, they still eat brownies, they're not into celery and carrots yet.* She was washing dishes at the sink and the girls were talking, for some reason, about semen. They had come up with some whimsical game of imagining colors for the semen of boys at school.

"Gus Smith's is definitely baby blue," Rachel had pronounced and Erica and Tara shrieked. Jennie had to agree. Gus was sweet, shy, easily embarrassed by his own voice.

"What about Jonathan Straut?" Tara asked, then answered herself. "He'd be kelly green. He is *so* kelly green."

"Yeah," Rachel agreed, then said, "No, I know. He's such a Republican. It's red, white and blue. Stripes, like that one kind of toothpaste."

The girls fell against each other laughing as they went on: tan for bland Timothy Stern, magenta for silly Peter Donofrio. And then suddenly they had questions.

"Is it true that semen's good for your skin, Mom?" Tara had asked. "Like Keri lotion?"

"If so, I sure could use some," Jennie had joked. "Softer, younger-looking skin."

"Trina Berry said so in gym," Rachel confided. "We didn't really believe her."

How innocent they were. Really. They had all been fourteen then, and as far as Jennie knew they were all virgins. They had gone to dances with boys, but never more than that; even Erica hadn't had a boyfriend yet. They were still so young then, and Jennie remembered thinking that sex was the promise the coming year would bring, or maybe the year after. None of them had yet encountered semen. It was an extraordinary mystery, something funny and tender that was part of the enigma of boys.

Jennie had taken note of that day. It was one of those moments in her life as a mother that she stored in her mind, like the first time she and Chris had held Tara's hands and done *1-2-3-wheee!* or the first time Tara let herself into the house with her own key. She had recorded that girlishness and fun, knowing how soon it would be that boys' bodies became real to them. She remembered how quickly she had progressed from giggling with Elizabeth *(Ooh! Would you touch one? How gross!)* to that night with Joel Tarn and she knew the same would happen for Tara, Rachel and Erica. The day would come, she remembered thinking, that one of them would point to her thigh or pat her flat stomach and say to the other, *Look! It was here. My first semen, my first sperm.* But until then, they would be girls together, entertaining themselves by inventing the male body according to their whims, merging the remnants of fairy-tale magic with the first stirrings of real desire, like this notion that a boy's character corresponded to the color of his semen.

Except now, Tara alone was spared by circumstance to grow beyond sixteen. Alone in the hospital, Alison in her arms, Jennie wept steadily for over an hour for Rachel and Erica, forever girls and forever gone, and for Tara, forever bereft.

MATT

H E DIDN'T GO to church that Sunday. For the first time he could
remember, no one in his family did. Since moving to Connecticut
they had spent their Sundays visiting different churches in town and just
a month ago had settled on one they liked. It was a newer church with a
huge congregation and five different ministers. Matt couldn't believe how
massive the parking lot was, how big the sanctuary. He had gone to the
youth group a few times, the kids went to Sunday school, and Dad was
getting ready to join the choir. It was interesting, but it wasn't like church
back home, where Pastor Tim had known all of them since they were
born, where after the service it took Mom an hour and a half to say hello
to everyone she knew.

Matt didn't want to go to church. He didn't want to step outside; he
could barely leave his room. He was waiting for someone to enter his
house and tell him it had all been a mistake, that Rachel and Erica were
recovering slowly in the hospital, but would be fine. He felt somehow if
he didn't leave his house, that still had a chance of happening.

Mom and Dad stayed home so he wouldn't be alone. They were not
the type to make exceptions. This was the first. They had been trying to
pray with him—for Rachel and Erica and for him—but he couldn't find
any words for such prayers. He knew he would go to hell for not praying
for them, but the words would not come. He had always found the words
before. He could say, "Here I am, God," as his parents had taught him
and with that offering the words of a prayer would squeeze out. But this
time, there was nothing to say.

Mom came up just before lunch to tell him the minister would be
coming to see him that afternoon. Matt didn't even ask which minister—
anyone who came would have a stranger's face.

He waited on his bed. He sat there on the edge of it, doing nothing for a long time and then later picked up a tennis ball to throw against the wall, over and over again for maybe forty-five minutes. Mom came up once and Dad twice to invite him down with the other children but he stayed by himself, throwing the ball, waiting.

The minister who came was the senior pastor, Reverend Linney. Gray hair, kind eyes. His hand was cool and dry when he shook Matt's hand.

Pastor Tim would have bear hugged Matt, not let him go.

"So you're feeling all right?" Pastor Linney asked. Matt looked at him incredulously and Pastor Linney clarified: "You weren't hurt at all in the accident?"

"No, I wasn't hurt."

"But inside I know you were hurt a great deal."

"Yes."

"These girls, your friends—it was terrible that they were killed."

"Yes."

"I know you must be feeling all kinds of things, blaming yourself, and that's natural, but you've got to turn it over to God. Scripture tells us, 'The eternal God is thy refuge, and underneath are the everlasting arms.' You've got to let those arms hold you, Matt."

Matt could not open his mouth to speak. The scripture made no impact. It wasn't as if he didn't believe what Pastor Linney was saying, but somehow he couldn't understand it. Things he had always known were now incomprehensible.

Pastor Linney had brought a Bible for him. *He doesn't know me at all,* Matt thought. *He doesn't even know if I have my own Bible.*

Pastor Linney marked passages for Matt to read, asked if there was anything he could do to help. Matt was not trying to be rude but he had nothing to say.

"You can call me anytime to talk," Pastor Linney said, "or if you think you need someone else to talk to, let me know that because we have some wonderful associate ministers."

"Okay," Matt said. "Thank you." He walked Pastor Linney downstairs. It was 3:00 in the afternoon and it was the first time he had left his room all day. He immediately returned to it, trying to pray again but prayers still would not come.

All that came was his question: how could this have happened? He kept returning to that. He had been right there in the car with them and he hadn't died. How could they have? He wasn't ready to believe it was as simple as the seat belts they weren't wearing and he was. They had all three been contained in that automobile, arm's lengths from one another. How could his body be whole, completely unharmed, while theirs no longer held life?

Right after the accident, he kept saying, "I'm sorry, I'm so sorry," over and over again. Erica had looked unhurt. There was no blood, no wound he could readily see, but she wouldn't respond when he spoke to her. She just lay there. Matt thought she must be in shock.

Rachel had been thrown into the front seat. He was unsure about the position of her body because it was so hard to see, but her face was only inches from his. He could hear her breathing. She moaned, "Help me." He reached out to touch her face and felt nothing but blood. She was bleeding from the head and he took off his shirt and gently wrapped it around her head without moving her.

"Help me," she said again.

"Just hold on," he said. He knew he needed to get help, and he was able to undo his seat belt and get out of his side of the car. He was running toward the nearest house when the front door opened and a man in pajamas ran down the long driveway toward him.

"Are you all right?" the man called.

"They need help," Matt had yelled.

"Don't move anyone," the man said. "My wife's already called the paramedics." The man ran back to the car with Matt and Matt crouched inside the upside-down wreck, speaking softly to the girls, telling them that help was coming. Rachel did not speak again except to moan and from Erica there was no sound at all. It was so dark out, and there were no streetlights—it was impossible to see the girls' faces. Within minutes they heard the ambulance siren and Matt remembered thinking—even now, he could recall his relief as he thought, *Everything will be all right now, this man is here, the paramedics are on their way.*

How could Rachel have died when she had spoken words to him? And Erica—she didn't have a mark on her? How could it be that he had killed them both?

Then he saw that that was why he couldn't pray for them. It was because there was no way . . . it just couldn't have . . . they couldn't possibly be dead.

JENNIE

Alison, three and a half days old, too small even for a Snugli or sling, wrapped in a blanket and pressed up against Jennie's chest, was attending her first funeral. Jennie hadn't wanted to bring her, but she needed to keep Alison with her in case she needed to be fed. Jennie's milk had come in the morning before and Alison suddenly wanted to nurse round the clock. Jennie's breasts were huge and throbbing, stiff as tree limbs and rock hard, her skin not just warm to the touch but hot. She could feel the heat through her dress, and even Alison's small weight against her made her want to scream.

Jennie sat near the back of the church, with the other parents. This was the first of two funerals; Rachel's would be the next day. Anyone who wanted to had been excused from school and a team of fifteen grief counselors would be on hand for the kids' return.

Tara had gone to sit up front with the students, hundreds of them filling the pews of St. Michael's. Jennie had no idea what being here might do to Tara. This morning on the way to the funeral she had shrunk against the car door silently until they reached the church parking lot. When Jennie turned off the motor and opened her door to get out, Tara had shrieked, "How can they be having a funeral already? She just died."

The sheer bewilderment on Tara's face broke Jennie's heart.

"Isn't there something else that should happen first?" Tara went on. "I mean, it's going to be over, she's going to be gone, before I . . . I . . ."

Jennie moved to take her daughter in her arms but Tara suddenly squared her shoulders and forced herself out of the car.

Tara had had no time at all to learn how to think about what had happened. With an older person, Jennie thought, someone with a terminal illness, you would see it coming. You would have at least some time to prepare, time for your mind to rehearse what you might feel before you actually had to feel it. You could go over it and over it before it happened and still it would be a terrible shock. With Rachel and Erica's deaths, Tara had nothing to draw upon but pure impact.

They had taken her up to Connaught Road again because she had done a painting that she wanted to leave for Erica and Rachel. She wouldn't let Jennie or Chris see it, and had left it rolled up at the base of the scarred sugar maple that the car had hit.

"They're predicting rain, Tara," Chris had told her gently. "It may get ruined out there."

"It doesn't matter. It's just for them."

The roadside was covered with bouquets of flowers, candles, notes, balloons, CD covers, poems, cookies. As they sat in the car waiting for Tara, another group of friends drove up to leave a large bouquet of daisies. Tara kept her distance, nodding at the girls but not exchanging words. She got back into the car after only a moment, as if it frightened her to be there. Since then she had cried day and night in her room, coming out dry-eyed and silent. She said little, didn't even bother to focus her eyes.

Now, Jennie craned her neck to try to catch a glimpse of her daughter at the front of the church but it was impossible. Too many people.

Instead Jennie turned to see Rachel's parents and brother coming up the aisle, walking heavily, up the steepest of mountains.

"Camille," Jennie said, and reached out to touch her arm. Rachel's mother, at seeing Alison, squeezed her hands to her chest, as if to hold her own heart in her hands.

After organ music the priest began to talk of tragedy. He called Erica's death a town tragedy, a collective tragedy, although to Jennie that over-simplified what had happened. It was collective only on the outer edges. What really mattered to each person at the church was utterly different. What did Camille and Kevin feel as they walked up the aisle, knowing that tomorrow would be their own daughter's funeral? Or Erica's parents, Chuck and Marilyn, who sat on opposite pews at the front of the church—they had lost their only child.

And Tara—Tara had lost the two best friends of her teenage years, maybe of her life. Her life would never be the same. As for Jennie, all she could think of was *what if . . . how close . . . what if Tara had died too?* No, she decided. There was nothing communal about what had happened. How could the deaths of young girls be mourned any way but personally?

Because Erica was so young, the priest said. That was the tragedy—needless death at a young age. But when is death needful? Jennie wondered. She wondered if the blessing of the dead is that they take everyone else with them, preserved as they were at the time of the death. For Tara, yes, Erica would be forever sixteen, but Erica would take the sixteen-year-old Tara with her too, leaving her to exist somewhere just as they had known her, sparkling and fun, unmarred by future failures or abandoned dreams. Jennie thought of her grandmother, who had died years ago. To Grandma Laura, Jennie would always be an eight-year-old, brilliant and reading three grade levels ahead, winning at the science fair, building factories with Legos. Grandma was the only one who hadn't lived to see Jennie make her big, early mistakes, to see her disappoint everyone by getting pregnant and dropping out of college. To know that she was preserved that way in a land populated only by souls had given Jennie hope sometimes when she needed it: the little-girl Jennie there, smiling with a grandma who saw only her dreams and achievements and nothing of what came after. This felt comforting to Jennie and she wondered if it might comfort Tara too. Maybe someday Jennie could tell that to her—not now.

After the priest finished, a few of Erica's friends spoke, but not Tara. She hadn't wanted to try to put words together so soon. Mrs. Lewison, Erica's English teacher, who had also been Jennie's own teacher half her life ago, read a poem Erica had written. She said, "I want to introduce this by saying that I had asked for an in-class essay on persistence and what I got were three stanzas about rainbows and dreams and dancing on air. That was Erica. Always doing the unexpected, but doing it with so much style you couldn't be annoyed at her for long." Here everyone laughed and Mrs. Lewison paused before she said, "These are the last words she wrote."

As Mrs. Lewison read the poem, near tears, Jennie thought of the English teacher's tragedy. Perhaps the paper had lain in her briefcase all weekend, unread and forgotten until she'd heard the news. Or maybe she had graded the papers quickly on Friday night, going through them at record speed in order to give herself a free weekend, and now she had to live with the B- she'd given the paper, maybe raised from a C+ for creativity. The poem would appear in the newspaper the next day—the last words of a dead girl; it would be printed at the back of the yearbook; pinned on Tara's bulletin board for years.

Was Tara ever to have friends like them again? Jennie wondered. Ten-page notes to each other every day, hour-long phone calls at night, that essential need to see each other, hear each other, that girl love that preceded romantic love. Jennie remembered how it had been between herself and Elizabeth all those years in middle and high school, knowing each other's every thought or movement, racing in from an evening out together only to talk right away on the phone. Elizabeth had been the first one Jennie told when she learned she was pregnant with Tara. Elizabeth even before Chris.

After the service ended there was a reception in the church basement. The teenagers clumped, some telling stories audibly, animatedly, others just staring past their friends at walls and windows.

Jennie went immediately to join the line of people waiting to speak with Erica's parents. Though long divorced, Marilyn and Chuck Linders stood side by side, receiving embraces and words of solace together. Chuck's new wife had the sensitivity to stay across the room.

Marilyn Linders had always terrified Jennie. When she and Chris had first moved into their house down the street from Chuck and Marilyn, Jennie was twenty-three and Marilyn in her forties, only a couple of years younger than Jennie's own mother and so like her—fashionable and sophisticated, always in a suit going off to some sorority alumnae function—that that's how Jennie had always thought of her. Marilyn Linders had succeeded in making Jennie feel like a kid, a dopey kid who had messed up her life. And Jennie had barely known Chuck; each time they had reason to meet it seemed he could not recall her from the time before.

Jennie could see now that Chuck had no idea who she was so she introduced herself as Tara's mother.

"Tara," he said. "Tara, of course. One of Erica's *good* friends." He shook Jennie's hand.

"Her *best* friend," Marilyn corrected.

"Thanks for coming," Chuck said, reaching his hand out to the next person in the line.

Jennie turned to put her arm around Marilyn while hugging Alison to her chest. Even under the circumstances it felt odd to do that, to hug Marilyn, and Marilyn's shoulder was unpliant against Jennie's hand.

"I'm so sorry, Marilyn," Jennie said. "We're going to miss her so much."

"We had tickets to the ballet tonight to celebrate my birthday," Marilyn said. Marilyn fingered the gold ballet slipper broach on her lapel. She looked as if she were going to the ballet, in her beautiful burgundy suit and silk scarf, her short blond hair perfectly arranged. Jennie wondered how they did it—not just Marilyn and Chuck, but all people captured by such unexpected grief. How had Marilyn even found the pin in her jewelry box, the very small concentration it would take to do that? How could she put on clothes, run a comb through her hair, form words?

"Erica and I treasured the ballet," Marilyn said. "It was one of the things we loved to do together. We had season's tickets. Now each month I'll go alone."

"I'm so sorry," Jennie said. "If we can do anything. . . ."

"Thank you, Jennie. Very kind of you." Jennie felt she would cry at Marilyn and Chuck's professionalism in the face of what must be screaming inside them.

She then went to speak to Rachel's parents, whom she knew better. She gave both Camille and Kevin ginger side hugs to avoid pressing against Alison.

"I loved Rachel," Jennie said. "She was such a kind, caring girl."

"She was," Kevin said. "It was there from the beginning. We were just talking about that last night, weren't we, Camille? She was the sweetest baby you could imagine. Just smiling all the time. You'd pick her up and she'd pat you on the back." He gave his wife a tender glance. His eyes were two black caves, his face the worst kind of wound.

"We were looking at baby pictures last night," Camille said.

Kevin said, "People always say they can never remember their children being little, but I can. As if it were yesterday. I can remember when she was—like that." He passed his eyes over Alison.

"Would you like to hold her?" Jennie asked.

Kevin's eyes flickered, but then he said, "No, no. I'm too shaky."

"How's Sammy doing?" Jennie asked.

"It's hard to tell," Camille said. "He's in shock. Right now he seems resolute but I think he's going to take it terribly hard over time."

"Hard on him being the only one left," Kevin said. "He and his sister were so close."

"Just the two of them, you know. Kevin would be at work and I would be at work but they always had each other." Camille stopped talking and it looked as if something had put a stop to her face. Then she continued, "We agonized over a third child years ago and it seemed so impossible then, remember Kev? We had such a hard time managing the two. Remember how they fought? I wanted to get back to work, it seemed I would be in diapers and bottles forever. Now I think, what was the big deal? Why didn't we have four, five of them. Why not eight?" Camille's hand went to her mouth and she said, "Oh God, not that losing Rachel would have been easier if . . . I just meant . . ." Camille turned to Kevin and he pulled her face into his chest.

"Children are so precious," Jennie said. "That's what you meant, isn't it? No one proved that more than Rachel." Camille was softly crying against Kevin's chest and Jennie could find nothing useful to say. Not a word.

From across the room Tara was moving slowly toward her, followed by a very tall bald man.

"Mom, this is Mr. Herndon from the pool."

"Mike Herndon," he said, holding out his hand. "Tara wanted me to see her little sister. My wife and I are expecting our first in a couple of weeks."

"Oh, congratulations."

Camille turned from Kevin to Tara and held out her arms. Tara went to her and Jennie heard her murmur, "I miss her so much."

Mike moved Jennie slightly away from the others. "Did you know the boy?" he asked her in a very low voice.

"I met him once or twice."

"A great kid," he said. "Reason I ask is I know Tara was a friend of his. I was talking to her about him. None of my business but he could use a friend. God, is he in bad shape. I've talked to him. Great kid. I liked him a lot, but Jesus, how do you get through this? That's the thing. You tell someone he's got blood on his hands you're sure to have his on your own."

Jennie was only slightly aware of what he was saying. She was starting to feel very weak on her feet. "He's going to need a lot of help," she said.

"That's for sure. This community doesn't rally around him it'll be as good as three kids in the grave instead of two."

"This community's not exactly known for rallying around anyone." Jennie hoped that didn't sound as bitter to him as it did to her.

"He's got a good family," Mike said. "He's got that in his favor. Good

family, good kid. I was going to give him a job this summer. 'Course now
I can't."

"Because?"

"Because of this," he said, sweeping his hand through the air.

"He hasn't been charged with anything," Jennie said, slowly awakening
to this conversation. "They don't know if he's to blame."

"Doesn't matter. It would look antagonistic to the community. If people don't bring their kids to the pool because of him it's not going to do
anybody any good. I feel bad. Haven't told him yet, actually. I need to let
some time pass. He was one of the few kids in this town who's willing to
work, who actually needs the work. Needs the money."

Alison was waking up now, soft baby cries. "Are you asking me to have
Tara talk to him?"

"Jesus. Don't know. Just thought I'd mention about the kid. I can talk
to him, but what does he need with an old man like me?" Mike grinned.
"She's got to do what's right for her, but I just thought I'd mention it."

"Thanks," Jennie said. She felt sure she was going to pass out from
standing for so long. Just then she would have given anything to be at
home in her bed, the baby lying by her side. "Excuse me, will you? I'm
sorry. I've got to go do something with my baby."

She left the church hall in search of the bathroom. She needed to sit,
she needed to rest. Her head was pounding and she was blinking to keep
her eyes open.

She managed a brief smile at the two women who stood at the mirror
in the bathroom and they gave her smiles back that apologized for caring
about lipstick and combs at a time like this. There was nowhere to sit but
on a toilet seat. Luckily Alison took the breast immediately, sucked away
frantically, then happily. Jennie's nipples stung and she bit her lip to keep
from crying.

She tried to keep her mind off the pain by turning her thoughts to
Mike Herndon. The pool guy, as Tara called him. What a decent guy. A
really decent guy. He was the manager of the town Y, though he probably
couldn't afford to live in town. Sheldrake was a town for lawyers and
bankers now, its tradespeople, even its schoolteachers and CPAs, driven to
its edges or out by the ever-escalating prices. Maybe, like Jennie and
Chris, he had managed to cling to the edges of the town he had grown up
in, overpaying for a tiny, poorly built house in order to earn safe streets,

low taxes, a good school system. Maybe, like them, he lived on one of the streets of tiny postwar ranches on the town's outer reaches, streets that to Jennie's mind guarded the town's wealthier inhabitants from the apartment buildings and dowdier neighborhoods of the surrounding suburbs in some feudal castle system. Sheldrake was her town—she had lived there for all but four months of her life—but she could not say she loved it with the smug pride of most of its other inhabitants.

Jennie felt that her strength was returning, but then just as quickly being sapped out again as she nursed Alison. She tried to breathe deeply, to relax. She listened to the conversation of the women she had passed coming in.

"They say he was drinking," one of them said. "It just hasn't been released to the paper yet."

"I don't know how they can keep this a secret. This has got to be public. Everybody has to know, that's the only way to get these young people to stop drinking."

"There's going to be a meeting at the high school next Wednesday night. To discuss this problem. Well, supposedly the problem of drinking in general, though this case will undoubtedly come up. We've got to do something about this before there are more dead kids."

"Of course that boy didn't even *go* to school. That's the thing. His family thinks they're too good for our schools, they try to shelter him and look what happens. *He's* the one who causes harm. *He's* the one who hurts our kids." The woman's indignation was matched in tone by that of her friend, who added, "Maybe if they'd let him grow up normally he would have gotten certain things out of his system. He wouldn't have acted so irresponsibly."

"Such a tragedy. Those lovely girls." Their voices trailed off as they walked out of the bathroom.

All weekend Jennie had been concerned with Tara, had been letting her grief go for Rachel and Erica, but for the first time, with almost as much grief, she thought of Matt Fallon. Jennie could see much of the town would share her mother's view: He was a weird boy from a weird religious family, and as a result he was guilty before any of the facts came out.

Where was Matt now? A room packed with people mourned Erica and Rachel, but Jennie could picture a room across town, empty but for Matt and his family. Of course he wouldn't be welcome at the funeral. Where would he be welcome now if he were already so condemned by the town?

Jennie had only met the boy twice in her life. The first time had just been an introduction, but the second time, Jennie had gone to pick up Tara at the Y and while she was waiting in her car, reading, Matt had seen her and come over.

"Mrs. Breeze?" he had said.

"Jennie. Yes."

"I'm Matt Fallon. Remember, we met a few weeks ago?"

"Of course. Hi, Matt."

"I just wanted to say if you're looking for Tara she left a few minutes ago with Rachel's mother."

"Damn, I was sure it was my day for pickup. My mind is really going."

"Sorry. It's lucky I saw you. My bike has a flat so I need to wait for Mom to come pick me up."

"Is she on her way?"

"I can't call her until six. She won't be home until then."

"Let me take you."

"Oh, thanks, but that's okay."

"I don't mind. I might as well drive someone home since I messed up with Tara."

"I live way over on the other side of town. By the main post office? I was going to start walking it and then call later."

Jennie was touched by his patience, pictured him slowly pushing his disabled bike across town in rush-hour traffic. "Don't," she said. "Get in. Really, I don't mind, Matt."

"Are you sure? Thanks. Thanks a lot." He lifted his bike up and popped it into the back of her Honda wagon.

Matt. She'd liked that he called himself Matt, not Matthew. It seemed all the boys Tara knew were Andrew or Benjamin or William, never Andy or Ben or Bill. When had that happened to boys' names, she wondered. She hated to think that way, but it seemed kind of *sissy* to her, all these Nicholases and Theodores and Christophers everywhere. *Sissy*, as in "Don't get dirty, Nicholas," or "Sit up in your seat properly, William." In her day (her day! God, she was only thirty-four!) boys were Nick and Ted and Chris—like her own Chris, whom she couldn't imagine ever calling Christopher.

Matt had picked up the copy of *Mrs. Dalloway* that lay on the seat between them.

"Is Tara reading this for school?" he'd asked.

"No, it's mine," Jennie said.

In quite a resonant voice, Matt said, "'It is Clarissa, he said. For there she was.'"

"You've read it?" Jennie asked, impressed. She was sure she had never before encountered a fifteen-year-old boy who had read Virginia Woolf. She instantly liked Matt, the boy himself, even more than his name.

"She was an autodidact," Matt said. "Jane Austen was too, but I like Virginia Woolf better. Mom put both of them on my reading list. She wants to show how home-schooling can create geniuses, but I keep telling her, 'Thanks, Mom, but I'm no genius.'"

"You never know," Jennie said.

"I think it's inborn, but not in me. I have to work much too hard." Matt laughed.

They crawled through traffic, terrible at this time of day. There was only one main road that cut across Sheldrake from east to west; everything else was tiny little streets or dead ends or cul-de-sacs. They passed the high school, set in its glorious acreage in the middle of town, and she asked him, "How do you like being home-schooled?"

"I like it," he said. "I don't have much to compare it with though. I went to preschool before Mom got on this home-schooling thing but I don't really remember it. Mom and Dad gave me the option of going to the high school when we moved here, but . . ."

"But what?" Jennie asked. "I'm just curious."

"I checked it out and it just didn't seem that . . . serious to me. I mean, I'm sure it's fine, I don't mean to put it down. I know Tara goes there."

"I went there too."

"Really? Sorry, I didn't mean to . . ."

"No, I'm not going to defend it." They hit a red light and Jennie turned to look at him. "I got a good education but not a great one. I never read Virginia Woolf in high school."

"See, that's part of it. I love to read and I'm sure I've read a lot more than I would have at school. Not just novels, but in my other subjects I've read a lot more primary sources. I mean I've read Socrates and Freud and Euclid, not just some anonymous textbooks."

Jennie smiled. He was no doubt parroting his parents' philosophy, but he did so earnestly. Jennie thought she would like to meet his parents, that they must be intensely idealistic, really passionate about education. She and Matt hadn't talked about religion that day, so she wasn't sure where that fit in, but what she had most remembered from their conversation was that she had been amazed by what he had read in his short life, and even more amazed at what he had to say about it. He had used words like *polemical* and *byzantine* and *juxtaposition* and they came out naturally, not as vocabulary words.

She wondered if this was what home-schooling did or if he really might be a genius. She had talked to smart kids before, but they were usually smart and nerdy or smart and shy. Matt looked you right in the eye and talked to you. Most of the Nicholases and Andrews and Williams she had met through Tara either patronized her as a *mother* or couldn't begin to make eye contact, say real words. With Matt, she felt as if she were talking to an equal.

Matt lived all the way on the western reaches of town in a narrow brick two-story house that shared a driveway with the house next door. After she dropped him off it took her twenty minutes to drive back home. She had gone into the house and said to Chris, "All right, that's it, he's the perfect boy. Tara can marry him."

And now what would happen to this perfect boy? Who would he be at the end of all this? Was he fragile, easily broken by what had happened, or would all that was different in him give him a strength that would only spread?

After Jennie finished nursing Alison, she returned to the church hall to see if Tara was ready to go home. Though people were beginning to leave, the room was still full. As she scanned the room for Tara, she could not keep herself from thinking of Matt. Nobody would mention his name, but they all knew he was the reason they were there.

MATT

THEY HADN'T CHARGED him yet. They were taking their time. Days went by with the newspaper saying, "The unnamed youth is under investigation."

The blood test came back showing that his blood alcohol level was 0.04, well within legal limits, but by then it didn't matter. That guy Sean from the party had told the newspaper he'd seen Matt drink five beers and a margarita and that's what everyone believed. They were probably all saying, *The tests were wrong, the kid was drunk.*

The newspaper quoted the police chief: "He's got these three strikes against him. He was too young to drink. He was too young to drive. He was driving too fast." Those three strikes played in Matt's head all day long, and all night. *Too young, too young, too fast.*

There was something about him in the paper almost every day, but since they wouldn't reveal his name, it seemed that it wasn't him at all. It seemed that the person in the newspaper was someone else, someone more real than he. At times he felt like shouting out his bedroom window, "It was me, it was me!" just so someone would know he was there.

He wanted to go to Erica and Rachel's funerals, but Mom had said he should stay away, that their families' grieving was too fresh for that. Mom thought he wanted to apologize, but he wanted to see for himself that they truly were dead.

Of course they were dead. It said so in the paper. The unnamed youth had killed them.

He started letters to Erica's parents, to Rachel's parents, to Tara, but ripped them all up. What could he say? *Dear Mr. and Mrs. Cleary, I'm sorry I killed your daughter. Tara, I'm sorry I killed your best friends.* How could he think of such a thing and what good would it do? Did he want their forgiveness? No. Because he had committed an unforgivable act.

"It's God's forgiveness that you must think about," Pastor Linney said when he came by again. "Only God can forgive you and He already has. Let's look at Ephesians. 'But God, who is rich in mercy, for his great love wherewith he loved us, Even when we were dead in sins, hath quickened us together with Christ (by grace ye are saved).'"

Dead in sins. Pastor Linney read on, but that's all Matt needed to hear. He wasn't dead in body, as they were, but dead in sins.

"God has forgiven you," Pastor Linney said. "The hardest part is for you to accept that."

"I can't," Matt said. "I can't accept that." How could Pastor Linney be talking about forgiveness when Erica and Rachel's bodies were just being lowered into the ground?

And always, privately, Matt would ask God, *Why, why has this happened? Why have they died and not I,* and he would offer himself, saying, *Take me; if you had asked me before I would have said, Take me and not them. But if not then, it's too late, if not then, now.*

Matt knew how futile that was because God wasn't a vengeful God; God wouldn't ask or settle for Matt's death as payment.

But what did God want?

How could God kill them and not Matt and then be so silent?

God hadn't killed them. Matt had.

God's power to forgive, which was one of the things that made God God, was now like a sword passing through both of Matt's lungs. He did not want to be forgiven. He wanted to be punished.

Why wouldn't God punish him?

Why wouldn't God tell him what he wanted?

Why wasn't God there?

The next time Pastor Linney came, he said, "You need to pray for yourself first, Matt, before you can pray for them."

"How can I do that?" Matt asked from his seat on the bed.

"God will help you. God hasn't left you, Matt. He's the closest one to you."

Mom and Dad said that too, but it wasn't true. Couldn't they see it wasn't true? God wasn't there. God had vanished.

He had always been taught that to be starving for food was a terrible thing, but much worse would be for your spirit to starve. To need God to live but not have God . . . and die. Die in all the meaningful ways a person could die, if not in the final way. *Dead in sins.* That's what he had always felt it would be like and that's how he found it to be. Only worse, because he realized that life without God was not only death, it was death with survival. A death which went on and on. And on.

Sometimes Matt felt he would go mad in his room. Sometimes he felt like standing up from his desk and hurling himself through the window. The glass or the fall would not be enough to kill him but that was all he could think of to do.

Instead, he would return to the physics video or pick up his Darwin and go on. He found that he could read several pages, go for maybe ten or fifteen minutes without thinking about Rachel and Erica, and then it would hit him with the force of the first time: What had happened. What he'd done.

He read a passage in Darwin that said, "Everyone has heard of the dog suffering vivisection who licked the hand of the operator."

Rachel: *Help me, help me.*

Erica: *Don't I deserve better than this?*

He threw the book against the wall.

His heart was going to detonate, explode from his chest like the time bomb it was.

Too young, too young, too fast, the police chief had said, but that wasn't it. Too lustful.

Too in love with the hint of her touch to keep his eyes on the road.

Now, to whom could he tell that?

JENNIE

CHRIS WAS PAINTING Tara's room. Jennie couldn't believe they'd agreed to do it now, but it was one of the only things she had asked for since the accident and there was no way they could refuse. It was the kind of thing Jennie's mother—if she had known about it, if she had been around, instead of in Africa—would have labeled outrageous, spoiling, indulgent, and perhaps she would have been right. Ever since she was small, Tara had this tendency to become fixated on things she wanted or needed to change, and she couldn't be calmed until they were taken care of. At age three or four she would lie in bed at night and cry for a balloon that had floated away hours ago. Or at eight, if she forgot her favorite doll at a friend's house, they would have to return for it that moment or there would be no peace. It wasn't brattiness, because it didn't occur that often and it wasn't mere *things* she was after. It was always at the time of some heightened trauma that it came out, like now, when two weeks after the accident she'd decided her room could no longer be yellow, it had to be plum.

"At least she doesn't want black," Chris said.

"Thank God she hasn't read Chekhov yet," Jennie answered.

"Why? What's in Chekhov?"

"It's . . . never mind," Jennie said, irritated that Chris didn't know what she was talking about. It had always disappointed her that her love of literature was, in her family, hers alone. "We shouldn't talk this way. It sounds like we're joking, joking about Tara's life."

Jennie had wanted to do the painting, almost desperately had wanted to stand on a ladder and listen to music and forget that her older daughter was in a deep place of grief she couldn't reach; that her younger daughter, born into this time of shocked sadness, wasn't getting all the attention a baby only days old required; that there was a boy across town who had to live with what he'd done. Jennie began the painting, but she barely got started before she felt weak or Alison wanted to nurse, and in an entire Saturday afternoon she had only gotten one wall edged. She gave up and let Chris do it the next day. He was such a perfectionist that when he started on something it took him over, and he would work hours until it was done. Jennie hadn't seen him at all on Sunday except for his trips on the way to the garage for a scraper or rag or to smoke a joint. By evening, though none of them had left the house all day, and though they had even had a couple of visitors drop by briefly to see the baby, Jennie had the strange feeling that she had spent the entire day alone.

Tara had been allowed to stay home from school the whole of the first week after the accident and there were days during that week when she didn't get out of bed or stop crying. By the second week Jennie and Chris insisted she go back. She made it through school each day, coming home drawn and silent, going straight to bed in a state of exhaustion Jennie hadn't seen since she was a little girl. She was behind in her schoolwork, and though the teachers were making allowances, there were only two more weeks of school, one of them for finals.

Tara was watching TV in the family room, which doubled as Jennie's office. The piles of folders and the computer that hadn't been turned on in days made Jennie hopelessly nervous. She was so behind in her work, barely had time enough to look at e-mails or go to the post office box since Alison was born. She didn't know how she was ever going to catch up.

Tara sat curled up on the couch in shorts and a tank top, her long hair greasy and pulled back in barrettes. She hadn't washed her hair in days. She looked so exhausted, so beaten down. One of the grief counselors from school had called on Friday to reassure Jennie that Tara was coping very well with the tragedy—those were the words, *coping very well*—but looking at her now, Jennie found those words absurd.

If only she would talk about it. If only she would let them know what kind of things she was thinking, whether it was sheer missing them, or blaming Matt, or blaming herself for hating them on the last night of their lives. Jennie supposed it was all those things and more, things Tara probably couldn't articulate to herself or to anyone else. Still, Jennie tried to place herself as close to her daughter as she could, hoping that if and when Tara was ready to talk, she would at least be nearby.

She sat down on the couch next to Tara and tried again. "So how're you doing?" she asked her.

"Okay," Tara answered without looking at her.

"Thinking about them?"

"A lot."

Jennie let a few moments pass and then said, "Anything you want to talk about?"

"No."

She patted Tara on the knee and asked, "Ready for school tomorrow?"

Tara snorted. "I have absolutely no memory of one single fact I'm supposed to know."

"It will come back to you. You'll see. You'll do fine." Jennie heard herself sounding like a *mother*, all platitudes and emptiness, and tried to change it, but what to say?

"I wanted to talk to you about Matt Fallon," she finally said. "I've been thinking about him."

Tara said nothing, and just as Jennie was sure this wasn't the right route to take, Tara said, "Me too."

"Have you thought about calling him?"

The eyes Tara turned on her were fearful. "What would I say?" she asked.

"Is there anything you'd like to say?"

"Just . . . that I'm sorry for him. It's not even his fault. It was an accident, just how it seems. Maybe it was the car. I'm sure he didn't do it." Tara's face turned ever so slightly from the TV toward Jennie and she was speaking with more feeling now. Jennie could see how much compassion Tara had for the boy and it filled her with pride.

She proceeded cautiously, trying to hold onto Tara.

"I'm sure it would make him feel better to hear from you. You know he doesn't have a lot of friends in this town."

"I wouldn't know what to say. It's strange. I don't feel angry at him, Mom. I feel like it's something that happened. But I can't imagine talking to him. It would be like talking to a ghost." Tara faced her, cross-legged on the couch. She'd actually called her Mom. To Jennie it felt like she had finally *caught* her daughter; for the first time since Erica's funeral, Tara was talking.

"Maybe Matt's feeling like a ghost," Jennie said.

"I feel really sorry for him. I don't know which way to think about it. The thing is, I was so pissed at them, all of them, and now they're gone and I'll never have friends like that again."

"Oh sweetie, your being pissed at them had nothing to do with the accident."

"I know that but—"

"Nothing!" Jennie said, more fiercely than she intended. "It was an accident. But I'm sure you wish more than anything that you could talk to them one more time."

"A hundred more times." Tara's lips and cheeks quivered and she slapped at her eyes as the tears started to come.

Tara had moved close enough for Jennie to sense it was now okay to hold her. Tara felt chilly and thin, almost lifeless as Jennie hugged her.

"Oh sweetheart," she murmured against the faintly musty smell of Tara's blond head as she cried. The feel of her daughter was different, both the smell and feel of her were different. Jennie read in those differences all that Tara had lost—not just her two best friends, but the part of herself gone with them. Rachel and Erica were her touchstones, as Jennie and Chris had once been, the people to whom she could say, "Is this weird?" or "Am I normal?" or "Is it all right that I feel this way?" To lose that now, during the most vulnerable years of her life—-what would she do? It was too late in her life for her to turn back to Jennie and Chris, much as they longed for her to. Nor could she find someone instantly to replace the friends she had lost. It could take months, years, for her to find that footing again.

Unwittingly, Tara's words made Jennie think of Elizabeth and all that she'd lost when their friendship died. That high school fervor, how intimately they understood each other's lives—it was something Jennie still missed, the thing she, as an adult, had never grown accustomed to doing without. She supposed family life was designed to replace passionate friendship, but it couldn't. It was something different altogether.

She held Tara for a long time, rubbing her sharp shoulder blades, wishing she could accept some of the immense hurt hosted by Tara's small body into her own. When Tara finally stopped crying, she pulled away and looked at Jennie with sad, scaly eyes, made bluer from the tears.

"I need them to live," she said.

"You have them," Jennie said, words rushing in to prevent the lump she felt rising in her own throat. "They're still with you, all the things you talked about, everything you did together. Their memories will be alive as long as you're alive."

Tara looked for a moment as if Jennie's words had some meaning to her, but then she said, "I don't want their memories. I want them."

"I know, sweetie. I know how much it hurts," Jennie said.

"How can you say that?" Tara interrupted with unexpected venom. "You *know.* Nothing like this has happened to you."

Tara pulled away from her grasp and Jennie quickly said, "You're right, Tara. I don't *know.* But I was thinking about my best friend from high school. Elizabeth. I still miss her. She's not dead, but the friendship is, and I mourn that."

"How can you think it's the same thing? You could call her up. You could just start talking to her. My friends are dead. They're *dead!*" Tara's fury set her upright again and she pulled farther and farther away.

"I didn't mean . . ." Jennie panicked, scrambled to save the moment. Suddenly they both heard the baby's cries from the other room, and though Jennie heard Chris call out "I'll get her," the cries of her baby sister were enough to send Tara to her feet, running out of the room in tears.

"Damn," Jennie hissed, at her own ineptitude. She heard Tara slam the door and suddenly felt exhausted, incapable of knowing or saying anything that made sense. If only she could get some sleep. If only she didn't have this new baby to tend to just when Tara needed her the most.

Tara didn't even have a room to storm off to, not while Chris was in there painting, so she had gone into the bathroom. Jennie knocked on the door and said, "Sweetheart?" She was greeted by silence. Added, "I'm sorry." Heard nothing. Offered, "I'm here. I'd like to talk." Got "No." "I'll wait," Jennie said.

She stood at the door for a full ten minutes, listening to the sound of Tara crying, wanting to go in. Finally, Tara said, in a voice calmer, fortified, "It's okay, Mom. I'll come talk to you later."

"I love you," Jennie said.

"Okay," she heard Tara say and she turned from the door to see Chris standing there with Alison. He had his little finger in Alison's mouth and she was sucking frantically at it. "I can't hold her off any longer, I'm afraid," Chris said. "She needs the real McCoy." He nodded toward the closed bathroom door, raising his eyebrows inquiringly, and Jennie shook her head and grimaced to show how little she'd been able to do for Tara.

Jennie took Alison into the bedroom, murmuring "ssssh," as she undid a nursing flap so Alison could eat. It had only been an hour and a half since the last feeding, but she settled in for another long session. She felt all she did was feed Alison, but she didn't mind—it was exactly what Alison needed and despite the pain and exhaustion, it was easy to care for her baby: some breasts, some arms to hold her, diapers and a couple of stretchy suits, a place to sleep. If only Jennie could meet Tara's needs so easily.

MATT

H E WENT THROUGH IT a thousand times a day, as if straighten-
ing the books and notes on his desk or packing the van for a
camping trip. If only he had refused to drive. If only he hadn't had a single sip of beer. If only Erica's boyfriend hadn't deserted her, if only she
hadn't made Matt feel she wanted him, if only he'd told them they had to
wear seat belts. If only his mother hadn't let him go that night, if only he'd
never met the girls, if only they'd never moved to Connecticut.

That was as far as he'd have to go to erase it all, and sometimes he felt
from wanting it so much he could succeed in making time go backward.
He would find himself concentrating on that desire, sitting at his desk,
handling it, turning it over like an object in his hands.

Moving from Oregon had been the mistake. If only they had stayed in
Oregon, where everybody knew his family, where Matt had lived his
whole life.

Dad had been born and raised in Eugene. Mom was the one who had
grown up everywhere, and liked the idea of Dad having small-town roots.
They met at Berkeley and Mom followed Dad back to Eugene when she
finished graduate school. They had lived there for twenty years. Twenty
years! It was where they belonged and when Matt traced it back, that was
where he always got: Oregon.

He could remember the day they'd decided to move to Connecticut.
His father had a friend out east who had recommended him for a job as
conservation director in Sheldrake. The town was suffering from threatening bacteria in the sound and on top of that they were dismantling an
old power plant that was going to cause all kinds of problems for the environment. They needed someone immediately and Dad was who they
wanted. He had a national reputation. After Dad had flown out there to
check it out they had a family meeting. None of the kids wanted to go at

first but they could see Dad was pumped up about the project. He was furious about what might happen out there; he kept talking about the water fowl and rehabilitating the site for healthy, sustained use. He had this way of being so outraged by injustice that he couldn't rest until he righted it. Mom sometimes called him Enviro-Man. They could all feel how much he wanted the challenge.

Mom said to be within commuting distance of New York City would be a great opportunity for the kids, with all the museums and historical places nearby. And it would only be a year, possibly two. "Look at it as one big field trip," Mom had said, and she asked the older kids to do research to come up with their own special reasons for wanting to go— Brian would get to go to a Yankee game, Pete wanted to tour the *Intrepid,* and Matt, who loved to act in the kids' community theater in Eugene, couldn't wait to see a Broadway play. Eventually, they'd all been up for it.

Now it almost killed him to think of their big old blue house, rented out to another family while they were gone. It killed him that these people were there, their eleven-year-old son in Matt's old bed at night with nothing to keep him from falling asleep. It could just as easily have been Matt in that room, where he belonged, looking out his window at the stars, thinking only of the book he had just read or what was on the chore list for tomorrow or of some girl he thought was pretty and was hoping to talk to or kiss.

JENNIE

ALISON LOOKED BLISSFUL after she nursed, moving in happy slow motion, stretching her long skinny arms and then bringing them back in, making these delightful little postsucking sounds that let you know she led the best life in the world. Jennie knew she should go try to talk to Tara again, but she lingered with Alison because it felt so deeply pleasurable to watch her and hold her, to smell the spiky wisps of hair that barely covered her head. Jennie was exhausted, yes—no more than five hours of sleep a night, and this broken into two or three little chunks—but these early days with Alison were still nothing like the first weeks of Tara's life, which Jennie still remembered with an almost palpable terror.

If it hadn't been for Elizabeth back then, Jennie didn't know how she would have made it through those awful days. Sixteen years ago, when Tara was born, Elizabeth had come home from her freshman year at Brown to a miserable summer job working nights, wearing brown-and-orange polyester in a coffee shop, earning a paltry salary and quarter tips. She wasn't one of the town's rich kids—her dad was a draftsman and her mother kept the books for a tool and die shop—so she didn't have the connections some of the other kids had to get prestigious summer jobs at their fathers' friends' firms. Each morning, after Chris and his parents had all left for work and Jennie was alone with baby Tara, Elizabeth would show up, smelling like eggs and smoke and old coffee, and she would stay all day. All day, every day, all summer long. Sometimes she would slip away and nap, but more often she'd tell Jennie to get some sleep. Jennie had had Elizabeth to help her mix bottles or go to the store, put in laundry or just say, "Give me her." They took long walks, pushing the baby in her carriage around the neighborhood, and they had talked, not of babies and gas and formula, but of friends, books, theories of life. Elizabeth had reminded Jennie, who was almost ready to admit otherwise, that she was human. In those months she was as life-giving to Jennie as Jennie had been to Tara.

Jennie had sometimes thought that if Elizabeth hadn't been there that summer she and Chris might not have lasted, Jennie's despair building up all day long so that when he walked in the door in the evening she would only be able to see him as the one who had caused it all. Instead, she was able to look at him with clear, hopeful eyes, and together they were able to care for their baby and their marriage.

After that first summer, Elizabeth was mostly gone from Sheldrake— away at college or on a summer program in France, an internship in Cleveland, off to grad school. As Elizabeth got busy with her life, she came home less frequently; months and months would pass without their seeing each other. Though Jennie kept thinking it was a lapse, that they would eventually renew their friendship, the truth was their lives had diverged completely, and it had now been four years since Jennie had seen or even talked to Elizabeth. She still missed her.

Jennie swiveled in her rocking chair to look out into the dark and quiet of her suburban backyard. That there was time in all of this for thoughts of Elizabeth amazed her. Nights like this you could so mourn the lives you hadn't lived that you couldn't take a step. Some nights, the absence of things were like cuts on the fingers upon which her mother would have told Jennie to count her blessings. "Stop feeling sorry for yourself," Fay used to say, adding her favorite line, "Get on with it."

Tara was right, it wasn't the same. Still, Jennie knew she understood the feeling of lives lost.

She got up and carried Alison into Tara's room, where Chris was still on a ladder painting, listening to The Jam. He turned around and flashed her a smile. "Hey girls," he said. "Tara went to sleep in the family room. I promised her I'd finish in here tonight so she could have her room back for tomorrow."

Jennie had to smile: playing out his fatherly devotion to the accompaniment of his "angry young man music." While he painted, Chris played all his favorite tapes and Jennie imagined he got to some place that made him feel he'd lived his other life, the one without the teenage marriage and child and enslavement to his father's landscaping business. Their lives were lived so close together now but their secret lives—the ones that came to them when they were each alone with a certain kind of music, maybe driving, free from household concerns, money worries—were so different that Jennie knew if they met now they'd have little to say to each other. Maybe that was true of all couples who marry young. In her alternate life Jennie would have graduated college in four years, gotten her Ph.D., become a professor. In Chris's other life, he was probably single, alone, driving around, maybe playing a lot of computer games, smoking more pot than he sneaked in now. He would have always taken care of himself, would have always made the people around him comfortable and happy, but Jennie sometimes thought what had happened to them had lured him into a more responsible life than he would have led otherwise, maybe even a better life. Who knew whether he would have felt differently? He wasn't the type to look back.

She watched from behind as he reached with the brush to paint a straight line of plum paint at the place where the wall met the ceiling. She loved the shape of him, the tautness of his arm, the ridge of his shoulder blade through his orange T-shirt.

"Was she all right?" she asked him. "We had a bit of a . . ."

"I know. She's fine. She was just tired."

"I just don't know what to do," Jennie said. "I spent all Friday afternoon at the library looking for books about grief but there's nothing for her. It's *Death of a Parent, Death of a Spouse, Death of a Sibling, Death of a Child.* Doesn't somebody realize how devastating *Death of Friends* is to a teenager?"

"It will be all right, Jen. It'll just take a while."

"I just can't . . ." Jennie felt her own tears come. "God, having all this at once . . . I feel like I'm hallucinating sometimes. I'm so tired and I can't keep track of what's coming out of my mouth."

"Why don't you get a little sleep," Chris said. He climbed off the ladder and gently took Alison from her. "Come on, she's ready to sleep. You take a nap and I'll watch her."

"I don't want her in with these paint fumes," Jennie said. "Just put her in the bed with me."

In her room Jennie lay down on the unmade bed. Chris laid Alison next to her. She looked at the baby sleep, her arms stretched out to her sides. Jennie registered each tiny pucker of baby skin, each little sigh.

"I thought we'd have more time for this," she murmured, feeling her own sleep on its way.

"Just the two of us sitting around watching her sleep?" Chris asked. He gave Jennie a wistful smile. "Yeah, me too."

She was hoping Chris would lie down next to them but he kissed her forehead, turned out the light and went back to his painting.

As she slept, Jennie fell into an old dream, one she used to have when Tara was an infant. In the dream, she and Chris and baby Tara were on a huge ship when suddenly Tara slipped from her arms and fell overboard. Jennie stood on the deck trying to decide whether to jump in after her. Could she possibly find her in that freezing, churning water, or would Jennie drown too? She was a very poor swimmer. The water was so rough, the ship moving so fast. There was no question of Chris jumping in; for some reason it was only Jennie who could do it. And that was the dream: standing there, trying to decide, agonizing, feeling each moment pass, wondering if she could possibly save her baby by jumping in, or whether they both would die.

In a half-awake state, so disturbed by the dream, Jennie thought, *I must be dreaming of Alison.* But no. Jennie looked into the dream and saw the baby falling from the ship's railing to the sea and knew the way any mother knows the differences between her babies, could identify any one of them by the weight of their hands, the way their mouths moved in sleep, the feel of their hair, anywhere, anytime, no matter how many years had passed—she knew the baby in the dream was still Tara.

MATT

NOT EVERY NIGHT, but almost every night there would be a border of gray light around Matt's window shades before he could sleep, and then it would be noon or later when he awoke, assailed by memory.

All night he lay awake thinking how he could do it. In his mind he put a gun in his mouth so many times he was sure if he had one he'd be dead by now. He would call the police and say, *In three minutes I'll be dead.* He would lock his door and the police would have to break it down to get in. They would be the ones to find him.

With no gun he thought of pills, or of hacking at the important arteries until he bled to death. Or going into the garage in the middle of the night and turning on the engine of one of the vans.

What stopped him, always, was who might find him. What if it was Katie? What if it was Em?

This particular night it was early, just after midnight, but he couldn't stand to be in his bed anymore. In his room. He opened his bedroom door to listen for Mom or Dad. He could see the light on downstairs and he went down. Mom was at the dining room table, a pink tutu in her arms.

"Hi," she said, pins in her mouth. "I'm shortening the straps on this thing."

"Katie's or Em's?"

"Em's recital tomorrow." She worked quickly, impatiently, and Matt wanted to apologize for all the trouble he was causing when she had so much else to do.

"Can't sleep?" Mom asked him.

"No."

"Damn!" his mother said. It was so unlike her to swear and she did it so loudly that he thought she had stuck herself with one of the pins. But then she went on. "It just seems that a fifteen-year-old boy shouldn't have anything on his mind to keep him from sleep at night."

"I'm sorry, Mom."

"I wish I could change it for you, Matt," his mom said. "I'd give anything for this not to have happened."

Sometimes he loved his mother so much he couldn't even talk to her. She was such a good person—strong, funny, never losing her cool. Last summer at church retreat in Oregon, the theme was "Love in Your Family" and one of the exercises was to list each of your family members and write the five qualities you admired most in them. He hadn't really thought about his family that way before. Mom was just Mom, his brothers and sisters what they were. Dad had been easiest because Matt admired his commitment to the environment, the way he never said no before considering every side of a situation, the way he would take on new challenges, like taking up Latin at forty or accepting this job in Connecticut. But it wasn't until he had to think about Mom that he'd actually separated out what made her different from other moms. He liked to tease her about everything being so *educational*, hanging posters of the solar system or the human skeleton on every free wall so they'd always be learning something. "Gee, Mom," he'd say, "do you think I could spend five minutes in the bathroom without having to study the Civil War timeline?" She overdid it sometimes, but she was so devoted to their education. She said it was because she was dragged around so much as a kid, never more than a year or two in one school, huge holes in her education. But Matt knew that she did everything full force and expected them all to be the same way.

He knew Mom was already imagining the worst. She didn't need to hear his fears and be reminded of how much he was disappointing her. He couldn't tell her the truth, that no matter what argument his lawyer, Mr. Finchley, would make—that the other two girls were drunk, as their blood alcohol tests showed, that he was the only logical choice to drive, that he had driven before with his father—it was still his fault because he had forgotten everything in the world for a moment and had taken his eyes off the road to look at Erica.

"Good night, Mom," he said abruptly, standing up.

"Do you need anything, Matt? Are you all right?"

"I'm all right."

He could see it in her creased face—the worry, her love for him, her desire to say something to help him. He couldn't be in the presence of all that so he said again, "'Night." He could see that she didn't want to say it, was fighting for something else to say, something that might make it all right, something that she felt a mother should be able to do for her children. But it wasn't there, there was nothing, and he almost felt her despair as she let out the words, "'Night then, Matt."

And he went to bed.

JENNIE

THE SCREAM THAT woke her was no mere baby cry, but a scream of absolute terror in a voice that knew what terror was. Jennie ran from her room into Tara's and found her daughter on hands and knees in her bed, no longer screaming but whimpering. Shaking violently. Jennie tried to hold her, but Tara cried, "No!" and batted her away.

"It's okay, honey," Jennie said. "You had a bad dream."

"No," Tara said. She looked at Jennie with crossed eyes and kept opening her mouth, as if there were really something she needed to tell her.

"What is it?" Jennie asked. She pulled Tara onto her lap, but Tara squirmed in her arms, trembling, not yet ready to be soothed.

"No," Tara said. "No, no, no. The glass."

"There's no glass, Tara. It's a bad dream."

"Don't sit on the glass!" Tara screamed. "Don't sit on the glass!"

"Sssh," Jennie said, patting her, patting her until she slept again.

The horror of Tara's scream echoed in her own heart and Jennie found herself unable to go back to sleep herself. She longed to do something utterly normal, something so boring and mundane that it might possibly dilute this ocean of terror and worry about her daughter.

She went into the part of the family room she used as an office and sat down at her desk for the first time in three weeks. Just turning on the computer made her feel defeated—the dozens of e-mails she needed to look at, the hundreds of entries she needed to make in her database. Just another anxiety creeping in. Her company was going to go down the drain unless she got some help.

An idea. Jennie had hired Rachel Cleary to work for her this summer, while Chris had lined up a summer job for Tara in the office of the landscape architect Chris worked with. But now, with Rachel gone, it occurred to Jennie that she could hire Matt Fallon instead.

She didn't know his family, but they had a lot of kids. She had this idea that they were young, his parents, maybe as young as Chris and she. Maybe because of the home-schooling, she pictured them as good, simple, religious people, probably without much money. She could give him a job, help him out, let him know someone trusted him.

Like all ideas hatched at 4:00 A.M., her plan seemed insane under morning light. She ran it by Chris, surprised by how nervous she felt expressing it even to him.

He immediately frowned, but it was a perplexed, rather than disapproving, frown. "Why?" he asked challengingly.

"Well, I've heard he's in pretty bad shape. I think he could use someone to believe in him."

"Does it have to be us?"

"Everyone else is being so hostile. Everyone's blaming him." She could have given him details. She could have told him what she had heard at the funeral; from her mother; at Marilyn Linders's house when she went to visit her the other day. She could have told him about the three-hour meeting at Sheldrake High to discuss drunk driving, virtually all of it spent indicting "the driver who killed Erica Linders and Rachel Cleary." She could have told him about the PR stunt they were planning for the afternoon before the senior prom: they would use crash dummies and one of the cars from auto shop to re-create the accident on the school lawn, driving the car into a tree with two thousand students gathered around to see what happened when you drank and drove.

She could have told Chris all these things, but she was tired. She didn't feel like pleading her case. She just said, "They're using him as the scapegoat for every bit of bad behavior that goes on at the high school."

Chris was shaking his head. "I don't think you should get involved with it, Jen. You don't know how messed up he might be."

"I know how messed up he's going to be if somebody doesn't take an interest. Imagine how much he must be suffering."

"It's not your job to eliminate all the suffering from the world."

"I don't think that way. I think that if we can do something for him, why shouldn't we?"

"What I'm saying is, you don't know him. You don't know how this is affecting him, you don't know what he's likely to do now."

"I've met him. I know what he's like. A good kid, a real star, and it kills me to think this might ruin his life. Chris, this could have happened to you or me when we were in high school. Remember driving on the beach in the pitch black, drunk out of our minds? Remember driving the wrong way up the entrance ramp on I-95?" Her heart lurched at remembering.

"I don't need to be reminded of what an asshole I was," Chris said, shaking his head, dismissing her words. "We got lucky. Nothing happened. But if it had, we would have been accountable."

"Think about how many times you've driven stoned. What if you had been stopped, what if—"

"I wasn't," he said sharply. He was quiet for a moment and then said, "Jen, let someone help him, sure, but someone who knows what they're doing."

But after all his arguments, in a very Chris-like reversal, he had gone in the other room for an hour, put on some music and then come back and said, "If Tara says okay, then okay."

Tara said okay.

When she awoke, looking as if she hadn't slept more than fifteen minutes, not remembering a thing about her nightmare, she sat at the kitchen table in her nightgown and frowned at the wall.

"I was wondering," Jennie asked her, trying to sound spontaneous though she'd been rehearsing it all morning. "Do you want to go out for breakfast, just the two of us?"

Tara pursed her lips, then shook her head. "I'll just have some cereal at home."

"Okay. What about lunch later? We could go to the Poppyseed."

Tara shook her head again.

"Sun Cafe?" Jennie prompted, smiling, trying to make it all sound fun and adventurous.

"No. I just want to stay here."

"Okay," Jennie said. She busied herself for a few moments wiping the kitchen counter, picking crumbs off the stove, then turned back to

Tara. She hadn't moved; her chin rested in her cupped hands, the swarm of her hair falling across one side of her face. Jennie fought the urge to tuck that hair behind her ear, to say, "You should eat," and bustle about pouring her juice and Rice Krispies. Instead she sat at the chair opposite Tara and said, "I've had this idea and I need your opinion."

The urgency in her voice had little effect on her daughter. Tara said nothing.

"I need someone to help me with My Old School this summer and I was thinking of asking Matt Fallon." The way Tara's eyes flew open almost made Jennie take back her words, but something made her press on. "It was just an idea, an idea, but I really wanted to know what you thought about it."

With panic in her voice Tara asked, "I don't have to see him, do I?"

"Not if you don't want to. He'll arrive after you leave in the morning and leave before you get home. But if you still don't like the idea, I won't do it."

"I don't care," Tara said. "I just don't want to see him, okay?"

"Okay, sweetheart," Jennie said.

Tara went back to her expressionless stare at the wall and with a despairing sort of guilt, Jennie felt relieved that she had jolted Tara out of her trance for a moment. Perhaps Tara would change her mind; Jennie would bring it up a few more times before she did anything about Matt; she wanted Tara and Chris and even herself to get used to the idea first.

Suddenly, in the soft, familiar Tara voice, the only time Jennie was to hear it all day, she said, "I think maybe it will help him, Mom." Jennie leaned across the table to embrace her daughter just as Tara got to her feet and left the room.

If only I could help you, Jennie thought. *If only you.*

MATT

TWO COUNTS OF reckless homicide. That's what they charged
him with. *Homicide.*

I am not a murderer, he wanted to shout after the charges were read
in court. The passage from *accident* to *homicide* had come so swiftly.

He was under house detention now, but as the judge explained
what this meant, Matt barely listened because the whole of his strength
was going toward keeping his eyes level, his face intact. He wouldn't
cry in court. He wouldn't cry in court. He tried to let everything pass
over him, tried to make himself numb, but that was impossible. If only
he could contain it, just keep it all inside until he could get home to
his room.

When the judge was done, Mr. Finchley, the lawyer Mom and Dad
had hired, hustled them out to the hallway. "I think there's a confer-
ence room somewhere around here we can use," he said. "We can talk
about the plea there, save another meeting."

"The plea?" Matt asked. His father had his hand on his shoulder.
Mr. Finchley was propelling them down the hall. He was a short man
with greasy brown hair and a mustache. Mom didn't like him. "I'm
sorry," Matt had heard her say to his father last night, "but that man
smells like butt." It was such an outrageously atypical thing for her to
say that Matt had almost laughed out loud, except that he wasn't supposed to be listening in the first place. Mom sounded so regretful when
she said it; he knew she was thinking, *If only we had the money to hire
someone better.*

"We need to talk about what happens if you plead guilty versus not
guilty," Mr. Finchley said. "Do we want to see you go to trial, that kind
of thing."

"I'm guilty," Matt said. "That's what I'll plead."

"That's my inclination," Mr. Finchley said. "Their investigation was thorough. They've got a strong enough case, and if there's a trial I believe they'll win. It will only delay sentencing, cost your folks more money. To tell you the truth, I'm not worried about the sentencing. They're not going to send you to jail. They've got plenty of criminals to send to jail. I'm sure we'll get you probation. Worst-case scenario? A juvenile home until you're eighteen but that's highly unlikely. Highly unlikely."

Matt stopped walking, which made all of them stop. "I'm guilty," he said.

"Matt," Mom said, putting her arm on his shoulder.

"Tell you what," Mr. Finchley said. His eyes darted from Matt to Dad to Mom. *Beady little eyes*—those were Mom's words too. "Let's let your folks talk to you and we'll all speak about it later. We've got some time. Another month. I've got another case. . . ." His finger stabbed the air and he set off down the hall.

"That's lawyers for you, son," Dad said. "They're either talking, or gone."

"Let's go home and talk about it," Mom said. Matt knew she was worried about leaving the other kids alone too long under the supervision of Brian, who was only twelve.

"We can talk about it later," Dad said in the car. "I don't want you rushing into a decision just because you think it will ease your conscience, Matt. Guilty or not guilty—this is all the legal talk, Matt. This is the legal side. What happened . . . the accident is something you have to come to terms with in your own way. The law is something else."

Matt didn't understand why they were trying to get him to say he didn't do it. Who was guilty if not he? It was as if he was being given permission to crawl through some legal wormhole and emerge in the galaxy of the blameless.

"I did it, Dad," he said with firmness. "There's no use talking about it."

From the backseat he saw Mom and Dad exchange barely perceptible looks, heads moving only fractions of millimeters toward each other. But he knew what the looks meant: *The boy is standing firm; let's try another time.*

At home, Matt went straight up to his room. While he was gone, this house had been transformed into a prison. Under the terms of house detention Matt could only leave to go to school, work and church. Because his home was his school and he had no work, that left church. One hour a week. Now that he wouldn't be allowed to leave, he suddenly felt an overpowering need to get out.

He hung up the suit he had worn to court and changed into shorts and a T-shirt. Em knocked on his door.

"Do you want to play Candyland?" she asked. "They won't play Candyland with me. They're poopoo."

"You're not supposed to say that word," he told her automatically. "Use nicer words."

Em brought the game into his room and they played on the floor next to the bed. She liked playing Candyland with Matt because he always worked it so she picked the Queen Frostine card. And Em was the only one of Matt's brothers and sisters he could stand being around now. At twelve, Brian was old enough to understand what his parents had told him and it had sent him into a silent shock. Pete, nine, asked too many questions, and Katie, five, kept saying, "Why was Matt in an accident?" Only Em, at three, knew nothing of what had happened. She loved him and *could* love him because she was not old enough to understand what he'd done.

"I stay with Mattie," she said after the game was done and he tried to send her downstairs. "I love this Mattie. I love this brother." She wrapped her whole body around his legs and he hugged her back and cried the tears that had wanted to come out in court.

JENNIE

I T WAS TIME for Alison's one-month checkup and Jennie was sleepless, harried and late. She had spent most of the previous night draped over Alison's bassinet, which she had pulled up tightly against her side of the bed, keeping the pacifier in Alison's mouth. Alison was quiet as long as she had the pacifier but as soon as it fell out she would scream again and Jennie would wake, frantically searching the blankets. At one point, she dimly recalled, she was actually shouting at the baby, "You must go to sleep, you have to go to sleep!" It was near dawn when Alison fell into a deep sleep, but what seemed like minutes later Tara let out a scream and Jennie had bolted from the bed to Tara's room.

When they got to the doctor's office, Alison was wailing with hunger because Jennie had rushed out the door without feeding her. She unsnapped Alison from the car seat and moved her into the well-baby checkup area. She noticed the sick area was filled with mothers and toddlers, but there was only one other person in the well area: Camille Cleary, Rachel's mother.

Jennie took a deep breath and stepped toward her. "Camille," she said.

Camille looked up slowly from the stack of closed magazines on her lap. It took her several seconds to recognize Jennie.

"Jennie," she said softly. "Is the baby sick?"

"No, no. It's just a well-baby visit."

"How old is she now?"

"A month."

"A month. Of course." So easy to measure: Alison's life, Rachel's and Erica's deaths.

Under both of Camille's eyes were a series of broken blood vessels and tiny red dots—damage from hours and hours spent crying. And the puffy area under her eyes seemed to have a different quality now, as if all those tears had altered the composition of the tissue.

"I'm here with Sam," Camille told Jennie. "He hurt his knee playing soccer. I have to wait outside though. He's too old to have me in the room with him." She smiled a labored, humorless smile. "Thirteen."

"I hope he'll be all right."

"Oh, he'll be—" Camille abruptly stopped talking and Jennie looked up to see if something had startled her, then realized it was just that Camille had trouble making it through a full sentence. Jennie sat heavily in the chair next to Camille and lifted up her shirt to start feeding Alison.

Camille sat impassively. Jennie had stopped by to see Camille twice since the accident, quietly anguished visits where Jennie had little idea what to say, but at least those times she had been prepared.

Camille drew in sharp, deep breaths. "How's Tara?" she asked.

Tara. Jennie immediately flashed on last night, Tara thrashing and moaning in the dark as Jennie tried to calm her. "It's very hard," she told Camille. "She misses them terribly, and along with the shock, the grief, I think she's just lost without them."

"Do you think she'd want to have anything of Rachel's? Her clothes wouldn't fit, I know. Tara's so petite. Maybe a sweater, anyway, or something from her room?"

"I think she'd love it, Camille . . . I can ask her—"

Camille interrupted Jennie and said, almost frantically, "We're leaving Rachel's room as it is for now. We aren't doing anything to it."

"No, of course not. You'll want all her things close by."

Camille spoke again. "Do you think Tara would like to come over and take a look through Rachel's things?" she asked.

Why hadn't Jennie thought of that? A visit from Tara might be of some solace to Camille. She'd thought about it the other way, as a painful reminder of what was lost, the way a woman who had just had a miscarriage might find it a torture to be in a room with one who was pregnant. Now she saw that Camille had lost not only Rachel, but Rachel's friends, Rachel's era; that whole realm of teenage girlhood had been ripped out of her life.

And Tara had always liked Rachel's mother. Jennie too. Ever since the girls were little she had wanted to count Camille as a friend, but the age difference—Camille was sixteen years older—and the fact that Camille went into Manhattan to work each day had always kept them at a distance—friendly, but not really friends.

The nurse came out and called "Elijah and Noah," and blond two-year-old twins went in with their mother.

"Which doctor do you see?" Camille asked, fixing her eyes on Alison.

"Dr. Fabry."

"Oh, she's wonderful. Very caring, very gentle. She took care of Rachel when we first moved here. Rachel came down with the chicken pox the day we moved in. The very day. She was six and Sam was three. God, ten years I've been coming to this office."

"Ten years since you moved in down the street from us."

"It can't be." Camille's eyes rounded in astonishment and then settled back on Alison.

Jennie nodded. "I can remember Rachel the first day we met her. She was out waiting for the moving van and Tara and I walked by, and in about ten minutes they were best friends. I can still see her with those long black braids."

"She's always had that thick, black hair," Camille said wistfully. "She came out with it."

"And she'd lost a tooth, as I recall," Jennie said. "That gave her great status in Tara's mind."

"You have an amazing memory," Camille said. "You remember that day as clearly as I do." Camille lifted her eyes from Alison and looked at Jennie with an expression of anguished surprise. Jennie was afraid that Camille, after a fond retreat into the past, was reliving the fact that her daughter was dead. In fact, it was something worse. "When I think how we moved here because we felt the city wasn't *safe* enough," Camille said. "This was supposed to be such a *safe* environment for children. If we'd just stayed in Manhattan she would have been riding the subway, for God's sake."

Jennie put her free arm around Camille's trembling shoulders. Quietly she said, "You can't think that way, Camille."

"I know I can't. But I do. I think every which way. Every possible 'if only this hadn't happened,' or 'if only we'd changed this one little thing.' I've thought of every single one."

"Then again, maybe it's the only way you *can* think," Jennie said, changing her mind. "Maybe it's the only way you can give yourself some power in a time when nothing you could have done or said could have changed what happened. If you just shuffle the events, in your own mind there's the relief of that exact thing not happening over and over again." She rubbed Camille's arm gently. "Because I can't even imagine how painful it must be for you to go through it again and again."

Camille nodded slowly, squeezing her eyes shut and pursing her mouth, as if trying to contain what longed to spill out. "No," she said. "You can't."

A tiny girl with two long ropes of mucous hanging out of her nose ran over from the other side of the fish tank and stopped in front of Jennie. "What's that?" she asked, pointing to Alison.

"That's a baby," Jennie said. "Her name's Alison."

"Miriam," the girl's mother said, picking her up and carrying her back. "Don't give that baby your germs."

"What is it with all these Old Testament names?" Camille suddenly asked. "Miriam, Noah, Elijah. All these Connecticut WASPs giving their blond-haired, blue-eyed children these names seems a little affected."

"I know a Jonah, an Isaac," Jennie said. "It's a fad. Inscrutable."

"Of course, Sam and Rachel have Old Testament names," Camille said, "but then I'm Jewish." She smiled the grim, straight line of a smile that was all she was capable of. "And it works the other way too. My Jewish friends in the city are all having Mollys and Spencers and Ariels."

"No kidding," Jennie said. "Though I'm one to talk. My kids' names came from *Gone with the Wind* and an old Elvis Costello song."

They were quiet again. Jennie was happy the conversation had lightened, but still felt anxious, almost wishing that the nurse would come and call Alison's name so she could leave the waiting room, leave Camille, for whom she could offer no solace, for whom she was perhaps a cruel reminder: *You lost your daughter, but I still have mine.*

When it was finally her turn to go in, Jennie gave Camille a hug. "I hope Sam's all right," she said.

"Tell Tara to come over. Anytime."

"I will. 'Bye, Camille."

It was a relief to be alone in the examining room with Alison, where she undressed Alison to the diaper, as the nurse instructed. Jennie watched her move her tiny naked limbs and dart her eyes as she lay on the examining table. Except for a few minutes each day during her bath, Alison was usually swaddled, just blankets and a face, and here she was, all long slithery limbs. Jennie felt she had so little time to do this—just watch her baby, just read her like a book. How could she watch more devoutly, how could she hang onto moments like this to have when Alison was fifteen or sixteen? What would she give to have a moment now with Tara as a baby? And Camille: What would Camille give for that of Rachel? She and Camille had both done the same things for their daughters, bore them, fed them, raised them, loved them, taken them to school, ballet, the doctor, soccer practice, every step of the way done their best and inexplicably Rachel had been snatched away while Tara survived. Jennie swayed at the thought that she might have lost Tara that night. How? How can you let your children die? What kind of mother could let that happen? How were you expected to bear it and go on living yourself, even if . . . *especially* if you had another child who needed you too?

After Alison was weighed and measured and pronounced a perfect four-week-old baby, Jennie dressed her again and left. Camille was gone from the waiting room, but out in the parking lot Jennie heard her call her name.

She peered into Camille's gray Volvo station wagon. "Where's Sam?" she asked.

Camille waved a hand. "Across the street," she said. "Picking up a prescription. Listen, I wanted to ask you, is it true what I heard, that they're going to restage the accident at Sheldrake High?"

Jennie nodded, vehemently. "On the school lawn, the afternoon of the prom. As a deterrent to drinking and driving."

"Assholes." Camille spit the word.

"That's what I thought," Jennie said, surprised to hear Camille use that word. "Didn't they talk to you about it? Didn't they ask your permission?"

"No, they didn't. No one said a word. What in the hell is it supposed to accomplish?" Camille asked. "It's only been a month. Don't they think it's fresh enough in people's minds?"

Jennie shook her head. "They've been wanting to crack down on drinking and driving among the students for years and I suppose they see this as their big chance."

"But Matt Fallon wasn't even drunk. He shouldn't have been driving, but he wasn't drunk. He was driving too fast. That's what caused the accident. God, they're turning them into some joyriding teenagers." Camille's words came fast, and with increasing anger, though Jennie was amazed at how even-handed she was being. If it had been Tara, would she have had anything but condemning words for Matt?

"They're turning them into symbols," Jennie said. "If they can scare the rest of the kids, that's what they'll do. I'm sure what they really love is that Matt Fallon didn't even go to Sheldrake. They can blame it on an outsider, maintain the integrity of their precious community."

"And continue to close their eyes to the fact that their own kids are stuffing coke up their noses at lunchtime."

Jennie nodded. She admired Camille's unwillingness to turn her daughter's death into an issue.

"What about that boy, anyway?" Camille asked. "What's he thinking of all this, all this anger directed at him?" After a pause she added, "Lots of it mine."

"I've been thinking about him," Jennie said cautiously. She wasn't sure which way Camille was going with this.

"He was arraigned yesterday. They're charging him with reckless homicide."

"Homicide!" Jennie chilled at the word. "What does that mean? What's going to happen to him?" she asked.

"I don't know. He has to enter a plea, then wait for a sentence to be passed. It could take all summer."

"All summer," Jennie said. She pictured him alone in that yellow brick house, just sitting and waiting all summer long. "I was thinking," she began with Camille. "He's so . . . alone. He doesn't go to school. I don't know if he has any friends. I wonder if he's getting any counseling. I had hoped Tara might call him. I don't know if she did. I was even thinking of . . . tell me if you think I'm crazy because I might be, but I was thinking of giving him the job Rachel was going to have with me this summer. To give him something to do, to give him a purpose and let him know . . ."

Something in Camille's expression made Jennie stop talking. She was afraid she had misspoken, gravely misspoken, and was about to recant when Camille said, in a tone hushed and weary, but kind, "Like I said, I would like to see that boy helped. I can't do it but someone should. It could have been my Rachel driving that car, or Erica Linders. They were drinking that night . . ." Camille's voice began to crack and she slammed her lips together.

"You're amazingly forgiving, Camille," Jennie said.

Camille looked grimly surprised. "Am I?" she asked. "I would never have described myself as a forgiving person. I was always the type to hold a grudge. I wasn't the second-chance kind of person at all."

"Maybe you just haven't had an opportunity to know that about yourself before," Jennie said. She winced at the word *opportunity*. What a terrible word to use.

"It's just how I feel," Camille said.

Camille's face, those embattled eyes, stayed with Jennie after she drove away, and as soon as Tara came home from school that day, Jennie told her about seeing Camille and about the invitation to visit. Tara had little immediate reaction, but ten minutes later she came into the kitchen and said, "I'm going over to the Clearys." Alone again, Jennie made a split-second decision. Because she didn't know when she would get to the phone again, or if she would change her mind, or whether Chris or Tara might try to change it for her, she went ahead and did it. She had Camille's and Tara's blessing, Chris's grudging assent. She called information to get Matt Fallon's number and then, without any pause for reflection, she dialed it.

MATT

H
E WAS REACHING up her body, finger-crawling over goose bumps and baby-fine hairs for her breasts. God, there they were. He reached them, one hand moving between them, just one hand—where was the other? He wanted both, wanted to grab fistfuls of breast and rub it, squeeze it, but it was just one, then the other. She had his penis, was pumping it with her hand. As he came his eyes opened and he saw that he was in his room, his own hand on his penis and she—the girl in his dreams—Erica—dead.

"Oh God, oh God, oh God," Matt said. He rolled himself into cat-backed position on the bed. The covers were on the floor. He dove onto the floor too, found yesterday's sock to wipe up the semen and then stayed there in a curl.

It was the first time he had masturbated since the accident and his physical relief was immediately slammed down by shame. How could he do this? What kind of hell gave him the girl he had killed as a lover in his dreams?

Hell, because it had felt like coming back to life for a few seconds and now he felt even more what it was like to be dead. Why did it have to be Erica? Why not Tara, some movie actress, a stranger, anyone but Erica?

"I know what I did, God," Matt whispered. "I know what I did."

The first day of his life that he had kissed a girl Matt had kissed three. He had given it no thought at all. He had this vague idea that things just *began* with girls. You would be this guy, this kid, and then all of a sudden you would become someone who kissed girls. He had expected to figure it out later. That day, that night, had felt like the beginning of things for him. He had the offer of a summer job. He had gone to a party and met people who might turn out to be friends.

Three different girls had shown they were interested in him. It had all ended because he reached for a girl in a car, not caring which girl it was. For treating the three as one, he had killed two.

He stayed on the floor and thought again of killing himself.

"What do I do, God? What can I possibly do? Is there a chance . . . is there a chance . . . ?" That was all of a prayer he could choke out, knowing what he'd done, how he'd sinned.

Pastor Linney said to call anytime but Matt knew he would quote more Ephesians, "For by grace are ye saved through faith; and that not of yourselves: it is the gift of God," or Romans, "For all have sinned, and come short of the glory of God," or even some passages from the Gospel of John, saying that all Matt had to do was to admit that nothing he had done or hadn't done could keep him from heaven if he admitted Jesus was his savior. These were Bible verses Matt had memorized in Sunday school and they had always made things simple for him before.

He didn't fault Pastor Linney for the absurdity of what he had to offer. Matt had believed it once too.

I T WAS THAT same day, though hours later, that Mom came to tell him he had a phone call.

"Who is it?" he asked. "Is it . . . ?" He knew no one who might call him. Aside from his relatives in Oregon, the only person who had called him was Mike Herndon, to tell him he couldn't give him a summer job. Tara hadn't called. Could it be Tara?

"It's Jennie Breeze," the voice on the phone said. "Tara's mom?"

"Mrs. Breeze?" Matt said.

"Jennie."

"Is Tara all right?" It was the first thing he thought of. Something had now happened to Tara as well.

"She's all right, she's . . . getting along. She's . . ." Jennie Breeze's voice trailed off and then she began speaking again, this time very quickly. "Listen, I was calling because Mike Herndon at the pool told me you won't be working for him this summer and I thought, well, I wanted to talk to you about working for me. Are you looking for a job?"

"I wasn't looking," he said very slowly. "But I need one." He didn't understand. She was calling to offer him a job? A job?

"I need someone to help me in my home office, just for the summer. I run a small business organizing high school reunions. It's a lot of grunt work. Basic things—data entry, stuffing envelopes, some phone work. Can you type at all?" She sounded almost like a talking classified ad. He struggled to keep up with her pace.

"I do all my schoolwork on the computer."

"Good. The other thing I need to know is do you mind being around babies? I don't know if you know this or not but I have a newborn so it's pretty chaotic."

"I have two little sisters. I know how to change diapers and give bottles, all those things."

"Don't worry! That won't be part of the job. I just want to make sure you won't mind being around a baby all day."

"No," he said. "I love babies."

"Great," Jennie Breeze said. She was silent for a moment and Matt felt perhaps he should have said more. He couldn't understand why in the world she would be offering him a job anyway. As if he were a normal teenage kid needing a normal summer job.

"Look Matt," she said, finally slowing down. "I don't want to pretend this isn't a terrible time for you. I know it is. I know what it's like to feel that things are falling apart." She paused and he heard her inhale deeply. The exhale was silent. "I don't know you that well," she continued, "but you struck me as very smart and hardworking and I'd love to have you come work for me if you want to but if you're not up to this right now, don't feel like you have to. We could try it for two weeks and see how it goes. Do you want to think about it and call me back?"

"No, no," Matt said quickly. "I don't want to think about it." He knew if he waited he would be too afraid to call her back. "I want to do it. Very much. Thank you. Thank you very much. I just need to talk to my mom first."

"I've already cleared it with her."

"Oh." Matt was slightly disappointed that she hadn't come directly to him—yet again people were talking about him, rather than to him.

After hanging up he went downstairs to find Mom anyway. It was the first time since breakfast that he had left his room; he had worked furiously on his schoolwork all day and had told Mom he needed to skip lunch to work on some history research. She was at the counter chopping vegetables, with Em wrapped around her legs while Katie sang "Old McDonald" and scrubbed potatoes.

Mom turned from the sink and asked, "So?" with a hopeful expression on her face. He had noticed how attendant she was these days to his every word or glance, always turning full attention to him if he entered the room. *I am here for you; talk to me.* It was too much. He would have rather been there at her feet, barely noticed, mildly annoying and mildly amusing but absolutely loved, like Em.

Then Mom made it easier by asking, "Are you going to do it?" so that all he had to do was say, "Yes." He didn't want to talk about it, didn't want his life to become evermore this thing about which people—his parents or Jennie Breeze or Mr. Finchley or anyone in the town—could say whatever they liked while Matt stayed in his room barely living it. He couldn't stand that he had become someone people spoke about, everyone with a label for him—*that reckless kid, that murderer.* None of it was private anymore, not a thing about his life was his except that thing he would not share—the reason they had died. His lust. His groping hands and eyes. And that he would never tell, just pay for.

"Do you want to work on deboning the fish, Matt?" Mom asked and Matt nodded, going to get the paper parcel from the refrigerator. This was the way his parents usually talked to their kids; this was the way he was comfortable with.

He worked on the fish then set the table, and there was time for a game of Candyland with Em before dinner. As he went about his chores he was suddenly seized with terror at having accepted Jennie Breeze's job. He was going to have to leave this house. After all that had happened, this house, with its rented furniture and wallpaper Mom would never have chosen, where they'd lived for less than six months, had become the safe place and now (was he ready, could he do this?) he was going to have to go back into the world.

JENNIE

THE DAY HE FIRST came into her house, he stood there in his ironed shirt and khaki pants and tie (her heart almost broke at that), holding all of his sadness and guilt in her foyer, saying not a word, and she was certain this had been the biggest mistake of her life.

What did she honestly think she could do for this boy? He was nothing like the boy she remembered. Of course he wasn't. She panicked at the responsibility she'd taken on, thinking the thoughts she had when she went into labor. *I've changed my mind; Jesus, this is too hard. This wasn't a good idea at all.*

The days since she'd offered him the job had passed at the same hobbling, sleepless pace of every day of life with a newborn, the indistinguishable hours of days and nights filling themselves with the attentive repetition of feeding, holding, rocking, bathing, changing, feeding, feeding, feeding Alison. By the time it came for Matt to actually begin working for her, it seemed she might only have dreamed that that was to happen.

Tara had by then struggled through her last days of school and taken her finals; it had felt like child abuse to let her go to school those last few days, her eyes sunken from so much crying, her skin a terrifying gray. On the last day of school she came home and went to bed at 5:00, sleeping all the way until noon the following day. After that, something changed in her, slightly, and for the better. Once she stopped having to walk the school hallways she had walked with Erica and Rachel; once she no longer needed to dig her books out of the locker they had all shared; once she was able to get up each morning and leave with Chris for her summer job instead of school, Jennie was sure that she saw a tiny fraction of weight lift from Tara's shoulders.

Matt was ten minutes early that first day. She realized how she must look now, dark crescents under her eyes, her hair piled up lopsided on her head. She was wearing yesterday's Oxford shirt, wrinkled and barely buttoned.

She filled the silence with her own talk.

"I've been up for hours," she told Matt, "but you can see how ready I am. This baby would not sleep all night and I'm trying to . . ." She motioned toward the living room floor where Alison, placed on a blanket squarely in the middle of the floor, arms flung out at right angles to her body, was suddenly fast asleep.

"I don't believe this," she said. "I've been doing waltzes around this room to get her to go to sleep and now she's out like a light. But come in, come in." After putting a blanket over Alison she led Matt into the kitchen.

"Does this need to be refrigerated?" Jennie asked, all but prying the brown paper lunch bag from his hands. She felt the weight of an apple, a reminder that he was someone's little boy.

"Please help yourself to soda, snacks, whatever. If I ever get to the grocery store again we'll actually have those things in our house and the offer will mean something. And the bathroom is just there, off the kitchen, or there's another one between the bedrooms. On the other side of the living room. And now you know everything there is to know about this house. Except for the office. It's just this way." She saw him eye the piles and piles of folders in the office, and said, "It's not as disorganized as it looks. I'm pretty meticulous about work. It's just everything else that's in shambles."

He still hadn't spoken except for his initial hello. He nodded politely, but his face, which she remembered as unusually expressive for a teenager, remained as impassive as slate.

"Where to begin?" she pressed on, wanting to get through as much as she could while Alison was asleep. Her nervousness and exhaustion gave her a kind of manic energy. She had Matt sit down at the table as she showed him her coding system. "Active means I'm corresponding with the reunionees now," she said, "at whatever stage that may be. I start a year and a half in advance, though I've got many more scheduled beyond that. The most pressing one now is Sheldrake '80. It's just a month away so we'll be doing a big mailing of confirmations later this week, plus there'll be lots of last-minute details with the caterer, the florist, the deejay, et cetera. But for now I thought I'd start you on St. Bernard's, class of 1950. That reunion's in September, just after Labor Day. I've got tons of responses to enter and acknowledge. Tons. You can't believe how far behind I've been, so I'm really glad you're here."

He continued nodding, but she had no way of knowing if he really understood. Once he was actually working, though, she could see how quickly he had picked things up. While he sat at the computer, entering details into the database, she went to work on retrieving the latest entries from her answering machine. She glanced over at him every so often and saw that he was working through the stack like lightning. She found his diligent presence somehow both calming and motivating, and she felt she was doing her first real work since Alison's birth.

"This is strange," Matt suddenly said. "St. Bernard's is in Connecticut but it seems every third or fourth guy lives in Arizona now. Do you suppose one of them went out there and encouraged the others to follow?"

"Ah," Jennie said. "They're all retired, you see. It's a golden reunion. They're sixty-eight years old, so they'll head for warm climates. You'll see something completely different with the Sheldrake '80s. They're thirty-eight, most of them hitting the peak of their careers, settling down with families. The majority are still on the East Coast, a lot of them here in Connecticut. A few are abroad, or elsewhere. California is popular. My sister's out there. It's her class reunion so I'm familiar with a lot of the names."

"Is your sister coming to the reunion?"

"Undetermined. You'll have to let me know if you get a response from her. Stephanie Northrop, Interactive Media Goddess."

Matt laughed.

"I'm serious. That's the name of her company. It's registered everywhere by its initials, IMG, but I swear that's what it stands for. Half the things she says are initials anyway. She's the queen of it. 'You got your VRIs and your IPOs and I've got to get in touch with every RSM' and then her cell phone rings. It's like having a conversation with alphabet soup."

Matt laughed again and then the phone rang.

"Connie, finally!" Jennie said when she picked up the phone in the kitchen. It was the Sheldrake '80 caterer, whom she had been trying to get in touch with for days. Jennie wound the phone cord into the kitchen and tried to block out Alison's wakeup cries while she and Connie talked about relish trays and hors d'oeuvres.

"Is that your kid?" Connie asked. "Do you need to get him?"

"No, it's okay," Jennie murmured guiltily. "What's the price per bite if we have four hundred there?"

The call lasted a long time, and when it ended, Jennie realized that Alison's cries had too. She went out to the living room to find Alison with Matt, on the couch. He held her on his knees and was singing to her. "Edelweiss," in a deep strong voice. Alison stared at him, transfixed. Something about the pose reminded Jennie of Chris. It was the way he used to hold Tara when she was a baby, on his knees like that. And Chris had been only a couple of years older than Matt when he held his first baby daughter in his arms.

"Thanks a million, Matt," Jennie whispered. "It never fails—the minute you've got an important call she wakes up." She spoke slowly as well as softly, just watching them.

"What's her name?" Matt asked.

"Alison. Alison Grace."

"Hello, tiny Alison," he said to the baby. And then to Jennie: "She's so unbelievably tiny."

"I know. It's so amazing when they're out in the world but still almost small enough to fit in your body."

"Does she look like Tara did?" he asked.

Jennie was surprised by the ease with which he mentioned Tara's name. "Not so much," she answered. "Alison has a different look to her. Her features are larger."

"My mom has these pictures of all of us at the exact same age hanging on the wall in our house—our real house, I mean, our house in Oregon, not the house here—and nobody can tell us apart except for Mom. Not even Dad."

Alison had seemed happy but now she squirmed a little, seeming more and more frantic.

"She hears my voice," Jennie told Matt. "I'm going to have to go feed her. If the phone rings, would you mind taking a message?"

"No problem," Matt said.

She stared at them a moment longer, then took the baby from Matt. He passed her over gently, supporting her head, smiling at her.

So this would be all right, Jennie was thinking as she lifted Alison in her own arms. The baby would carry them through. It hadn't been a terrible idea. They would all be fine.

MATT

JENNIE HAD CALLED IT drudge work but it wasn't so bad. His fingers flew over the keyboard and he liked reading what people had to say about their lives. He was always interested in the little patterns he saw. "Look," he'd call to Jennie, "six of the Sheldrake '80s have become engineers and married dental hygienists."

He learned quickly that Jennie had a fascination with names and tried to point out the interesting ones to her. The St. Bernie's class of 1950 was good for little-old-man types of names, names that sounded to Matt like they should be from some Flannery O'Connor or Eudora Welty story. *Ambrose Clemmo. Byno Thibaud.* "Look at this," he said. "A Schmeckabier and a Schmeckpepper in the same class."

"Big German population, I guess," Jennie said.

She loved the names that sounded medieval or Shakespearean, romantic in a way. He found a Gabriel D'Arcangelo for her, a Serenissima Luce, a Jacob Caliban. "Oh my," Jennie said, "Mr. Caliban must be destined to speak in rhyming couplets."

Matt's favorite task came when Jennie let him track down lost alumni, calling all seven Sue Johnsons in Hartford, Connecticut, to find out which one had graduated from Hill Top High in 1981. Jennie made him keep a log of how many phone minutes it took to find somebody. She wanted to know exactly how much everything cost.

Jennie was a funny combination of being really meticulous and organized about work and very lax about her house, which was always a mess, with dishes in the sink and a laundry basket on the couch and baby spit-up cloths draped everywhere like doilies. Half the time he was sure she wore yesterday's clothes. It was oddly sexy to him. He pictured her dropping her clothes on the floor when she got into bed and then stepping back into them in the morning. Sometimes he was sure she must have slept in them. She was so different from Tara, who was so tiny and neat. Jennie was curvy with these astounding breasts.

And of course Matt never actually saw Tara herself at Jennie's. He didn't know if she purposefully planned to miss him or if that's just how it turned out. It didn't feel right to ask Jennie about Tara. At first he was burning to know things about Tara—if she liked to stretch out on the couch where he sometimes sat with Alison, which chair she sat in at the kitchen table, which of the CDs piled next to the stereo were hers—but as the days started to go by, he thought of it as Jennie's house or his office, the place where he worked, together with Jennie and Alison, eight hours a day, five days a week.

Jennie had an amazing collection of books, all stuffed into bookshelves that lined each room, and she began loaning them to him— books he would have never known to read, books they talked about when they took their lunch break each day.

He was glad Jennie Breeze's house was clear on the other side of town, because it meant a long ride each way, every day, five days a week, the colors of the houses snapping at his senses, the arches of the trees that lined the older streets tunneling him to a possible future. It felt fantastic to be on the bike, riding through town, seeing more than his backyard or a dim view down the street from his bedroom.

All in all, she gave him long bike rides and work to do, a baby to hold occasionally, books to read, two hundred dollars a week and Mom's optimistic face when he walked in the door at the end of the day and she asked, "So how was work?"

And that was his life now. Not his old life, nothing like that—but *a life,* which was far more than he deserved.

JENNIE

J ENNIE'S HANDS SHOOK as she let herself back into the house, and once inside she leaned against the door, trying to steady herself before going any farther. Her heart, every pulse point, beat together, loudly, rapidly, audibly she was sure. No matter how many times she said, *I'm not going to let her get to me,* her mother always did.

She had just been out to lunch with Fay, and they had had a fight that began when Fay found out that Jennie had hired Matt.

Jennie hadn't wanted her mother to get hold of this fact, but Fay kept pressing *(Who was it that answered the phone? Where did you find him? What's his name?).* It occurred to Jennie to lie, but how could she do that? Make up a name?

"You've brought him into your *home?*" Fay asked when Jennie told her. "A drunk driver? A messed-up kid, at the very least. And a *baby* in the house!" They had been sitting at one of Fay's favorite restaurants and Jennie felt just as she did when she was nine years old and being scolded for wearing the wrong shoes with a dress.

"What do other people think about this?" Fay continued. "After what he did? He came from that sheltered lifestyle, that home-school deal, so of course he's going to let loose when he's out in the real world. He hasn't had a normal upbringing, he's not going to act normal and now look at the devastation he's brought on this community."

"That may be the way some people see it," Jennie said calmly, quietly, "but that's not how it is." Fay held a forkful of endive midair, shaking her head.

"Jennie?" Matt asked now, appearing in the hallway where she still clung to the doorway. "Are you all right?"

"I'm all right," she said. Matt took the baby seat from Jennie's arms and set it gently on the floor.

"You seem sort of shaky," he said.

"That was my mother," Jennie said. "She does this to me." Jennie crossed the floor to the couch and sank down on it. Matt followed her.

Jennie had tried to end the discussion with her mother by saying, "Look Mom, I'm sorry you disapprove, but I don't think this accident should ruin his life. It's as simple as that. He's young and it's a terrible thing, but I'm trying to help him through it."

"Well, that's admirable," Fay had said, "but sometimes people do do things that ruin their lives and you can't help them." There was a pause and then Fay said, "Look at you. Pregnant at eighteen and look what that's done to your life."

"I didn't . . . ruin my life," Jennie had struggled to say.

"Tell me this is what you'd be doing, this little reunion deal, living in that boxcar house, married to a gardener? Is this how you would be living if you hadn't gotten pregnant?" Fay delivered this blow with a voice so calm there was no way Jennie could match it.

"You're really good at that, aren't you, Mom?" she had said, voice thick and desperate. "Just trash my whole life, why don't you?"

"Don't put any responsibility for that on me, Jennifer. You took care of that yourself." For the first time in her life, Jennie feared she would actually slap her mother, slap that placid smile right off her face. But it was something she had never done. Could never, ever do. Her mother wouldn't have stood for it. What would Fay do if Jennie blew up at her? It wasn't difficult to imagine her mother calmly walking away. Too much bother; she had another daughter; she had other commitments. Appointments. Reservations.

Recalling Fay's words brought tears to her eyes and she blinked rapidly, trying to make them evaporate. She couldn't believe herself, falling apart in front of the boy she was supposed to be helping. "Sorry, Matt," she said, "you're seeing my childhood awfully close to the surface."

"It's okay," Matt said. Jennie wished he would just go back to work. This was absurd. She knew she should get up and walk into her bedroom, collect herself there instead of in front of Matt, but somehow she couldn't move. And he didn't either.

She remembered something Matt's mother, Belinda, had said when Jennie first talked to her about hiring him: "I wouldn't let him come if

I didn't know he was strong enough to handle it. Matt's a special kid. We may only have been able to see him for sixteen years but he's got a soul that has been around much longer than that."

"You're very lucky," Jennie said now, to Matt. "To have such a close-knit family. You may not realize it yet but it's rare. A real gift."

Matt opened his mouth to say something, then let out a little sigh. "I know I'm lucky," he said, but with more resignation than pride. "Mom and Dad have dedicated so much of their lives to making us . . . well, Mom once told me that she didn't think people should abandon their children to the vagaries of the world. Once Pastor Tim—this was at our old church in Oregon—Pastor Tim gave this whole sermon centered around that phrase, 'It takes a village'—you've heard that, right?—and while he was talking, Mom wrote 'baloney' down on an offering slip and handed it to me." He smiled at the memory. "She said the village doesn't care, that maybe it used to care, but now parents are the only ones who care enough, or should care enough, will do enough and sacrifice enough for their children. She says it was different in preindustrialized society—if you talk to my mom for more than five minutes you'll hear her say something about the industrial revolution—but now, she says, if you depend on the village you'll end up with vagrants and tramps."

"Do you agree?" Jennie asked. She was feeling a little bit like a villager at that moment.

"I haven't decided yet. My parents aren't trying to make us robots or anything, little repositories of everything they believe. On the contrary, they're always trying to get us to think for ourselves. They're always saying, 'God gave you a brain so you wouldn't have to use mine.' It's just that they expect a lot. I mean, they give a lot too. They give *everything,* but they expect us to do the same thing." Matt leaned his head against the back of the couch and closed his eyes. "They talk in capital letters a lot. Truth. Honor. The Spirit."

"Ah," Jennie said quietly. This was the first time he had opened up about his family. She didn't want to interrupt him now that he was going.

"I think that's why they just don't know what to do now that the accident . . . happened. They can't figure out what to do for me. They never planned for anything like this and now that it's happened they just can't believe—" He suddenly stopped, changed tacks. "I was doing this report once on domestic violence and what I could never understand was why women would stay with men who beat them. It just didn't make sense. I couldn't understand it at all—these reasonable, intelligent women, most of them with children, letting these men beat them. The more I thought about it the more I couldn't understand. Then I came upon the idea that they just couldn't believe it was happening. That's why they couldn't leave, because there was no way it could be happening to them." Matt paused again. "It's the same with my parents. They just don't know what to do because they never dreamed one of their kids could do something so awful."

"Oh Matt, they just want to protect you, rescue you. Like all parents, they want to keep you from harm."

"I'm not saying that they're angry at me. They just can't believe it's happened and they want me to tell them what to do, how to act, but I don't know either. It's not fair to them. They've put so much into me and I've tried to do what they wanted and now I think, What have they got left? They're going to have to pay all these legal bills and we may have to stay in Connecticut and everything . . . it's all ruined."

"It's not *ruined*, Matt." Jennie sighed and said, "Listen, my mom just used that phrase on me. And she was totally wrong. It's not the same thing at all, I know it's not the same, but when I was a couple of years older than you I got pregnant with Tara and there was no question for me at the time of abortion. No question. And, well, I can't tell you how much it changed my life. I was at the University of Chicago. I was ambitious, I had all these plans, and having Tara changed everything. I did all sorts of crummy jobs and it took me eight years to get through a second-rate college and another five years to get a master's and my life today is nothing like I had planned, but the point is"—and here Jennie felt herself arguing with her invisible mother—"my life was not ruined. It changed. Totally. But it's not like your life is some perfect pristine thing, some line from point A to B and things that happen, mistakes you make are little bumps shooting off to the side. They're part of your life. They determine your life." *Oh God,* Jennie thought, *just stop talking. It's the same thing you do with Tara. Just keep your mouth shut about your own damned life.* "What I think," Jennie said, "what I think is it will take a long time for you to get *through* this.

You'll never get *over* it and it will change you in ways you or your family would never have imagined but you'll always be you."

As soon as Jennie stopped talking, she felt, rather than saw or heard, the shaking of his body. Like the tremors signaling an earthquake, they were detectable, not threatening.

He was gripping himself by the shoulders and she studied his hands, thick-fingered and strong, as they tightened their hold. He had large hands, larger than hers: a man's hands. She wondered for maybe the first time what it would be like to have a son instead of daughters, a son who had grown up into a man but was still a boy. You took your daughters into your arms. But what about mothers and their teenage sons, she wondered absurdly, what did they do?

She put a hand on his shoulder and it seemed to her that was the thing that made him let go.

"That's it," he said, and with the words came a heaving sob. "I could go on, sometimes I feel that I can go on. I could have this . . . *life*. But they can't. They *can't*."

"Matt, refusing to live your life isn't going to bring them back," she said.

"No, but it makes it more fair. If I go to jail . . . I need to pay. I need to pay for what I did."

"Oh, you're paying, sweetie. You're paying."

He was weeping now and Jennie, mother of two daughters, opened her arms to him and held him like a son. His head was against her breastbone and she felt his tears soaking through her shirt. How he clung to her, this boy who felt like a man. This boy who desperately needed a mother, and anyone's but his own would do.

MATT

H E HELD ALISON on his knees and let her pull at his pinkies with her fists. She grunted and strained, as if she were trying to do tiny sit-ups. She was so strong already. That she had been born on the day Rachel and Erica died made him feel forever connected to her. He wanted to know her all her life, see how she grew, what she turned into, help her with problems she might have. It was a feeling he couldn't name, different than the one he had for his little sisters, because with them, of course, he would know, he would be there, it was obligatory, while with Alison he'd have to decide to stay in her life.

Alison just would not give him a moment to work this afternoon. It was something to do with her eyes: He could put her down but he couldn't break eye contact or she would immediately jut out her lower lip and prepare to cry. Her eyes were so wide open, lenses collecting every bit of light there was to be had. She fixed on his eyes with a frenzied, groping attachment. He had read somewhere—maybe in one of Mom's old baby books—that infants developed one sense at a time. If so, Alison was definitely working on sight. She looked and looked and looked.

He hadn't done much since Jennie left for her doctor's appointment. He'd gotten good at working at the computer with Alison on his lap, and he was able to sort mail or stuff envelopes and still hang onto her, but with the eye contact thing it was impossible to do anything except answer phone calls. Jennie had said, "Don't worry about anything. If I come home and she's happy that's all I care about," but he still felt guilty for not getting any work done.

Alison was looking at him as if she were waiting for him to tell her the secret of life.

"I'm trying, girl," he said. "I'm trying. You're just asking too much.

Here, look out the window. See the pretty birdie? That's a cardinal."

That seemed to delight her for about seven seconds. She paused for a moment to take it in, legs kicking, arms rolling and head bobbing, that big gummy smile that made her kind of look like a retarded person who didn't realize that the other kids were laughing at him, not with him. The kind of smile, in other words, that broke your heart.

Alison noticed right away that Matt's eyes had strayed from hers and she started to wail.

"Okay, okay, I get it," he said.

He wondered what she was thinking. *If* she was thinking. He had read something last night about there being no difference between the place before life began and the place after it ended. "A brief crack of light between two elements of darkness," the author Vladimir Nabokov had said. *Speak Memory.* Jennie had loaned him the book because he had mentioned that he loved biographies and she said she preferred memoirs or journals because they seemed truer. She had given him *Speak Memory* and *The Journals of John Cheever* and a volume from *The Diary of Virginia Woolf,* but he had started with *Speak Memory,* and he loved it, right from the opening line: "The cradle rocks above the abyss."

Matt wondered if the place Alison had come from was indeed the same place Erica and Rachel had gone. He wondered if they'd brushed by one another that night, those two dead girls and this baby. And what was his place in it? He'd read somewhere—Norse mythology? Homer? the Arthurian legends?—about warriors taking on the souls of all those they had killed in battle, the bravest as heavy as ships moving through the sea.

The connections between the dead and the living had never troubled him so much before. It had seemed so clear, always, the way he was taught in Sunday school and at home: that to die was to be reunited with God. He imagined he must have asked Mom and Dad the questions he heard Katie and Em ask them now: *Where will my face be when I die? Can you talk in heaven, 'cause I know I'll want to talk? Is it the same heaven for Oregon and Connecticut?* At some time he had just come to accept it all, but the problem now was two problems. What happened if death came too soon? It wasn't God's will that they had died. He knew that. Not God's will but his own stupidity. And now, if he had a life, which it seemed he did again, what was it to be like for him when he died?

Alison's eyes, perhaps from staring at his for so long, had finally closed. He decided to risk putting her down so he could get back to work, and he quietly carried her down the hall to her bassinet. The bassinet got wheeled from room to room all day depending on where she needed to be, but now it was in Jennie's bedroom so he put her in there. He felt a little strange going into Jennie's bedroom while she was gone. The bed was unmade but the shades were open so he walked across the floor to close them. He felt uncomfortable being there, because even for the bassinet and the changing table wedged in a corner and the piles of clean and dirty baby clothes and spit-up cloths and diapers, he still thought of it as Jennie's bedroom. Jennie's bed. The place where Jennie and her husband slept together. Made love.

He had never met Jennie's husband, Chris, but there was a picture of him with Jennie on their dresser. They looked so young. And so happy. She had on a white miniskirt and her hair was curlier than now. Her legs were brown and her bare arms too. Chris had on a peach shirt and was even more tanned than she. They held amber bottles of beer and they looked at each other with the biggest smiles he had ever seen—looked at each other, not at the camera, yet the camera had captured those smiles. From the clues he deduced that they were at a party, it was summer, and it was a long time ago—maybe when they were first in love, maybe even all the way back in high school. They looked young and happy and Matt feel deep swords of longing in his groin. He wondered, was it possible to miss something you'd never known? But that's what he wanted, to feel whatever they must have felt as they looked at each other; he wanted it so badly and yet he didn't even have a taste of what it was about. It was something he wanted, but now a way he'd never feel, a life he'd never live.

He tiptoed out of Jennie's room. With Alison sound asleep he'd finally be able to get some work done. But first.

But first he stepped inside Tara's room, another thing he'd never done before. It was a dark pinkish-purple room and smelled recently painted. Nothing was hung on the walls yet but on the floor, leaning against the walls, were a mirror and some plaques and one of those photo collages ready to be hung. He crouched down to look at the pictures. Tara and her parents, Tara and Rachel, Tara and Erica. There was one of the three of them—Tara standing up with a curling iron, curling Erica's hair, Erica sitting in a chair curling Rachel's. How much he had already forgotten their faces; how comforting it had been to picture them vaguely instead of exactly.

Where Jennie's room made him want to linger, Tara's felt like a tomb. Perhaps because he had not seen Tara since the accident he had come to think of her as dead too.

He went out to the office again, started checking the e-mail, finishing in no time and turning to the mail. He realized he was waiting for Jennie to breeze in. He always thought of it that way, like a Tom Swiftie: Jennie Breeze. It was sort of a made-up name anyway. Jennie had told him that Chris's last name was Brezione and hers was Northrop and when they got married she hadn't wanted to change her name for feminist reasons but hadn't wanted to keep her old name "for reasons of disinheritance," so they had together decided to anglicize Chris's Italian name and become Jennie and Chris Breeze. He liked that a lot.

When Jennie did come home he showed her the three last-minute Sheldrake response cards he had opened and asked, "Are you still accepting these? I know the deadline was last Friday."

"You have to have deadlines or they don't respond at all. We even accept them at the door if they've got cash. You wouldn't believe how many people try to crash their own reunions. The losers." When she picked up the three responses she said, "Hey, this is from my sister. She didn't even write a note. Typical. At least she's coming."

"Oh, I have another name for you," Matt said. "John Midwinter."

"Oh my. Oh my. Please tell me he's sixty-eight and an insurance salesman. If you tell me he's a twenty-eight-year-old painter I'd be forced to divorce my husband for him sight unseen."

"He's a St. Bernie's."

"Oh, thank God. John Midwinter. Isn't that gothic and puritanical."

"Like 'In the Bleak Midwinter,' " Matt said, and started to sing the song.

"You have a gorgeous voice, young Matt," Jennie said.

"Thanks. I used to sing in the choir back home."

"Is there anything you can't do?"

"Drive a car," Matt said, realizing instantly that his attempt at a joke had failed. How self-pitying he sounded. Just yesterday he had wept in her arms and she had been so comforting, her inherent kindness rising to the surface like a human breath, up like warm air. He didn't want to do this again. He had to get a grip on himself. She was his boss, after all.

"Can I ask you something?" he asked quickly.

"Sure."

"It's about *Speak Memory*. There's a line you had marked and when I came to it I wondered about it too. 'The spiral is a spiritualized circle.' I've been trying to work it out."

"Just because I underlined it doesn't mean I understood it. It probably means I didn't." Jennie paused. "I remember that line ringing in my head for a long time though. He talks about his life in three stages, right? Thesis, antithesis, synthesis?"

"Yes, twenty years in Russia, twenty years in exile in Europe and then twenty years in America."

"But it's the exile years he wrote about most?"

"Right. It reminded me of a kind of triptych. That's how I could visualize it. Mom took us to look at some at the Cloisters when we first got here. Have you been there?"

"No."

"They have an amazing collection of religious art, medieval art. These triptychs I can visualize, three separate pieces of art, yet functioning as one. The spiral image I just don't get. You know how something sounds so good sometimes but you just don't quite get it?" He knew he wasn't expressing himself very clearly, but she was nodding, agreeing.

"That's exactly how I felt about that image. Still do. A colored spiral in a bowl of glass or something? The spiritualized circle. I always felt my own definition of spiritual was lacking somehow and that was my problem with the quote." She smiled. "I guess you'll just have to go to some top-notch college and have some brilliant professor explicate it for you and come back and tell me all about it. I'll probably still be here, stuffing envelopes." Jennie laughed that great laugh of hers—the one that made you want to do anything you could to hear it again.

"Have you ever thought of going somewhere else? Besides Connecticut, I mean?"

"All the time. I have lived here all my life, you know."

"Where would you go?"

"My dream is to do a Ph.D. program, just pick up and move everyone to, I don't know, Ann Arbor or Berkeley or Chapel Hill, North Carolina."

"Why don't you?"

"Complicated." She seemed reluctant to say more and sighed. "Tara has two more years of high school for one thing, and Chris, he runs his landscape business here. You can't move a business like that and start over, it would be . . . ridiculous." Jennie dropped her eyes; she was speaking almost as if they were someone else's words in her mouth. "It's not that easy at this point to change things, at a moment's notice. It would have made more sense for us to break away years ago, when we first got married. It just didn't occur to us then . . ." Her voice trailed off and she turned back to her work.

They heard Alison's cries from the other room and Jennie said, "How long did she sleep?"

Matt looked at his watch. "Just under an hour."

"Not bad." Jennie went in to get Alison and brought her back, rocking her gently in her arms.

"I think she's hungry," Jennie said.

Alison was making that mouth like you'd just hurt her feelings, then opening and closing it like a little bird. And then she started to do that eye thing again so Matt smiled at her and bent down to kiss her cheek.

He wondered how much of loving someone was just learning to recognize her gestures and expressions, so that each time a familiar one appeared you were drawn in deeper, each one taking you closer to love.

JENNIE

A DATE. Jennie hadn't been out alone with Chris since Alison's birth and she found herself remembering even the hours they shared when she was in labor with great fondness.

She was nervous, in a way, about tonight: what dress to wear, what earrings. She smiled to herself as she nursed Alison because she knew something that Chris didn't.

She had gone to Dr. Perrin that afternoon for her postnatal checkup. "Your cervix is completely back to normal," Dr. Perrin told her after examining her. "You'd never know you had a baby seven weeks ago." Jennie had scoffed, looking down at her stomach, the brown line from her pregnancy rising over the bulging terrain of her belly, picking up again on the other side of her craterous belly button. "Inside, at least," Dr. Perrin said. "The cervix is so resilient. It's a prime feature of the female anatomy."

"So everything's okay?" Jennie asked. "We can start having sex again?"

"You've got the go-ahead," Dr. Perrin said, laughing, "if you can find the time."

And all day Jennie had carried this around, one of those rare tingly secrets of the long-married, wanting to save it as a surprise.

But at the rate they were going, their date would start at midnight. Before they left, Jennie had to finish nursing Alison, express milk to leave for the next feeding, find some clothes to fit her body, put on makeup and get Alison to sleep.

Chris popped his head in and asked, "About ready?"

Jennie rolled her eyes. "I think she's done if you want to try to put her down." When he bent down for Alison, she took in a deep whiff of the cologne he always wore when they *went out.* It was the same bottle of Aramis she had given him in high school and it had had about a half an inch in it for the last seven years. Always, every time, it stirred her.

She went to the bathroom to put on her makeup and for the first time in weeks, she spent more than ten seconds looking at herself in the mirror.

In general Jennie did not feel old, and thirty-four did not sound that old to her, but when she looked in the mirror all she saw was a collection of flaws that told her she was no longer young. She could remember when aging had set in like slow erosion. At twenty-six, those lines stretching from her nose to the corners of her mouth. At thirty-one, the first hint of lines around her eyes that didn't go away once she'd stopped smiling. Crow's feet—how she hated that term. And now, since the baby had come, she had what looked like coffee stains under her eyes. She had persisted in thinking a good night's sleep would make them disappear but it seemed as if the pigment in her skin had actually changed. The girl behind the cosmetics counter at the drugstore had shaken her head sadly and said, *Mother's mask*—she couldn't remember if it was permanent or if it faded, and Jennie was too depressed to try to find out. The girl sold her some powder, which helped only slightly.

You'd never know you had a baby seven weeks ago, Dr. Perrin had said. *Ha,* Jennie said to the mother's mask in the mirror. *Ha ha.*

Only seven weeks. Seven weeks since Alison's birth and Jennie's body had healed to the point where she could have another baby. Seven weeks since Rachel's and Erica's deaths and Tara's wounds were just opening, would continue to open for months and years, would possibly never heal.

How could it be that the human body was so different from the human heart? Had God expended all the intricacies of healing—the bruises and scabs, the shrinking and swelling and regeneration—all the tricks of the trade only He practiced, before He reached that organ?

Jennie had a sudden surge of love for Tara that made her want to run to the other room and hold her. But Tara was so far away—even farther now, gone all day at work and then absent in another way when she was home. Evenings, she lay on the couch and watched TV. If she went anywhere it was to Rachel's parents' house, returning in such a tranquil state that Jennie wanted to weep for whatever Tara was telling Camille but could not tell her.

It plagued her, this not knowing, this not having any window into her daughter's grief. Chris was no help. *She'll be all right,* he said again and again when Jennie pummeled him with questions about what Tara did, what Tara said, how she *seemed,* each day at work. *You can't go through this for her,* he kept telling Jennie. *She has to go through it herself.*

Jennie had always found that one of the hardest parts of being a mother—allowing Tara distance to live her life. She was amazed that this life she and Chris had created out of pure nothing had grown into one they knew almost nothing about. Progressing from knowing each time your daughter pooped and peed and cried and moved her limbs to not having access to a single thought or feeling she had was almost unbearable. Children taught you how to love them and then began to leave. Jennie thought it would make more sense for it to work the other way so that as your ability to love deepened, so did their need for it.

Chris knocked on the door again.

"Five minutes," Jennie said. She finished her makeup and sat down to pump milk for Alison.

Would there be a time when every good evening, every happy or frivolous thought wouldn't be undermined by a serious one? Would she ever be able to plan an evening with Chris or tend to Alison or look at herself in the mirror without feeling that tide of worry for Tara rush in too?

At least tonight Tara had a friend coming over. Jennie had suggested it when she asked Tara to baby-sit and to her surprise, Tara said yes. Jennie let her heart go wild at the thought of Tara and Danielle making popcorn, watching a video, painting each other's toenails.

When Chris popped in again, she told him, "I'm so sick of this. Milking myself and smelling like animal fat."

He gave her a comical grimace. "I'll come back later," he said.

As always when she was in a hurry, the milk came slowly. Finally she yelled out the door to Chris, "Go. Sit in the car. I'll be there in two minutes."

He was sitting in the driver's seat drinking a beer, singing with the radio, when Jennie finally emerged from the house. She smiled tenderly. That was one of the hundreds of small things she loved about Chris—the way he always launched into harmony with whatever song came on.

They went to one of the only places in town where you could eat outside. Jennie would have preferred a sidewalk cafe in some romantic European city, but she settled for this table overlooking the brick fountain plaza of an office center. The evening was beautiful, warm, not humid, the kind of perfect summer evening there aren't enough of in Connecticut. It was just turning dark and the maître d' came around to light all the candles at the tables.

The luxury of sitting face-to-face with Chris somewhere that wasn't their messy, crowded little house made Jennie feel elated at first, and also a little shy. So often recently she had seen him only peripherally, coming and going, taking the baby or handing her a spit-up cloth. Now, it was the whole man confronting her. He looked gorgeous, his tan already deep by this point in the summer, his thick blond curls slightly bleached. He wore a faded denim shirt that was the same color blue as his eyes. As he reached across the table to take her hand she stared at the strong, dark forearm leading from his rolled-up sleeve. That had always been one of her favorite parts of his body.

"So," Chris said, "you're my wife?"

"I am," she said. "I haven't forgotten. I just haven't seen you in a while."

"Well, I'm seeing you now, and you look great."

"Thanks for saying it. It's nice that it's so dark you can't see the black circles under my eyes."

He smiled and said, "You look great, Jen. Really."

She was again surprised at her shyness, as if this were a blind date—something she'd never even had.

"How many times were you up with her last night?" Chris asked.

"Midnight. Two-thirty, four-thirty, but then she was *up,* up. She didn't nap until ten, and then only for about twenty minutes. Matt got her to sleep for an hour this afternoon though. While I was out." Jennie added this last line cautiously. She hadn't told Chris about the doctor's appointment, partly because she wanted to keep it a surprise, but also because she didn't know how he'd feel about Matt as a baby-sitter.

He frowned at her words, started to say something, frowned again, then spoke. "Do you really trust him that much? With Alison?"

"He's great with her. He knows exactly what to do. He's had all these little sisters and brothers, and on top of that I think he really just loves babies." Jennie was looking at Chris, trying to catch his eyes, but while she talked he was stirring his drink, staring hard at it.

"I've kind of stayed out of this, you know?" he said, taking his hand off of Jennie's. "This whole Matt thing. I know you think highly of him, but what if he has post-traumatic something-or-other and decides to snap one day when my daughter is with him?"

"He's not going to *snap*, Chris," Jennie said, irritated. "If you knew him, if you met him, you'd see. I'd trust him with Alison's life." As she spoke, Jennie was all too aware of how odd it must sound to Chris, how strange things had become this summer, when she could more accurately assess Matt's emotions—the feelings of a virtual stranger—than she could those of her own daughter.

Jennie reached for her napkin, crisp and pleated, dark maroon. It seemed the antithesis of her life.

Jennie felt the ever-present thump of worry for Tara grow louder, more insistent. "What about Tara?" she asked Chris.

"What about her?"

"How was she this week?"

"It's so busy at Martin's office that I don't think she has a chance to think about them all day."

"Well, that's got to be healthy," Jennie said, with more sarcasm than she intended. "I mean, doesn't she say anything to you in the car? On the way there, on the way home?"

"We talk about lots of things, but I don't think she mentions Rachel and Erica much."

"You *don't think?* Aren't you paying attention? Don't you ask?" Chris's nonchalance stoked her own anxiousness through her body at furious speed.

"Listen, Jen, you're leaving our baby daughter in the care of Mr. Reckless Homicide. I wouldn't worry too much about how I deal with Tara if I were you." The anger gathered like a cloud over Chris's eyes.

"Oh God," Jennie said. "This has turned disastrous pretty fast."

"Thank God the waiter's coming to save the day." As he spoke, Chris was half rising from his seat, gesticulating wildly toward the waiter who was paying them no attention. They both laughed and when Chris sat down again Jennie took his hand back in hers.

"I'm sorry," she said, putting his hand to her lips. "I love you and I'm sorry I sound like such a shrew."

"I'm sorry too," Chris said, and she saw that he meant it. This was a thing having children gave you. You might be quicker to temper, but you were always quicker to forgive.

"You don't have to worry about Matt, really you don't," she said. "I'm just on the defensive about him because I saw my mother yesterday and you can imagine the earful I got when she found out who he was."

"I hope you gave her an earful back," Chris said.

"I wish I could," Jennie said. She was still holding his hand up to her face and she nuzzled it a little bit. It smelled like soap and Aramis. The best smell she had ever smelled. She breathed him in deeply, feeling that ache and jump in her pelvis and thighs. She was tempted to say, *Let's skip dinner and go home to bed.*

The waiter came, finally, with menus and a basket of bread. Jennie was starving—it was almost nine o'clock. "Look at these seeded rolls," she said. "And they're hot too."

Chris laughed. "I guess we haven't been out in a while."

Jennie was almost glad they had gotten all the tense moments out of the way up front, because now they could chat, laugh, pass back and forth the dozens of little facts they had been saving up for when there was time.

Later, they walked arm in arm from the restaurant to the parking lot, and when Chris went to open the car door, Jennie pushed against him and gave him a deep kiss. His arms went immediately to her butt, her breasts, and they kissed against the car for a while, until Chris said, "God, Jen, you're killing me. What are you doing to me?"

"Want to go home?" she asked.

"Yes," he said quickly. "But I promised Frank we'd meet him. And we're late already."

"Why do you suppose they want to see us so urgently?"

"Maybe they want to tell us they're getting married," Chris guessed.

"No way. How many times have you heard Frank say he needs his freedom? He's only had like twenty-five girlfriends in the past five years."

Chris shook his head. "He's not that bad anymore. I think he's getting ready to settle down. Maybe Janet's the one."

In the bar, Jennie saw immediately that Chris was right. Janet ran toward them, flapping her ring hand in front of their eyes.

"Hey, look at that rock," Chris said.

"Congratulations, sweetie," Jennie said to Frank as he gave her one of his strong, full-armed hugs.

"We're doing it, Jen," Frank said. "We're really doing it."

"Have you set a date?" Jennie asked.

"Hold onto your hats," Janet said. "July fifteenth."

"This year," Frank said.

"Isn't that like in a couple of weeks?" Chris asked.

"Three," Jennie said. "That's the night of the Sheldrake '80 reunion."

"Oh, Jen, do you have to be there?" Frank asked. "We've put the deposit down on the hall. We wanted to ask Chris to be the best man."

"Maybe I can make the wedding, but I've got the reunion all night. Sorry."

"I know it's so—*instant*," Janet said, "but when we decided to do it we just decided, why not now?"

"Are you pregnant?" Chris asked.

"See, I told you everybody would think that, Frank," Janet said, punching him lightly on the arm.

"She's not, she's not. It was my idea, mostly," Frank said. "I know you guys are thinking, what has happened to this guy, believe me, but all of a sudden I knew I couldn't risk letting her get away. I just had this feeling one afternoon. What am I saying? It wasn't a feeling, it was a moment of complete and profound knowledge. I was at work and I left in the middle of the afternoon and drove over to her office and asked her. I just had to do it right then."

"But it's all worked out so perfectly," Janet said. "We had this vacation to Cape Cod planned already, so we'll just have the wedding the weekend before and call it a honeymoon."

"And Janet's lease is up August first. We were thinking of moving in together anyway but her mother would kill her for cohabiting, so if we get married there's no problem."

"I'm really happy for you guys," Chris said.

"It's going to be one hell of a party, I can tell you that," Frank said. "Hey, let's start now. Beer, Chris? Beer, Jen?"

Jennie and Chris sat on bar stools holding hands, drinking beers, hearing about the wedding plans and the honeymoon, talking about restaurants in Cape Cod and jet skiing and the beach. They didn't talk about Alison at all, they didn't talk about Tara or the accident or Matt. They were just one young couple out with another, celebrating, talking, toasting to future happiness. Frank and Janet seemed giddy with a happiness that helped Jennie to momentarily shed the anxiety and fatigue she had worn like a winter coat all summer.

Jennie would readily admit that marriage was a complete mystery to her. She had no idea why her own had succeeded, but only that when she looked up at Chris in the bar, feeling a little drunk, she wanted him so much she couldn't curl her fingers around her mug of beer. There was the physical attraction that had been there from the moment she first saw him in the halls of Sheldrake High, and there was the weight of all those years they had shared. And there was his utter ability to surprise her, as now in the bar when Frank asked them for advice about marriage. Jennie immediately said, "Beats me," but Chris asked the waitress for a pen and earnestly began a numbered list on a napkin. What was he writing? Jennie peeked and she saw he was taking his assignment seriously. It was dim in the bar but she could still read number one: *Don't sleep with anyone besides your wife.* So practical and sweet, so perfectly true in all its simplicity. So Chris.

At home, after Jennie nursed Alison she found Chris in the bedroom with two bottles of beer.

"I thought, why not just one more?" he asked.

Jennie took one of the beers and bent to kiss Chris on the lips.

"Do you want to make love?" she asked him.

"Can we?" he asked, eyes widening, his expression pure, undisguised desire. And then suddenly her marriage didn't seem a mystery at all, just a miracle in the way it could charge on without you for days or months and then suddenly reclaim you both for it, your love for each other hitting you again full force. Your marriage could separate itself from your family, from every crisis you both faced, and when you entered back into it that way, it was the sweetest next breath you could take.

MATT

W ASHING THE VANS had always been a family activity, all of the Fallons on the driveway with hoses and sponges and buckets—in warm weather, squirting and splashing until they were soaked to the skin. Katie and Em usually started with the interior because they were small enough to climb under seats looking for gum wrappers or hair barrettes. Then Brian or Matt would go in with the vacuum while Katie and Em got a bucket of warm, soapy water to scrub the floor mats. Peter liked to do the inside of the windows and somebody else would wipe down the seats before they closed up the vans and began the free-for-all outside. They were very thorough in their fun, and cleaning both vans took the better part of a Saturday morning, usually rewarded with Popsicles on the back patio afterward.

This Saturday, though, it was just Matt and Dad and one van in the driveway. Mom had taken the other kids to the beach. When Dad suggested they wash the green van, Matt was happy to have something to do, to be outside in the sunshine with a purpose. Matt got so edgy on the weekends. Mondays to Fridays were fine, filled with work that he enjoyed, but the weekends felt like a return to a cage after a reprieve for fresh air.

He was sweating like crazy inside the van. The weather had been in the nineties three days in a row and today promised to be no exception. He would give anything to be in the ocean right now, or a swimming pool, but all he was allowed was the sprinkler and Em's kiddie pool in the backyard. He missed swimming, missed those breaths that gave you no time to do anything but work on earning the next one.

After he finished with the vacuum he closed the van's doors and took a water break.

"Hot enough for you, Matt?" Dad asked, that question to which there was never any reasonable answer. When he nodded yes, Dad turned the hose on him full blast. Matt gave a yelp, then spun around to let the water cool him off.

"Thanks, Dad," he said.

"No problem." Dad joined him on the stoop. "So how are you doing, son?"

That was Dad's usual intro for a father-son talk. Matt felt more irritation than dread.

"I'm doing all right, Dad," he said slowly.

Dad nodded thoughtfully, as if Matt had said something worthy of consideration.

"It's hard for us to know . . . your mother and I . . . what's going through your head at times. You know we're here whenever you want to talk."

"I know," Matt said. "I'm all right, really. Just waiting, I guess." Matt usually had to say something in order for Dad to be a great listener, but he couldn't find anything to say now.

He had always brought his problems, his questions to Dad. When he was a kid, back in Oregon, he and Dad cleaned the leaves from the gutters in the late fall so the snow wouldn't collect and crack them in winter; they put in storm windows for the winter and screens for the summer; they hoisted the wrought-iron patio furniture up into the rafters of the garage after the first frost. He saw now that these occasions were as much for him to help Dad as they were for Dad to listen to whatever was on Matt's mind. *Dad, but how does the baby get inside Mommy's tummy? Where is the sewer system, Dad? Dad, if a man in a coma needs to have an operation, does he need anesthesia?*

How Dad must have secretly laughed at all Matt's solemn, childish questions. But he always answered everything seriously, thoroughly, and if he didn't know the complete answer, they would write the question on a Post-it note and stick it on the computer so they could search the CD-ROM encyclopedia later. Matt realized what a labor this had been for Dad, to make sure all of Matt's questions were answered. He knew whatever questions he asked now would be examined with every resource Dad could muster. But Matt couldn't ask anything. He couldn't begin. It was as if some chamber had closed off shortly after the accident. To open it now, to even utter some of the things he was thinking in the presence of Dad was impossible.

Dad was already worried enough about Matt's court date next week. During their last meeting with Mr. Finchley, Dad had slammed his fist on the table and said, "Why does it have to drag on? He's just a boy." Dad and Mom were always talking like that, as if Matt were the victim, as if these things were being done to him with a mean spirit and for no reason. Matt didn't care so much about the time dragging on. Jail or no jail, detention center or probation—none of that would change what he'd done.

Matt turned his eyes to the green van, ready to get back to work.

"Dad?" he asked, allowing a question to form on his lips before he could stop himself.

"Yes?" Dad's eyebrows went up, his face looking the way Matt always saw it in his mind: kind, attentive and stern.

Remember? Matt wanted to say, but didn't say. *Remember driving out here?* Even that was too much to bring up with Dad, so he said no more and turned the hose on the van. The Jolly Green Giant—that's what they had nicknamed it during their road trip out here. And the white van had been the Abominable Snowvan.

Was it just six months ago that they drove the three thousand miles from Oregon to Connecticut? It was hard to believe that they'd done it, crossed through eleven states, half of them mountainous, in the middle of winter, with both vans. It had taken them a week of driving twelve-hour days, only stopping for gas or the bathroom, not even for lunch. If it had been summer they would have camped, but it was January so they stayed at Holiday Inns and Best Westerns along the way. A couple of them had indoor swimming pools, even saunas and Jacuzzis, and it was a great reward for a whole day spent in the car playing twenty questions, eating packed lunches and listening to books on tape.

It had felt a little like a wagon train going in reverse, from west to east, to a new land for all of them. They had hit some terrible weather. In Colorado some snow had come upon them without warning; one minute they had been singing *ting tang, walla walla bing bang* under a clear blue sky and the next they couldn't see ten feet in any direction. He was in the Abominable Snowvan with Mom, Katie and Peter when it happened. Mom reduced her speed right away and kept checking the rearview mirror for signs of the other van. "I can't see a *thing*," she'd muttered, which Matt knew meant, *I have no idea where they are.* She'd made the decision to crawl along despite the snow because she was afraid the van would get snowed in if she stopped.

She couldn't have been going more than ten miles an hour when the car just seemed to slip off the road. It was so silent—there was no crash or thud, just a smooth, sideways glide, and then they were stuck. Matt and Peter got out and tried to push while Mom stepped on the gas, but the van was going nowhere.

They waited for an hour. Not a car came by, not a single one. At first it was kind of fun. Mom had them sing more songs, and they played some cards. Katie was the only one to say she was scared, though Matt was running through every blizzard story he had ever heard: *trapped for days, only snow to eat, all of them perished.*

When he could no longer stand it in there, he got out of the van to stand on the road. He was scared and he was praying, and after five or ten minutes he saw two dim headlights coming slowly, slowly toward them. He watched the lights creep closer until finally he recognized the Jolly Green Giant.

Dad got out of the van and put his hand on Matt's shoulder. "I always wanted to drive cross country, son, but I sure wish we didn't have to do it in January." Mom came out and threw her arms around Dad and it was only then that Matt could tell how afraid she had been.

And then together Mom, Dad and Matt had rigged up a chain, and the Jolly Green Giant had pulled the Abominable Snowvan out of the ditch. Matt recalled being proud that day of being able to rescue the van without the assistance of a tow truck or the highway patrol, of being able to go on their way without having to call anyone else for help. It was what Dad and Mom wanted them all to strive for—self-sufficiency, independence, resourcefulness. It was the way his family had always operated.

Remember? he still wanted to say to Dad, but the shame of what he'd done to his family since then made saying anything impossible.

He was scrubbing the headlights when he heard a car rev its engine and screech down their block. He looked up in time to see two black garbage bags catapult from the sun roof of a small gray car. Garbage flew from the car, spilling across the front lawn.

Somebody in the car shouted something but Matt couldn't hear what it was.

Dad ran down toward the street. The car picked up speed and then it was out of sight.

"Did you see the license plate?" Dad called back to Matt.

Matt shook his head.

"I'm going to call the police."

"I don't think you need to. . . ."

"Yes," Dad said quietly. "I do." He surveyed what was on the lawn—orange peels and tea bags and milk cartons. Ordinary garbage, nothing more.

"It's just garbage," Matt said.

"Just leave it all for the time being," Dad said. "We'll clean it up after the police have a look. It's not just garbage, Matt, it's not just vandalism. It's an act of vigilantism. Intimidation. You don't know who it could have been?"

It was only logical, but Matt couldn't spit out the words except in a whisper. "I would guess they are friends of . . . Erica's and Rachel's," he said.

"They're going to have to learn more appropriate ways of expressing their grief," Dad said.

"I don't think it'll do any good to call the police, Dad. Let's just clean it up and forget about it."

Dad gave Matt a final "no" and went into the house. Matt's face burned with shame as he imagined a police officer crouching on the ground to examine the garbage. Couldn't Dad just say *damned kids* and leave it alone?

Matt turned his back on the garbage. As he held the spray gun of the hose his hand shook with anger at Dad.

He didn't know who it could have been in the car, or how they knew where he lived. It could have been anyone from the high school; there were hundreds of kids he hadn't even met who had reason to hate him.

JENNIE

O N THE WEDNESDAY before the Sheldrake '80 reunion, Jennie
had three significant phone calls. The first was from her mother,
who called to tell Jennie her sister was getting married.

"To whom?" Jennie asked. This was a stunner. She didn't even
known Steph had a boyfriend.

"His name's Jerry. He's in the same business, something to do with
computers."

"Have you met him? What's he like?"

"This is the first I've heard of this particular fellow. I imagine we'll
find out all about it when she arrives. Are you sure she hasn't called
you?"

"She doesn't call me."

"Can you get Chris to pick her up at the airport? We have a commitment."

"Well, no," Jennie said. "I can't. He's got the rehearsal dinner for
Frank's wedding, and I'm too busy getting ready for this reunion."

Fay sighed. "I don't know what we'll do then."

When Jennie hung up the phone, she was surprised by how much
the news hurt. She and Stephanie weren't close, but Jennie liked her
sister—every time she saw her she was pleasantly reminded of how she
enjoyed spending time with her. Somehow they still remained useless
to each other. Despite their closeness in age, she and Steph seemed to
have had almost entirely separate childhoods, each designing her own
route, never learning to depend on each other in any way at all. As
adults, neither of them had made a move to change that.

Jennie's phone conversation with her mother was short, but it
would have been longer, and much more heated, if the second phone

call had come before the first instead of right after. The second caller was Marilyn Linders.

"I always give people the benefit of the doubt," Marilyn said. "I've been told that you have Matthew Fallon working for you as a baby-sitter. A baby-sitter! In your home. This is what I've heard and it sounds impossible to me but I always withhold until I know the truth."

"I did not hire him as a baby-sitter," Jennie said. "I hired him to help me with my business." Marilyn said nothing and Jennie struggled to go on. "It was the job Rachel Cleary was supposed to have," she said haltingly. Silence again. "I thought that Matt was someone who really needed this sort of an opportunity to keep him going. I'm sure it must sound shocking to you. I just saw an opportunity to maybe help him, make him see that he's not a monster, not an outcast because of the accident." Another silence was unbearable, so Jennie rushed on. "I talked to Camille Cleary. I meant to talk to you too, Marilyn. I called you once but you were out. Did you get the message? I guess I should have waited to talk to you."

"What the hell are you talking about?" Marilyn said. "What kind of person are you?"

Suddenly Jennie recalled every complaint, every uncharitable word Erica had ever said about her mother. She said, "Marilyn, what would you have him do? Pay with his life? Rot in jail?"

Marilyn's instant, unequivocal answer of "yes" made all of Jennie's compassion race back.

"Well, he's in agreement with you on that," she said quietly.

And though it would have been right for Marilyn to do so, Jennie was the one who let her voice swell with emotion.

"I'm sorry, Marilyn. I'm so sorry. I know there are hundreds of ways that this must hurt you but I honestly didn't think it was a disgrace to Erica's memory. I wouldn't have done it if I thought it was."

"I'm not buying any of this, Jennie. No rational person would do this kind of thing. I can't accept this. That boy was reckless, he was drunk and careless and he killed my daughter. It's unjustifiable. If you can't see that then you must be twice the deviant he is. Twice because you're twice his age. You should know better."

Jennie let some time pass before she answered. "I'm sorry, Marilyn.

I can't say I'd feel any differently in your place. I can see why you'd want to write him off. But everybody can't. Somebody has to be on his side."

"Heaven help you when your daughter is killed and some ignorant stranger wants to sing the praises of *her* murderer."

Jennie listened to the click and the silence. She laid the phone against her pounding heart and tried to dry her eyes on the collar of her shirt.

"I don't even have to ask if that was about me," Matt said. He was behind her.

Jennie hid her face in her sleeve. "Between you and me and this baby, this is certainly the house of tears," she tried to joke, but it sounded feeble and completely wrong.

"I'm sorry," he said.

"Don't be sorry," she said, finally turning around to look at him. His eyes glistened, just short of tears but heavy with them. Alison was in his arms.

"I'm sorry that I've made you get involved in my life," Matt said.

"You didn't make me do anything," she said. She hung up the phone and instinctively reached out to take Alison from him. He then seemed not to know what to do with his empty arms. They remained outstretched between his body and hers until he crossed them over his chest.

"But why did you do it, Jennie? I mean, there was no reason for you to help me. You hardly knew me."

What she should say now was something light and diplomatic, something like, *I just thought of how it might be for you all summer, nothing to do, worrying this out.* But the look on his face and the boy that he was demanded a more serious answer. The true answer.

So she said, "I had a summer in my life that was very hard for me. A summer when I was sure my life—as I knew it, anyway—was over. For various reasons, most of the people in my life couldn't or wouldn't help." She didn't say *the summer Tara was born,* she didn't go into specifics, but she was sure he understood. "I had this friend, Elizabeth, and she came to my aid. She kind of gave me a purpose for the summer, she gave me something to do every day, and once I'd made it through that summer I found I could make it through the rest of my life. She was my temporary angel." Jennie was rocking Alison as she spoke, rocking her for no particular reason because the baby was entirely placid. "Not that I'm calling myself an angel, but I was thinking of that summer when I hired you. Don't think I didn't know there was something in it for me. I knew you were smart. I knew you'd do a great job."

"I appreciate what you did," Matt said slowly, uncertainly. "But you shouldn't have to fight my battles. Erica's mother should be yelling at *me*, not you. And I've never even met her. I could walk right by her and never know." Matt's eyes dug into Jennie's with a fierceness that bordered on feral.

What did I really think I could do for you? she wanted to say. *How can I possibly, possibly help?*

She handed Alison back to him and he held the baby to his shoulder.

L ATER THAT AFTERNOON, while Jennie agonized over Matt's every twitch and sigh, feeling that he was on the edge of tears or one of his impassioned speeches, Joel Tarn called.

"Jennie Northrop?" the voice on the phone said. She would have recognized it anywhere, even after all these years. "I thought we'd just run into each other somewhere but we haven't."

"It's not like this is a small town," Jennie said.

"In my mind it had turned into one. After L.A., I guess. I've been here all week. Going out of my mind. I've been seeing a lot of movies but there aren't that many around I can take my mom to. Can we get together?"

"I'd like to, but I'm really busy getting ready for this reunion."

"Could we just meet someplace?"

"What? What place?" Jennie's eyes went to Matt, who was no more than four feet away from her. It was embarrassing to have this conversation in front of him. She heard herself switch back and forth between her Professional Reunion Organizer voice and something resembling Slightly Flirty Old Flame.

"Okay," Joel said. "How's this? Tomorrow, lunchtime?"

"A brief lunchtime. I can manage that. Where?"

"Wherever you say. It's your town."

"I wouldn't call it mine," Jennie said. "Let's see, the restaurants are always super crowded at lunchtime unless you go really late."

"Let's not go to a restaurant then. All those ladies who lunch. How about just getting sandwiches and meeting somewhere."

"The beach?"

"No, too many mothers with toddlers."

"Is there any place in this town you'd actually be willing to be seen?" He was irritating her. He'd made the call, he'd made the contact, but it was to be Jennie who was to make the plan. She wouldn't play.

"Wait a minute," he said, finally sounding decisive. "What about that creepy playground near school where we, where *people* used to go to get high?"

"Behind the Mobil? Very sinister."

"Perfect. I'll meet you there at one tomorrow."

"Okay," Jennie said and the plan was made before she really had time to think about why Joel Tarn wanted to see her. She hadn't had much time to ponder it these last weeks but when she had envisioned *the moment* it had been at the Sheldrake Hilton, in the ballroom, or maybe in the lobby just outside as he stepped up to the table and she handed him his name tag. She hadn't in a million years expected him to call.

When Jennie first started organizing reunions she had held all these romantic notions about them—that lovers who had somehow missed their chance in high school would now see each other across a crowded room and destiny would run its course. That men and women who were the *wrong people* in high school would now, at twenty-eight or thirty-eight or forty-eight or fifty-eight or sixty-eight, be free to fall in love, madly and soulfully. But it was never like that. Sometimes people would go home together but she rarely heard reports of relationships blossoming after the reunion—at least in the ten- or twenty- or even thirty-year reunions. It was only a possibility at a fortieth or fiftieth reunion where maybe there were early widows or widowers seeking the comfort of someone who had known them in happier times. At one of Jennie's golden reunions, a man and a woman who had had fourteen children and three dead spouses between them saw each other for the first time since high school and three months later Jennie got a postcard telling her they had gotten married. But that was the exception. In general, there were more cheap and tawdry moments in the parking lot than earth-shaking declarations of love.

"Interesting," Jennie said, aloud. She and Matt were on the floor cutting and gluing old yearbook pictures on name tags.

"What's interesting?" Matt asked.

"Nothing," Jennie said. "Just someone I used to know."

That evening, Jennie talked Tara into going to the mall with her. She really wanted to get something for the reunion, and seeing Joel was going to involve something new to wear too. All summer long she had worn shorts and loose tank tops or Chris's old button-down shirts.

"I don't know," Tara had said at first. "I'm kind of tired."

"Well, you know what will happen if you let her go by herself," Chris had said helpfully.

"She'll end up spending the whole time in the bookstore and looking like a bag lady at the reunion," Tara said.

"See?" Chris said. "She needs you."

"But *Dad*," Tara said. "Have you ever been there while she debated whether or not she should even *try on* a pair of pants?"

"Been there," Chris said. "That was me, wasting my life away making faces at myself in the triple mirror at Lord and Taylor."

The way they were talking reminded Jennie of when she was pregnant and they would discuss her in the third person in front of her. Then, it had irritated her. Now, hearing Tara joke with Chris warmed her heart.

"Okay, okay," Tara said. "I'll go."

How long had it been since she and Tara and gone shopping together? They had never been mom-daughter girlfriends, like some Jennie knew, trying on clothes and makeup together, buying matching earrings, but even so, until Tara was twelve or thirteen it had been a ritual for them to go shopping once every month or two, after school, stopping for dinner together at Friendly's afterward. Jennie had enjoyed those days; even though she hated shopping for herself, finding clothes for Tara was a lot of fun.

But then Tara became old enough to get dropped off and picked up at the mall with her friends and she did that instead. Tara and Rachel, and later Tara and Rachel and Erica, would spend an entire Saturday shopping together and come back with only a hair scrunchie and a half-eaten soft pretzel in a bag.

Jennie felt grateful to be able to do this ordinary thing, go shopping with her teenage daughter, but she worried that for Tara this outing might only remind her of what she had lost. In the dressing room, Jennie touched Tara's arm and asked, "You doing all right?"

Tara nodded. She was slumped on the stool, silent and pale, with a lapful of clothes. Everything Jennie tried on looked terrible, but Tara cheerfully took out the rejects and brought in new things for Jennie to try.

"What about this, Mom?" she asked shyly, returning with a very pretty moss green dress.

She was back on the stool while Jennie put on the dress, then jumped to her feet to zip it up.

"Perfect," they both said at the same time, then laughed. Jennie's eyes met Tara's in the dressing room mirror but when she turned around to smile at her, Tara had disappeared. She returned with something else for Jennie: a light brown minidress with thick embroidery all over the front. Jennie would wear that tomorrow to meet Joel.

"This has been the most satisfying shopping experience of my life," Jennie told Tara as she put her own clothes back on. "And the quickest. Will you become my on-call personal shopper?"

Tara smiled. Her face was a little pinched looking. "See, Mom?" she asked. "Something else I'm good at. Shopping."

"You're good at everything you do," Jennie said.

Another tired smile.

"Should we get ice cream?" Jennie asked. "A Coke?"

"Too tired," Tara said. "I'd just like to go home."

"Okay," Jennie said, disappointed. The evening bore all the marks of a successful mother-daughter outing and she was reluctant to let it go so quickly. She didn't want to go home, where Tara would retreat back into her room, but home was where Tara wanted to go.

Tara had started to look a little pink now, rather than pale, and she was quiet most of the way home.

"I feel sick, Daddy," Tara murmured when they walked in the door to their house. "I think I'm going to go to bed."

"What's wrong?" Chris asked.

"Let me feel your forehead," Jennie said. "I think you've got a fever."

Tara was sitting on her bed in her nightgown when Jennie returned with the thermometer.

She clicked it in Tara's ear. "Oh my God," she said. "It's a hundred and one. Lie down. Do you want something to drink?"

"Some grape juice," Tara said. As if she now had permission to be sick, she lay down on the bed. "And Mom?"

"Yes?"

"Can you bring me some cold cloths for my forehead. Like you do."

"Of course, sweetie."

Jennie rushed to tend to Tara, feeling the relief and deep pleasure of finally being able to do something for her. Bring her juice. Bring her pillows. Bring her Tylenol.

"There's no way you're going to work tomorrow," Jennie said when she came back in the room. But Tara didn't answer. She had already fallen asleep.

Jennie set the juice and Tylenol next to her bed, gently slid the pillows beneath her, covered her with a sheet and cotton blanket.

Chris poked his head in the room.

"Do you think she's okay?" he whispered.

"It's like one of those fevers she got when she was little. Remember how they came on so suddenly at night? She'll probably be all right in the morning."

Chris left the room, but Jennie lingered, smoothing pillows, feeling Tara's forehead again. She felt she was seeing a five-year-old Tara or a three-year-old, not this growing teenage girl. She looked as young as that in her twin bed. Really, was there any difference in that clear skin, the small features of her face, the fine blond hair that they'd been waiting for years to thicken but never had? Was there any difference between Tara at six and Tara at sixteen? She was taller, but she had the same long string-bean shape, the same thin shoulders and long legs.

She was still a child. Watching her sleep you couldn't deny that. How could it be that her eggs were ripe and ready now, that her cramps each month were so bad Jennie had taken her to the doctor? Could all that truly be happening in this tiny girl? Jennie tried to imagine, and couldn't, the weight of a man on this body, this body giving entrance to something the size of a man's penis. A *boy's* penis; it sounded less terrifying that way. Jennie had been sixteen when she first slept with Joel Tarn and Tara was sixteen now. Sixteen had seemed so different from the other side.

Jennie felt that childhood should last twice—no, three times—as long as it did. You should have decades to play and ride bicycles and learn to read. To go from feverish babyhood to age sixteen took eons when you were living it; the blink of an eye when you were watching, as a mother, from above.

Jennie bent and kissed Tara's hot forehead.

"Goodnight, little girl," she said, and left her to sleep.

MATT

H E PLEADED GUILTY to two charges of reckless homicide. Guilty: as if there was any other option. He'd done it. He was the one who had driven the car into a tree and killed Erica and Rachel. He was the one driving too fast, without a license. Saying it in court made him feel that the weight of a barge had dropped from his heart but the doors of a real prison had opened.

It took barely any time at all. An hour to wait for the judge to call the case and then just minutes, really, to enter his plea. The judge gave him a sentencing date of August 22nd and Matt could not believe that he had to wait six weeks to find out what was going to happen to him. Mr. Finchley said they wouldn't send him to jail, that the worst that could happen was a juvenile home until he was twenty-one. He was sure that Finchley had said eighteen before. Now he was saying twenty-one.

"Let's just wait for sentencing," he told Matt outside the courtroom, and added, "I've filed the juvenile delinquency petition and I'll let you know what I find out."

Dad said, "Is there any chance they can change the sentencing date—make it sooner?"

Finchley's head went back and came down in kind of a sympathetic scoff. "Sooner?" he said. "Keep our fingers crossed they don't put it off. Usually do once or twice."

"In view of Matt's age," Dad said. "To wait all that time is . . ."

"You don't have to convince me, believe it," Finchley said. "I'm going to try to make this date stick. Of course because of his age. You don't like to put the young ones through that hell of waiting." Finchley shook hands with Dad and then looked at Matt. Finchley always seemed to think Matt was some little kid he could pat on the head or something, always seemed surprised that he was taller than he was.

It was only 11:30 in the morning and Matt didn't want to spend the whole rest of the day at home. He could read or do yardwork or help the kids with their sea life mural, but he didn't want to. He had taken the day off work, but work was where he wanted to go.

He knew it wasn't just the work, though he enjoyed it and it kept him busy—tracking down other lives, ignoring his own. It was also Jennie herself because everything about her seemed to forgive him, and in her house he could feel he was someone worth that much forgiveness. Ever since she had used the word *angel,* then denied it, he saw that's what she was.

At home he went upstairs and took off his suit, put on shorts and a polo shirt and went back downstairs. Dad had already left for the office but Mom was outside on the deck with the kids, pots of paint everywhere, smashed-up tissue paper, fluorescent card stock, gold ribbon scattered around them.

Mom stood up when she saw him. "Matt?" she asked. She had a tiny pink jellyfish stuck to her knee.

"Em keeps saying she wants an elephant," Katie said. "There are not elephants in the sea, right Mattie?"

"I like elephants," Em said. "They are big, big elephants." She stood up and held out her hand to Matt. "Come," she said.

"I'm sorry," he said. He put his hand on Em's soft curls. He hated saying no to her. "I can't. I'm going to work."

"Oh, Matt," Mom said. "I thought you had the whole day off."

"I do. I mean, I did but I didn't know it would be over so quickly. I might as well go in."

"But is she expecting you?"

"She's swamped with the reunion on Saturday. She'll be happy to have the help."

"You sure you don't want to take it easy instead? We could use your underwater expertise." Mom pushed the hair out of her eyes and smiled encouragingly at him but he took in the whole scene and didn't see himself in it. With him gone they could do the mural, maybe go to the beach later, or the park, or anywhere. Places he wasn't allowed to go. Places where no one would throw garbage at them.

He had begun this weeks ago, envisioning his family without him.

Sometimes he could see their whole future, Brian becoming as old as Matt was now, then Peter, then Katie, even Em, all of them growing into teenagers and then adults, the family easily intact without him. They were all together, and he was alone. It took no effort at all to edit himself out of his family.

Riding across town he felt the despair gradually displaced as it always was when he went to Jennie's. But when he knocked on the door, it wasn't Jennie who answered but Tara.

What seemed like his whole life had passed since he'd last seen her. She took him backward in time.

Neither said a word. Matt's mouth was open but there were no muscles to close it.

Tara's eyes flickered big, then small. "Mom said you weren't coming today," she said finally. She looked pale and deep-eyed, her hair in two braids.

"It took less time than I thought," he said. Then, after silence: "I thought she might need me."

"She just left."

He stood there, just looking at her until he could say, "I'm sorry."

"No."

"I'll just go home." He turned quickly away.

"No, it's okay."

They were both speaking so slowly. They sounded like two of Katie's windup dolls, batteries running low, words stretched out long and deep.

"You probably don't want to see me," Matt said. When Tara said nothing in return, he said, "It's okay if you want me to just go home." He found himself squinting at her the way you had to when you looked at the sun. She was staring at her own finger scratching circles on the screen door.

"Mom had to go somewhere," she said. "I'm home sick. I mean, I'm not sick now. I was sick last night so I stayed home. From work. Today." She was looking at him as if she had forgotten he was a real person until now, as if since the accident he'd been frozen somewhere, an experiment in cryogenics only now coming back to life. Abruptly she said, "I wanted to call you, Matt, talk to you. I really did." There was nothing convincing in her voice. She splayed her fingers across her face and said, "God, this is so strange. You're in my house every day, all this time and I've never even seen you." She paused again. "Since then. Since . . . it happened."

"I . . . you . . ." There was nothing to say. He wanted to turn and run but now she was holding open the screen door for him.

"Come in," she said. "Please." She wasn't holding the door open wide enough, but when he went to pull it open wider she stumbled out the front step toward him.

"Sorry," Matt said.

"Oh God, sorry," she said, speaking at almost the same time as he. She had to turn her back to him and step back into the house and the screen door slammed before he could grab it.

Once he was finally inside, they continued as before, staring and speaking slowly, just without the door between them now.

"I didn't know what to say to you," Tara said. "That's why I never called. I must have seemed so . . ." She shook her head. "I just didn't know what to say."

She was as lovely as ever, though pale and maybe even thinner than he remembered. He could see the small points of her shoulder bones next to the straps of her orange tank top.

"Are you all right?" he asked her.

"I'm not sick anymore," she said, though that wasn't what he meant. He didn't know what he meant. "I woke up fine," she said.

From the other room he heard Alison crying. "Is something wrong with her?" he asked.

"I think she's hungry or something," Tara said. "Mom promised me she would sleep the whole time but she woke up a few minutes ago and I don't know what to do."

"Did she leave a bottle?"

"Yeah, but I wasn't really listening how to give it to her because I didn't think I'd need to."

"Want some help?"

"Please."

Matt went to the bedroom to take Alison out of the bassinet. She was doing her square-mouthed yowl, the one that meant she was hungry, and when Matt picked her up she cried even more because he wasn't Jennie.

"Sssh," he murmured. In the kitchen he handed her to Tara so he could warm up the milk but Tara looked in danger of letting Alison drop from her arms. It didn't seem as if she had a clue how to hold the baby. He took Alison back and held her against his shoulder with one arm while using the other to get a bottle out of the refrigerator.

"Mom said you had to go to court today," she said. She was sitting on the counter, watching as he warmed the bottle.

"I did."

"What happened?"

"I went there to enter my plea."

"Your plea?"

"I had to plead guilty. To . . . what they charged me with." He couldn't bear to say the words.

"Oh my God. Oh Matt, everyone knows you didn't . . ." She stared at him for a few seconds then raised up her knees and laid her head on them. "What did they do? I mean, how long . . . ?"

"I don't know how long or where or when. I don't find out until August."

"Don't you want to know? Why do they have to wait so long? What do you think will happen?" These questions came in an almost shrill tone, in rapid succession, and then she whispered, "Are you scared?"

He was shocked by all these things she was asking him and in the end he only answered the last. "I wouldn't call it scared." No, that wasn't right. Why was he trying to sound so stoic? "I mean, of course I'm scared. I just don't think about it much, about what's going to happen. I think about what *did* happen. That night, I mean."

"Me too," Tara said. She hugged her arms to her chest as if cold. "I should have been there, you know."

"No," Matt said, feeling a flash of anger at what sounded like glibness. "Don't say that."

"I should have been there and I would have been if Alison hadn't been born that night. Maybe it would have made a difference."

"What do you mean?"

"I mean, was Alison born that night just so I wouldn't die? Or if she hadn't been born and I had gone with you instead, maybe there wouldn't have been an accident. That's what I want to know. Did she save my life or was she the reason they died?"

Matt looked down at Alison, falling asleep as she sucked on the bottle. It surprised him, because usually she fought the bottle.

"I wouldn't say Alison had anything to do with it," he said softly.

"I don't mean her, the actual baby. I mean the idea of her. The expectation. I really wanted to go that night. Even with my mom having the baby I would have gone . . ." Her eyes looked up at him and then quickly down. "With you . . . if my dad had let me. I was mad that you all went without me."

"Why?"

"Because I . . . wanted to go too."

Matt lifted his eyes from Alison's face to Tara's and thought he saw what it had cost her to say that. She had her chin on her knees, her whole body curled up like a snail. She looked so young. So small and so young. He wondered if what she was saying was that she liked him still. He was so good at getting things wrong that there was no value in even speculating. That kiss was from another boy's life.

"My whole life has been this," Matt began to tell her. "Just since the accident. Nothing more."

She lifted her head from her knees and nodded. "Me too," she said and kept nodding. "Everything from before was wiped away."

"You must miss them so much."

"They were my best friends. I told them everything. Everything." She cocked her head to one side and rolled her lips inward, making them disappear. "Now that they're gone, it's not just that I don't have anyone to tell, but now there's nothing *to* tell."

So she was feeling as dead as he'd felt her to be. That's what he had succeeded in doing. Guilty of three counts, not just two.

Tara slid off the counter and hugged him. "I've missed you," she said. It was awkward—he was still holding Alison and the hug was one-sided. "I can't believe I was so afraid and now we're talking like this."

Matt simply nodded, everything about him jarred by that hug. Jennie had hugged him yesterday. Perhaps they were a hugging family, perhaps that's just what they did. His parents hugged their children, but Matt had never seen them hug anyone else.

He suddenly felt very self-conscious in Jennie's house. What if she were angry? Matt would do almost anything to avoid letting Jennie down because she was the one who had taken him on, taken him in, when no one else seemed to acknowledge he was alive.

"Maybe I should go after all," Matt said.

Tara raised her eyebrows in surprise.

"I really don't know what Jennie would want me to work on and she might not have anything for me to do right now." He just wanted to go. Alison was sucking the last milk out of the bottle and he burped her and went to hand her to Tara. But Tara didn't hold out her arms.

Matt kissed Alison's head and set her down under her activity gym. At the door, Tara hugged him again.

"I'm sorry," she said, ". . . about everything. About not calling, about everything."

As he got on his bike in the driveway she called out, "Matt, are you going to that reunion Saturday night?"

"Yeah. Jennie needs me to help because your dad has to go somewhere. A wedding or something?"

"Yeah. I'm going too, so I guess I'll see you there?"

"Okay," Matt said. "See you there." She was leaning against the door frame and he gave her a wave. These normal gestures, any kind of regular words—there was no way they could pass between him and Tara.

He took off down the street on his bike. He couldn't stay at Jennie's house and he didn't want to go back home. With these the only two options, anywhere else could get him in trouble. If he broke the terms of house detention who knew what would happen.

He kept on riding and he was almost there before he realized where he was going.

He had never seen it in the daytime but it wasn't hard to find. He laid his bike on the grass and walked immediately toward the tree. Its sad, ruined bark was broken off in a big wound at waist level with horizontal gashes below that. It was an old tree, a sugar maple, massive but brittle, possibly dying, but not because of the accident. *Perhaps if it had died earlier. Perhaps if it had been taken away by the town.*

No. He wouldn't let himself do that.

He would instead fall to his knees and finger the grass, touch the remnants of what had been left there—dead bouquets of flowers and one live one, ribbons and candles and stuffed animals, cards and letters that had suffered from nights of rain, paper soggy and falling apart. But one letter was new: a pale yellow envelope leaning against the base of the tree. He looked around to see if anyone was watching but the road was as deserted as it had been the night of the accident. He couldn't help himself. He was starving for it. He opened it and read.

To my little one. I know this is not where you rest but it is where I come to say good-bye. And good-bye and good-bye. I love you always, Mom.

Rachel or Erica, he didn't know which one it was addressed to, but it could have been either. They had both been their mothers' baby girls, and now they were dead.

He was careful to return the card to its envelope and place it exactly where it had been left. He did that calmly, meticulously, and only then did he begin to weep. For them; for himself and what he was feeling; and for knowing that he would feel this way over and over again for all that remained of his life.

JENNIE

J OEL WAS THERE waiting for her, sitting cross-legged on the metal merry-go-round, one of those rusty pieces of playground equipment you never really saw children playing on. Jennie had never associated this playground with children anyway—that old metal made your hands smell. It had always been a secluded spot where teenagers hung out, redolent with broken glass.

Under normal circumstances she might have tried to be fashionably late, but as it was she had missed their meeting time by a full half hour. She walked toward him with a step she hoped looked light and casual, attempting to erase the morning spent agonizing over whether Tara, now fever free, would be able to look after Alison while she was gone. She still wasn't convinced she should have left her two daughters alone and she was certain that worry showed.

Joel stood up as she walked across the asphalt toward him. He wore a short-sleeved gold turtleneck and black jeans, a dopey sort of straw hat that he removed and waved at her. He was smiling and she smiled back but it was awkward to sustain that smile and the accompanying eye contact as she covered the ground between them. He did not meet her halfway or take even a step; he just stood and waited for her to reach him.

"Mrs. Breeze," Joel said, as soon as she was close enough. His ironic tone of voice came back to her instantly.

He held out his arms and they met for what was more an embrace than a hug, accompanied by a soft, puckerless kiss on her cheek.

"Please," Jennie said, stepping back. "You act as if this is news. I've been married for years and years."

"Two-point-two kids, a house, two cars, a dog."

"No dog. A very small house and no children beyond the decimal point, thank you."

"People around here seem to do that, get married. Marriage occurs frequently."

"People in Los Angeles don't get married?"

"Not the people I know."

They both sat down on the merry-go-round and Joel gave it a little spin. Half of their lives had passed since she had seen him. She'd forgotten things: that he was a little shorter than she was, that his broad shoulders were part of a stocky build. Also he'd changed. His dark hair was thinning. The lines in his forehead—part of his ironic look—had become permanent. He still had bemused eyes, a dark look, a nice jaw.

And what did he see in her? Probably her twenty-five pounds, fifteen still from the baby, ten real ones since high school. Again she wondered why he had wanted to see her.

"I brought sandwiches," he said. "And some great-looking chickpea salad."

"Thanks." Jennie had completely forgotten about the actual lunch part of seeing Joel and she watched him unfold several napkins with a flourish, assembling them into a tablecloth.

"So, how's good old Sheldrake?" Joel asked.

"I don't suppose it's changed that much over the years. I should be asking you about good old L.A. Your questionnaire said you're a filmmaker?"

"That's what it said." Another ironic smile. "I'm trying to get my film made now. I'm working on funding. It's a drag. You either need a grant or some decent family money and I've got neither."

"So what do you do? I mean, how do you live?"

"You don't want to hear about my money job, believe me. Not that it's sordid and illegal, just small and depressing. I'd much rather find out about your life here."

She got distracted by his eyebrows. They were moving up and down in a way Jennie remembered, always in motion, even when the rest of his face was still. Those eyebrows had won him a lot of character roles in high school drama productions.

"Oh," Jennie said. "My life." She shrugged and took the sandwich he was offering her. "Why is my life so fascinating? You grew up here. You know what it's like. Getting more expensive by the nanosecond. Stocked with smug people thrilled to death that they 'bought in' to the community."

He smirked. "Such a fetching portrait you paint," he said.

"Yes, but it's true. A lot of people say in the reunion books—you'll see on Saturday—'I never would have believed I'd be living in the same town a mile from my parents, blah, blah, blah.' I guess I should admit that I'm one of them."

"See, that's so shocking to me because the only thing I was sure of, growing up here, was that I wanted to leave."

Jennie felt a brief, sharp pang of jealousy. That he had known that. That he had gotten away while she had let the events of her life determine that she stay. "How did you know that?" she asked him. "How could you know that?"

"Just knew it wasn't for me. I wasn't one of them."

"That's what people from godforsaken towns in Kansas or somewhere think. Not those fortunate enough to live in Smugville."

"I'm sure I wasn't the only one. Surely other people from our class felt the same way."

"We're not from the same class, Joel. Remember? I was a freshman when you were a senior."

"Really? I didn't remember that."

"You should pay more attention to details. They come in handy in filmmaking, I'm sure, especially when you're looking for funding."

"Touché, Mrs. Breeze." He looked amused but in an admiring sort of way, as if she had just scored some points in whatever game he liked to play.

"Sorry." Jennie had no idea why she was being antagonistic. She had a feeling her life was being mined for a documentary about a return to Ye Olde Hometowne.

"So why are you so involved in this reunion if you aren't even in my class?" Joel asked.

"It's my job," she said impatiently. "I'm being paid to do this."

"So you're just being nice to me because it's your job?" he asked, effecting a pouty tone. "And I only came because you wrote that cute note on my invitation."

"I wrote lots of cute notes, Joel Tarn," she said, smiling. "Get over it."

As he passed her a sandwich and some salad, she said, "It was my sister who was in your class, don't you remember?"

"Ah, the strong and strident Stephanie. Is she coming out for the reunion?"

"So she says. It's hard to know until she actually shows up."

"Where does she live?"

"San Diego."

"No kidding. I'll have to look her up."

Jennie concentrated on eating her sandwich but when she looked up, Joel was staring at her. "It's really good to see you, actually," he said. "I had no idea it would be this good."

"Why is that, do you suppose?" She heard her own voice taking on Joel's ironic cast.

"I'm not sure," he said. "I never really knew you that well, and as you recall, the last time I saw you I didn't behave very well."

"That was a long time ago," Jennie said. She tried to maintain the irony, keep the flirtiness in her voice. "It doesn't even seem like those people were us. You and I sitting here, I mean."

"Thanks for saying it, but I've been having one of those 'wasn't *I* an asshole?' flashbacks. I mean, going back to L.A. and never calling you? After you'd given me your virginity?"

"Oh," Jennie said, "so you're the one who's had it all this time? Are you here to give it back?"

Joel threw back his head and laughed. She must have caught him off guard because this was the first genuine laugh she had heard from him.

"C'mon," he said, "were you really so forgiving back then?"

"I shed a few teenage tears, but you didn't break my heart." She smiled, surprised at how close to the truth that really was. "The thing is, you do occupy a more significant position in my life than you realize," she added.

"I know I was your first. That's why I felt like such an asshole."

"Not just that," Jennie said, wondering why she felt she needed to tell him this. "Let's just say that while you've slept with a hundred women or whatever since then, the only other guy I've ever slept with has been my husband."

He looked completely incredulous. "You're joking, right?"

"It's not like that's how I planned it," she said, suddenly defensive. "That's just how it worked out."

He was shaking his head. "I'm just amazed at your restraint. Notwithstanding the fact that I do feel privileged." Those eyebrows were at it again. Along with his voice, it was his way of looking at you. This "just say the word and I'll be all over you" look. What had she and Elizabeth used to call it? The Rhett Butler "undressing you with his eyes" look.

She kept wanting to feel something for Joel. Not that she wanted something to happen, but to have to fight something off would be nice. To feel some turbulent rush of emotions, to feel something that took her back to that June night in 1982—secretly, she supposed she had been hoping for that.

Joel started the merry-go-round spinning again and brought out the package of biscotti he had brought for dessert.

"So why this sudden interest in your old hometown anyway?" Jennie asked him.

"It came to me in a dream," he said. "No, really, the thing is, when I left twenty years ago I was happy to leave, dying to leave, but suddenly, I don't know, faces of people and places I literally hadn't thought about in all that time started coming back to me. I want to find out why. I developed my attitude about this place years ago. I mean, maybe I resented certain people for x years, say six years, three actively and three dormantly, and then suddenly I didn't think about them at all, ever, for maybe eight years and then now, who knows why, but I'll wake up thinking about Charles Delan—"

"A lawyer," Jennie interrupted, "married, working in England, three boys. Not coming to the reunion," Jennie said.

"Or Sue Gifford and Roger Moran . . ."

"Sue's a flight attendant and part-time shoe model, single. Roger's married, living back in Sheldrake. You'll see them on Saturday."

"You are a veritable font, Mrs. Breeze."

"It's my line of work."

Joel's head bounced up and down for a moment or two. Then he said, "There's something else. I've probably lived in fifteen different apartments in the twenty years since I left and I get these Christmas cards from friends—the few that can find me—and some of them have had the same address for eight, ten years. I'm just so curious about them. To stay in the same place. You know, they've put down roots. Installed water filters on their faucets and all that." He flashed a smile.

"Just because they're in the same place doesn't mean they want to be there," Jennie said.

"Maybe not, but most of them seem pretty happy. They seem so settled and, well, nice." He offered that last word with some embarrassment.

She echoed him. "Nice?"

"I know, that would have been the kiss of death from me twenty years ago, but now I've come to value nice people, decent people."

Well, bully for you, Joel, she almost said. This antagonism was really taking her by surprise. "They're not all decent," she said. "Jimmy Fitzgerald got busted for selling cocaine a year or two ago."

"You know what I mean, they work hard, raise their children right, become part of the community. Stay planted."

Planted. She wondered if it would be possible for him to use a more unflattering word. "Are you including me in that group?" she asked.

"I suppose."

She gave him an annoyed look, then laughed. She suddenly felt nothing but impatience. She wanted to get home and check on her daughters, she wanted to get back to work.

She wasn't much interested in talking to Joel anymore. Not *this* Joel, anyway—the same way she would rather not have to be *this* Jennie. She would have liked to talk to the old Joel, the teenage Joel, to feel the intensity and passion he'd had when he was the boy who had to get away, before he became the man who had forgotten why.

And yet she hated to think that it was just youth she was talking about. Was youth so gorgeous that she should worship it so much, mourn its passing?

Jennie and Joel walked to their cars and kissed good-bye—on the lips this time, though nothing much passed between them. Jennie saw that she was a reunion organizer who had fallen prey to her own myth: that magic would happen when you stepped back into your past. Irony again, because the magic would be there only if you really could step back, which of course you couldn't. You could only look.

MATT

THE GRAY HONDA AGAIN. He must have been waiting for him, must have known exactly when he would leave Jennie's house, because Matt had cycled only three blocks toward home that Friday afternoon, the day before the reunion, when the Honda darted in front of him. He had to run his bike onto the grass to get out of the way.

He struggled to untangle his legs and pull up the bike but he was on one knee in the grass when he heard, "I've been waiting all summer to do this, asshole."

It was Jeff, Erica's boyfriend. Matt felt a sick pounding in his chest as he tried to free himself from the bike. No sooner had he stood up than Jeff lunged at him, using a sequence of punches to push him back from the road into the thick patch of trees that shielded the houses behind.

"Look," Matt gasped. Jeff's face was sheer, gray fury. Jeff was almost exactly the same size as Matt and they would have looked eye to eye if Jeff had been looking ahead. Instead, he was looking down, at Matt's arms, his chest, as if seeing no more than a bundle of bones to break, flesh to batter.

"Look," Matt tried to say again but Jeff threw a punch at his face that immediately bloodied his nose. That blow, its absolute enmity, made something switch over in Matt. Instead of trying to stop Jeff, he now struck out with his fists at Jeff's arms, his chest, his shoulders. Not his face. He wouldn't hit his face.

Jeff seemed giddy that he had Matt before him. In his heavy, panting breaths was something that sounded like laughing. Matt could make a run for his bike, could possibly get away, but he found himself charging back at Jeff, hitting harder and harder and harder. For as long as he fought back Jeff would keep hitting him.

Those were his breaths, that was his laughing.

With his bike helmet on he couldn't see what was coming and he tried to yank it off but arms up he was vulnerable, and Jeff barreled straight at him, knocking him to the ground and then throwing his weight on top of him.

Matt crushed Jeff's fists with his own to keep them away from his face. Jeff's knees were digging, digging into his chest and he felt his lungs squeeze close.

He sucked in enough air to say, "I'm sorry."

This made Jeff angrier and he squeezed Matt's whole torso with his knees, fought to pull his hands free.

"You asshole," Jeff said, "you son of a bitch," but he drew back just long enough for Matt to heave him off of his chest.

"You . . . loved . . . her," Matt said, the words coming out as heavy, stertorous sounds. "I'm . . . sorry."

"Did you fuck her?" Jeff asked and Matt's eyes distended with horror. Erica had died, and this was what Jeff wanted to know?

"Did you?" Jeff asked, his voice a snarl. Their arms battled from side to side, arm wrestling in the air. "Did you?"

Jeff tore his right hand free and used it to strike Matt on the chin, but as he geared up for another punch Matt was able to rise up and knock Jeff over. He threw himself on top of Jeff with a loud groan, pinning his arms and legs. Matt's face hung inches above Jeff's and they both panted, trying to recapture breath. For the first time, Matt could look Jeff in the eyes and he searched there for what he hoped to find—searched for shame, for guilt, for love—but all he saw was rage. It was a rage that incited a rage in Matt and his instincts were to pound on Jeff, to pummel and beat him until he became part of the mud and leaves in which he lay.

He fought it. He fought that rage. If he didn't move, just stayed with his eyes on Jeff's—still searching, not finding—the rage would subside.

Finally Matt released him.

"God help you," he said and got to his feet. Jeff sat up, breathing hard, staring at the ground.

"I didn't fuck her," Matt said quietly, as he turned from Jeff. "I killed her."

He listened for sounds that Jeff was following him, but there were none. Apparently Jeff just sat there until Matt was gone. Matt never knew—he didn't look back. Trembling, he picked up his bike and walked it back to the road.

He reached up to wipe the sweat off his face and came away with an arm wet with blood. He looked down at his chest, his arms and legs, and saw how covered he was with blood and dirt.

When he was out of sight of the Honda he stopped and rested a bit, trying to decide what to do. He couldn't let Mom see him like this, couldn't let Dad call the police.

There was nowhere to go but back to Jennie's. He walked the bike the whole way, still feeling too unsteady to get on it. He was grateful that no one passed by and saw him.

When Jennie opened the door, saying, "Oh my God, Matt, what happened?" he tried to make her see that he wasn't badly hurt.

"It looks worse than it is," he told her.

"Come in, come in." She held her arm out to him. "Did you crash on your bike? What happened?" She was leading him by the hand back to the bathroom.

"It was a fight."

"Somebody attacked you?" she asked, shocked. "Do you know who it was?"

"I know who it was," Matt said.

"Who?"

"Just some other kid."

"We'd better call the police."

"No!" He put his hand on her arm almost frantically, trying to stop her. "No, you can't. I fought back. When you fight back, I don't think you can call the police."

Jennie looked as if she were about to cry and when Matt saw himself in the bathroom mirror he could see why. It wasn't just his nose that was bleeding. His lip was cut too, and he was caked with mud and leaves. When he took his shirt off he saw a deep gash in his left shoulder. She took his shirt from him and threw it in the bathtub, then wet a washcloth for him to wash his face. She hovered over him while he was at the sink, looking so concerned that he said again, "I'm really all right. See?" He held out the washcloth to her. "Just a lot of blood."

"There are some cuts," she said, and he felt her fingertips on his lip, on his chin. "Sit down."

He sat on the edge of the tub while Jennie knelt in front of him to dab antiseptic on his cuts with a cotton ball.

"I'm really sorry to bother you with this," he said. "I know you have so much to . . ."

"Ssssh," she said, and as her lips formed that sound he wanted suddenly to kiss them. It was a desperate feeling, desire that took him just to the edge of hysteria. He almost felt he would cry.

"You're right," she was saying softly. "It's not that deep. Just a lot of blood. I'll get you some of Chris's clothes to wear home and throw yours in the wash."

"You don't have to do that." He was embarrassed by what he was feeling for her, and more embarrassed that she might know somehow—as if the mere proximity of her face to his would allow her to read his thoughts.

"*Please,*" she said. "I only do about ten loads of baby clothes a day. I'm used to it."

"Thanks. I . . ." He had to move his eyes away from hers. What was the matter with him? It was as if this fight had stirred up all these feelings in him and now they all were coming out in the wrong order. He moved his head slightly so that he was staring at the faucet on the sink behind her.

He cleared his throat. "I don't mean to ask you to lie, but I'm not planning on telling my parents about this, okay? I'll just tell them I fell off my bike or something."

Jennie sat back on her heels on the bathroom rug and considered what he said. "I don't think you should keep things from your parents," she said. "And the police need to know. What if this affects your sentencing? The fact that you were attacked?"

"I just want to let this one pass," Matt said, trying to sound casual, as if he had been in hundreds of fights. "I think this guy and I are even."

"What if he comes after you again?" Jennie asked, those two little points between her eyebrows creasing as she frowned.

"I don't think he will."

She worked on tucking a loose strand of hair into her barrette, something she always did when thinking. He regretted the situation he was putting her in.

"How's this for a deal," she finally said. "I don't completely understand why you want to keep this quiet, but I'll respect your decision if you promise me . . . *promise me,* if it ever happens again you'll tell them. Your parents, the police, everyone."

"I promise," Matt said. "I promise."

"Okay," Jennie said, sighing a resigned sigh. She didn't look all that happy about it but Matt knew he could trust her.

When he left, wearing one of Jennie's husband's T-shirts and a pair of his jeans, Jennie said, "Listen, I'll understand if you don't feel like coming to the reunion tomorrow night. I can manage without you. Tara said she would come and help out."

"I know," Matt said. "She told me."

Jennie raised an eyebrow. "She did?"

"Yes."

"I didn't realize you had talked to her."

"Only yesterday. When I came around after court to see if I could be of any help. Didn't she tell you?" Matt suddenly felt he had blown it. Was Jennie angry? Was he getting Tara in trouble?

"She didn't mention it," Jennie said.

"Oh," Matt said.

"Just call if you change your mind," Jennie said.

"I won't," he said quickly. He couldn't wait for it. It would be the first time he had been out in more than two months.

She reached out and patted his arm as he walked out the door. "Take care," she said. "Tell your mom Alison threw up on your clothes or something."

"Okay," Matt said. "Thanks." She stayed in the doorway until he had put his helmet on and mounted his bike, making sure he was okay. He gave her a thumbs-up signal and began pedaling down the street.

It was all very strange. Yesterday, when he had left Tara and ridden to the tree on Connaught Road, he felt thrown right back to the first days after the accident, the days all he wanted to do was hurl himself from the window and make it all end.

But today, when this fight, Jeff's hatred, his own aches should clearly have made him feel even worse, he didn't. He felt the pride of having fought his own fight, an alarming excitement at having Jennie tend to his wounds. This fight, coming face-to-face with Jeff, had done something to him.

Later he would think of it as the time he started to harden his heart against what he had done. When you committed an unforgivable act, you could either end your life or you could continue it, feeling forever as he had at the tree yesterday, letting what you had done melt you into a pool of sorrow and guilt. Now he saw there was a third way. You could decide—yes, *decide*—to harden your heart and go through with your life, allowing yourself pleasure and plans, allowing yourself *life*.

JENNIE

PEOPLE GOT MARRIED for all sorts of reasons. Jennie's sister, Stephanie, who blew into town Friday night for the reunion on Saturday, told Jennie she was finally doing it because she wanted to know with absolute certainty whose pubic hair was curled around the bar of soap in her shower. Chris's best friend Frank had been at work one afternoon when it seized him that he didn't want to eat dinner alone anymore and he immediately drove to Janet's office to ask her to marry him. Sometimes when Jennie thought about it, the fact that she and Chris got married because they were expecting a baby didn't seem so foolish, though people usually pointed to it as the single most foolish reason in the world for marrying. It was, after the test of time, as good a reason as any, and perhaps not even the truth; Jennie had been away from home for the first semester of college, vomiting all day long and not making friends, and that, when she looked back, was the real foolish reason they'd married.

She had missed Chris achingly—he still at home with all the familiar people and places—and she had been terrified. It seemed to her that when she fell in love with Chris he had shown her the warm heart of family life that had been missing in Fay and Leo's house, and she pined for that so in Chicago. It was with some relief that she returned to it.

Though underneath it all—and they never questioned it for a moment—was the simple fact that she and Chris loved each other, there were still these strange arbitrary reasons for a life—Tara's—to be lived rather than unlived. But examining them now, they seemed no more or no less arbitrary than other reasons she saw around her.

"So I hope you've got more than the pubic hair thing going for you," Jennie said to Stephanie. It was the morning of the reunion and

Stephanie was helping Jennie load up the car with boxes of programs, name tags and party favors.

"We have the same interests," Steph said in answer to Jennie's question. "We work out together, we run, we're both avid skiers, vegetarians, we like to play golf."

"Oh. It sounds like you met through the personals."

Stephanie nodded. "I think our similar lifestyles will take us a long way together. It's not going to be moonlight and fucking forever, you know."

"I know that. Boy, do I know that."

"The thing is," Stephanie said, "I'm thirty-eight years old and I can't wait forever to feel a way I've never even felt before. I love Jerry, we have a lot in common. He doesn't want children either, thank God. We have our work. We go to the opera. It's great."

"You sound like you're convincing yourself."

"Do I? I suppose I'm on the defensive because I'm imagining what Mom would say."

"Since when has Mom ever disapproved of anything you did?"

"Please," Steph said, giving her a sideways glance. "I just have to deal with it less often. Why do you think I live so far away?"

"The weather?" They both laughed. Stephanie was masterfully packing the trunk of Jennie's car. That was a thing about Stephanie. She didn't show up often, but when she did she was happy to put herself into whatever situation was in progress.

"So why didn't you bring him with you?" Jennie asked. "Don't want him to meet Mom and Dad?"

"He couldn't get away. Plus I didn't want to have to entertain him at this reunion thingy. I just want to see who's there and what business they're in, what their Internet needs are. Ha!"

"Oh, so this is a business trip."

"Any consultant will tell you it's the best way to build up your business. Starting with people you know in whatever tenuous manner is always better than trying to start from scratch."

"All right," Jennie said, slamming the trunk. "Want to ride over to the Hilton with me? I'll drop you off at Mom's after."

"Sure."

"Chris, we're leaving," Jennie called into the house. Chris came to the door with Alison propped against his shoulder. He was still in his pajamas. He'd been out late the night before at Frank and Janet's rehearsal dinner, which had metamorphosed into a sort of bachelor party afterward.

"When you get back will you listen to my speech?" he asked. "Alison's helping me with it."

"Promise," Jennie said. "Wake Tara at noon if she's still sleeping?"

"Okay."

"How's Tara doing?" Stephanie asked when they were on the road. "Mom told me about her friends."

"I honestly don't know," Jennie said. "I can't tell if she's getting anywhere at all with this."

"Is it depression?"

"It's . . . lots of things. She'll wake up in the middle of the night and cry for an hour, inconsolable, then go back to sleep. Or she'll be really manic, wanting to build a bookcase for her room or go shopping for clothes *right now* and then she won't take a shower for three days or comb her hair."

"Is she seeing someone?" Stephanie asked.

"You mean like dating?" Jennie immediately thought of Matt. The fact that they had seen each other two days ago, would see each other tonight, terrified her in a way. What would the two of them come up with together?

"No, like a shrink," Stephanie said.

"They had these grief counselors at school. She went once or twice but she didn't want to anymore."

"Suggest it. It might help."

"You suggest it," Jennie said. "She won't listen to me. I'm her mother."

"Well, we never listened to our mother, did we?" Stephanie let out a hoot. "Of course she never tried to tell us anything."

"Except 'use birth control.' That's the only thing I ever remember her telling us. And see, I didn't listen."

"Oh, the old wounded child thing." Stephanie rolled her eyes. "Don't dust that one off, Jennie. Maybe you should be seeing someone too."

"In all my free time," Jennie said.

"Listen, can I talk about Jerry again or is that in bad taste?"

"No, it's okay." Jennie smiled. She and her sister hadn't seen or talked to each other in a year and a half but she was enjoying spending time with her. She always did, but whenever Stephanie went back to California, Jennie's letters or e-mail would go unanswered and they'd forget about each other until the next Christmas.

"The thing about Jerry is this," Stephanie was saying. "You remember that guy from high school. Joel Tarn?"

"Yes." Jennie felt a tremor. "I just saw him the other day," she said, speaking slowly.

"No kidding."

"Yeah, he's home for the reunion."

"You know, I went out with him for about three minutes—maybe three weeks—in high school. He was my first boyfriend and a lot of the reason I broke up with him was I really liked him but I thought there must be something more."

"And?" Jennie asked tentatively.

"Well, I went on to date about one million other guys, but that way I felt about Joel, it's the same way I've felt about two or three guys since, and it's the same way I feel about Jerry. It's a pleasant, somewhat committed, but not entirely rare feeling."

Jennie wanted to be clear about this. "So you think you should wait until you feel something more?" she asked.

"Hell no." Steph scoffed. "I'm saying just the opposite. I know now this is as good as it gets. After all that experience, that's what I know. It just makes me wonder if I should have stayed with Joel. I mean, that's absurd. All the different types of guys and all that was great but I'm still left with the same feeling and I think, was it worth wasting all that time when I could have just settled on the first guy."

"Except you wouldn't have known that unless you had the experiences of these other relationships."

"That sounds like Glinda in *The Wizard of Oz* telling Dorothy that she had the power within her all along to get home but she just had to learn it for herself."

"I guess," Jennie said.

Stephanie snorted. "No place like home fucking home. God, I hated that movie. I would have been so pissed if I were Dorothy. I would have said, 'Why couldn't you just tell me, goddamn it?'"

"Geez, sorry, Steph. *I'm* not Glinda. Anyway, you'll see Joel tonight at the reunion if you want a second chance."

"That is entirely beside the point. I'm not saying he was the one. He was just *a* one. One of a handful. That's all."

Jennie felt a tightening in her throat when they used Joel's name. Not that she wanted him but she *wanted* to want him.

"What are you going to do the rest of the day?" Jennie asked Stephanie later when she dropped her at Fay and Leo's. "Seeing any of your old pals?"

"God no. I'll see them tonight. If I see them today I'll have to live through the painful story of how they found the perfect Mexican tile for their bathrooms. Smile through the obligatory tour of their starter homes. No thanks. I'm going to just hang out at the pool at the country club. Want to join me?"

Jennie had a familiar flash of envy. "I've got a million things to do today," Jennie told Stephanie.

"See you tonight, then."

What Jennie didn't tell Stephanie was that she and Fay had had a blowup on the phone the evening before. Jennie blamed her mother's gossip for the fight Matt had been in—how else would anyone know Matt was working for her?—and right after Matt left her house she had called her mother and chastised her. It was tricky; she had promised Matt she wouldn't tell about the fight, and she didn't want to give her mother a new round of information to pass on. Instead, she told Fay about Marilyn Linders's call. Of course Fay denied telling anyone "of consequence" that her daughter had "that Matt Fallon" working for her this summer.

"It doesn't matter who you told, Mom," Jennie had said. "This is Sheldrake. Things get around. Marilyn Linders was absolutely livid. If she knows, anybody might know, and I'm concerned about Matt's safety."

"His safety? This isn't the wild, wild west, Jennifer. They're not going to send a posse after him."

"You're so convinced you live in the center of the civilized universe, aren't you, Mom? Do you know how many of your beloved bankers and lawyers and stockbrokers have guns in their houses? Do you know how many of them have teenage kids who are completely unsupervised? Who have plenty of money for alcohol and drugs and whatever they want and if they have a hankering for Daddy's gun, well why not that too?"

"I think you're exaggerating now. No one's going to go out and shoot the boy." The finest trace of a laugh in her mother's voice sent Jennie over the edge. She didn't know why she had embarked on this tirade about guns but it had gotten her so heated that her voice cracked in anger and desperation. "Why couldn't you just *listen* to me? I asked you to keep it to yourself and you had to gossip all over town. It was one small thing I asked of you, Mom."

And then Jennie had hung up. She had never, in years and years of wanting to, hung up on her mother. Always before when they fought on the phone she felt she had to find a way to make everything nice again before they said good-bye. This time, she didn't care.

She didn't tell Stephanie any of this, though Steph would probably have said, "Way to go!" when she heard. She didn't want Stephanie involved, didn't want to hear her big-sister lectures. On more than one occasion Stephanie had said, "Did our parents give us enough attention? Of course not. Are they cold and self-involved? You bet. Are you going to get them to change? Absolutely not. So just get on with your life." Which is what, after all, Stephanie had done, very well, and Jennie admired her for it. She knew the distance helped immeasurably.

At home, Tara was still in her pajamas, watching TV on the couch, Alison was taking a nap and Chris was in the bedroom putting on his tux. "Frank wants me there at two now," he said. "Do you have time to listen to my speech?"

"Sure." She sat on the bed, with its usual mess of tangled sheets, burping cloths, shed clothes, and Chris picked up a notecard off the dresser.

"That's your whole speech?"

"It's not really a speech. It's more like a toast, I think. Okay, here goes." Chris cleared his throat, shifted his feet and began: "Since I'm the longest-married person he knows, Frank naturally wanted to draw on my experience and wisdom by asking for my advice about marriage. Well, I wrote it all down on a napkin which he then used to wipe up some spilled beer in a bar and now I can't remember anything I said, so instead I'm just going to tell a story to let Janet know that the guy she's marrying isn't a complete buffoon. How's that so far?"

"Good," Jennie said. "What story are you going to tell?"

"About our wedding," Chris said. "Remember how when it was time to go in I was nervous and my mouth was all dry so I got that cherry soda from the vending machine . . ."

"And when you opened it, it squirted all over."

"And Frank said I couldn't get married in that red-speckled shirt so he gave me his, and then he just wore his T-shirt under his leather jacket." Chris had up to now been telling the story jovially, a smile on his face, but Jennie could see the emotion overcome him and he had to choke out the last words: "Well, I just wanted Janet to know that she was marrying a guy—who—would—give—you—the—shirt—off—his—back." Chris wiped at his eyes and said, "That was supposed to be the punch line. That was supposed to be *funny.*"

Jennie stood up and put her arms around him. "It's great," she whispered. "You tell a good story." There was a quiver in her own voice too. She was touched, not just by his memory of their wedding day, but also by the tender respect his story paid to their marriage. "I love you," she said.

"And I love you."

They stood in the center of their bedroom for a long time, just holding each other. She felt they were a snapshot of what marriage was: two exhausted, hurried people taking a moment in their shambles of a bedroom to remember love.

Over Chris's shoulder Jennie caught sight of her very favorite picture of the two of them, one that had stood on their dresser for years. It wasn't from their wedding day, but from the day Tara was conceived.

She didn't *know* (they had been having sex all the time then, every day in each others' cars, or basements, or spare rooms at other people's parties) but she *knew.* That night, at Elizabeth's going-off-to-college party, they had begun for the first time to say good-bye. Jennie was leaving for Chicago in a couple of weeks and they had been ignoring that fact all summer, pretending that things would carry on forever between the two of them. But that night (who knew why—the mood? the moon? the inevitable collapse of pretending?) they had used words they had avoided all summer, words like *letters* and *visits* and *Christmas,* even the long-avoided *other people.* Jennie was headed for four years of college and probably grad school afterward, and he was staying in Sheldrake to work for his father. Long-distance romances never worked, people told her—her mother, her sister, Elizabeth, all her friends—especially when one of the people simply stayed behind.

And maybe it wouldn't have worked. If they had just gone home that night, instead of sneaking into Elizabeth's bedroom and locking the door and making love and making Tara, maybe there would have been frantic phone calls at first, lots of letters, then fewer, some visits and then a painful but graceful and permanent end. Instead, as Jennie was finally feeling her way toward letting go, the cells and fluids inside them were working to keep them connected forever.

"We did the right thing, didn't we?" she whispered to Chris now. "By getting married?"

"You're asking that question now?"

"I guess it's rhetorical."

"I was thinking that you can't really say *right* or *wrong* after so many years. It's who we are, Jen. You're my . . . life." He bobbled his lips against her cheek and added, "I mean it as a compliment."

FRANK AND JANET'S wedding was in Sheldrake's beautiful old Congregational church, packed with flowers and candles and guests. How different this was from Jennie and Chris's. They had gotten married in the county courthouse with Frank as best man and Elizabeth as best woman—she had insisted on calling herself that—"I'm no one's maid," she had said. Jennie's parents wouldn't come and Stephanie wasn't home from college yet, but Chris's family was there, and a few of their friends. It had been three days before Christmas. Jennie had worn an emerald green velvet dress and was four months pregnant.

It seemed more than slightly amazing now that they had done all that—two eighteen-year-olds, frightened but in love. They had been so desperate for guidance then, but there was none. Every decision they made could easily have gone the other way.

Frank and Janet's wedding seemed to be over in no time—some inaudible vows, a kiss and the soloist singing the latest Disney movie love song—but then Jennie was so distracted by reunion plans that she wasn't paying much attention.

The minute the ceremony was over she ducked out of the church and went home to feed Alison. As soon as the sitter came, Jennie and Tara left for the reunion, picking Matt up on the way.

Matt came out of his house in a suit and Jennie thought she noticed a slight stiffness in the arm that he had injured yesterday. His face looked fine though, with just a little redness around the nose. She had been feeling increasingly uncomfortable about agreeing to keep quiet about the fight. What if this guy, whoever he was, or some other guy, decided to come after him again? It would be Jennie's responsibility, plain and simple, if anything happened.

Matt's mother, a small, boyish woman, waved from the doorway, and Jennie felt a little pang for knowing something about her son that she did not.

Matt sat in the back and Tara twisted around to say a shy hello. Jennie had the odd feeling that she was chauffeuring them to the prom. She tried to will herself invisible so they would be more comfortable with each other, but it didn't work. They didn't say much in the car, but once at the hotel, where Jennie gave them the name tags to lay out and programs to distribute around the tables, they seemed to relax.

The Sheldrake '80 class president, Missy Foley, arrived early, looking much the same as she had as homecoming queen twenty years ago. Blonder hair, deeper tan. She wore a strapless red dress and she stuck her name tag on her bare skin as if that was the funniest thing in the world. While Jennie answered Missy's questions, Matt and Tara unpacked the reunion favors—beer mugs engraved with SHELDRAKE TIGERS—STILL ROARING AFTER ALL THESE YEARS. It had been Missy's idea and inscrutable to Jennie.

Missy had a playlist for Jennie to give the deejay; topping the list was "Lady in Red" and Jennie wondered just who Missy was targeting with this seduction plan. For Missy, this seemed a little like a "find

Missy a husband" event, but then Jennie had already discovered that most people had a hidden purpose behind going to their high school reunions.

"Hi, Aunt Stephanie," Jennie heard Tara say.

"How're you doing, Tara? Sorry I missed you this morning, sleepyhead." Stephanie frowned at the name tag Tara handed her—she was wearing a strapless gown too, a yellow one—then stuck it on her purse.

Stephanie's eyes shifted to Matt and she put out her hand. "Stephanie Northrop," she said.

Matt shook her hand and Jennie saw him move his lips to keep from grinning. *Interactive Media Goddess,* he was probably thinking.

"I'm Matt Fallon," he said. "Nice to meet you." The smile still wobbled a bit and his eyes met Jennie's.

"Well, Steph," Jennie said, "aside from the reunion committee, you're the first to arrive."

"Of course," Stephanie said. "I came all this way. Do you think I want to miss a minute of this thing?"

MATT

FOR MATT, the reunion began with the deep pleasure he felt in meeting all of the people whose names he had learned over the summer, deep pleasure that they could exist in real life and not just as details on a filled-out form, entries in the computer database. He couldn't really explain why this was encouraging to him, except that the intersection of these lives—those that were described, written about, reported on; and the real ones, fueled by the soul—made him feel hopeful about his own life. That while another person might know the facts of your life and make judgments about who you were, you could be somewhere else, living your life and proving them wrong.

He and Tara were in charge of the welcome desk, handing people their name tags and seeing how their faces matched or didn't match the pictures he and Jennie had cut out from the yearbook. For the first hour or so they were very busy but then it quieted down. Jennie brought them out plates of dinner, pausing to count the unclaimed name tags. It amazed Matt that some people hadn't bothered to show up. He knew the tickets cost eighty-five dollars each.

Tara looked great in her short peach-colored dress, her hair on top of her head like a ballerina. It looked as if she were wearing makeup and that gave her a certain embery glow she hadn't had when he saw her on Thursday. A gold chain hung at the base of her throat. She had the highest collarbones Matt had ever seen. It looked as if the softly rounded points were pressing up, trying to break through her skin.

It was hard being with her, but at least the reunion gave them automatic things to talk about. Tara was reading aloud from the reunion bulletin, most of which he'd typed. She was most interested in what people listed in their "my advice to high school students now would be . . ." column.

"They're so conflicting," she said. "One person says 'live it up' and the next one says 'study hard.' This guy says 'finish college' and this one says 'get the GED as soon as you can.'"

"I suppose they're telling you what worked for them."

"Or what didn't. Now here's something really useful: 'Stock up on hall passes.'"

Matt started to read over her shoulder. "This one makes the most sense: 'Never listen to older people who tell you what to do.'"

"A lot of people say 'follow your dreams,' but then look at what their jobs are." She started flipping through the pages. "Food technologist. Electroplater of zinc/cadmium. Service revenue clerk. Audit manager. Analyst. What are those things? Could they be anyone's dreams?"

"I don't know. Maybe they're saying follow your dream because we didn't."

"Or maybe they're still following their dreams and this is just what they're doing in the meantime."

"Or maybe their dreams involve something totally different from work, like running marathons or building a house from the ground up." It wasn't hard for Matt to think what his parents' dreams might be. His father's: to help the world sustain itself a little bit longer. His mother's: to give her children the education she wished she had had herself. But would they have said these things in high school?

"What would you say your dream is?" he asked Tara, a bit hesitantly. They were finally talking naturally and he hated to jeopardize it by being too serious.

"My dream. My dream. Hmmmmm . . ." Her eyes searched the ceiling and then turned to him. "When I was a kid, I always used to want to be a dancer."

"That's funny," he said, "because I was thinking you looked like a ballerina."

She reached up to touch her hair. "Yes," she said. "I'm a bunhead. But I've kind of stopped dancing. Now I was thinking I'd like to illustrate children's books."

"That's neat." Matt immediately pictured the book he had read to Katie and Em before bed last night, one about a fisherman who found a pearl and became so rich he no longer needed to fish. One day, a thief broke into the man's house and robbed him of everything he had. The fisherman set off to tell the police but on his way found his old fishing pole and instead returned to the happiness of his old life as a fisherman. He caught many fish and returned home to a good meal and a nap. Later, when the police came to tell him they had found his belongings, the fisherman said, "I am a fisherman. It is true I am a rich man, but nothing of value has been stolen from my house." Whenever Matt read that last line his voice always faltered and Katie and Em would pat him on the arm and say, "It's not sad, Mattie. See, it's not sad."

He told Tara, "The best children's books are not just for children, I think. Do you know what I mean?"

"Kind of." She sat pensively for a moment and then asked, "So what's your dream?"

Matt shook his head, which was to say that he did not think of dreams anymore. She kept that pert, inquiring expression on her face, so he finally said, "I'm not sure." She looked away then and he felt bad, as if he had set her up.

Jennie came out again, this time to tell them they didn't have to stay at the table anymore—anyone who hadn't arrived yet was officially a no-show—so they went inside the banquet hall and listened to Missy Foley read out the senior superlatives. There were the ones you would expect, like Most Likely to Succeed, Best Athlete and Best in Drama, but also stranger ones. Most Self-Centered. Most Spacey. Strangest Laugh. "I know who would get that from my class," Tara said.

As their names were called, men and women went up to take a bow and get their pictures taken with Missy. Jennie's sister Stephanie had won both Biggest Smart Aleck and Best Party Giver. Missy won Most Secretly Admired and Best Hair.

"Wouldn't it be weird," Tara whispered to Matt, "if the guy who got nicest hair was bald now? Or if the best in dancing was really fat?"

The Best-Matched Couple from the class of '80 officially opened up the dance floor by dancing to the Sheldrake '80 theme song, some slow song from twenty years ago. The man was tall and stiff in a dark gray suit and the woman seemed to wince at every word of the song. *Sometimes when we touch,* went the words, *the honesty's too much.* Matt wondered if it had been their song, hers and this man's, and now it hurt to hear it again.

When others started to join the Best-Matched Couple, Matt suddenly felt someone grab his hand. It was Missy and before he could say no, she pulled him onto the dance floor. She was singing along with the words of the song, so off-key he couldn't stand to hear it: *I want to hold you till I die, till we both break down and cry.*

"I'm sorry," Matt said. "I'm here to work." But she wouldn't let go. She squeezed his sore shoulder and he winced and had to push her away. But then Jennie was there, saying, "Sorry, Missy, Matt's already promised this dance." Jennie pulled him away from Missy, and he put his arm around her waist in order to dance.

"Oh no," Jennie said. "Don't worry, you won't have to dance with me. I'll get Tara." She led him by the hand off the dance floor and he kept his head low so she couldn't see how red his face had turned over this clumsiness.

"Sorry to be so patronizing," she said when they were a safe distance away, "but she's ripped and I don't want your parents thinking I've dragged you into some den of iniquity." She was talking right into his ear to be heard above the music and a strand of her loose hair tickled his neck. He could smell her perfume—a dark, cinnamony scent she normally didn't wear—but underneath he could smell *her,* not something artificial but the smell that he had come to recognize over the summer.

"It's okay," he said.

"Tara," Jennie called, motioning her over to them. "Sweetheart," she said, "Missy Foley is the thirty-eight-year-old female equivalent of a dirty old man and I need you to save Matt from her. Okay?" And she disappeared so that they had no choice but to dance.

Thankfully it was a faster song now, a Blondie song he recognized. He had no idea it was twenty years old. He was glad he didn't have to worry about where to put his hands, how close to stand. Tara's dress had such thin straps that there would be no place but skin to touch.

He felt a flare of anger toward Jennie. Was she setting them up? He had the feeling that he and Tara were just another reunion she was trying to organize.

Tara looked right at him as she danced, smiling as if she were having the best time. She seemed to dance more for him than with him. She was especially great on the fast songs. Matt was not very confident on those, but he'd learned to waltz and polka and cha-cha-cha for a community theater production he had been in once and he tried to use those steps. The steps of slow dancing were easy enough, if only his hand wouldn't sweat so on her waist.

From time to time he would search for Jennie, drawing radar circles with his eyes until he found her—talking to someone, laughing with someone, giving someone a hug—and then he would let his eyes return to Tara.

Once they had begun dancing, they didn't leave the dance floor all night. It was fun, that was part of it, but Matt also felt that if they stopped dancing, even for five minutes, to have a Coke or rest their feet, it would be so monumentally hard to begin again—to walk toward each other with smiles and find the beat and place their hands on each other's bodies—that they wouldn't be able to do it. They had to keep up the momentum, keep dancing until they were told to stop because any pause would mean the agony of starting all over again.

JENNIE

S HE HAD SAID HELLO to Joel at the door but they were now two hours into the reunion and she hadn't gone over to speak to him yet. She didn't know what she was waiting for, or afraid of. Looking across the room at him, she felt like an eighth-grader at her first dance and that kept her away, though he made no real effort to work his way over to her either.

Joel had shown up wearing white linen pants and a turquoise shirt, looking a little *Miami Vice*-y, but because he hadn't done deliberate maneuvers with hair gel or sideburns it didn't look too put-on. *Okay, what the hell,* Jennie said to herself, *he's a sexy guy. So what?*

Joel ate dinner at Stephanie's table, she noticed, and afterward he stood at the bar while Stephanie bulldozed through the room. Stephanie was the only person Jennie had ever seen who could use business cards as weapons. At one point she brought someone over to Jennie and said, "Jim Storvak. Who would have thought? He's got a custom auto parts shop. Mail order all over the world and no Web site." She slapped him on the back and flitted off, and Jennie was left to listen to Jim Storvak, whom she remembered only vaguely from high school, tell her about the house he was building in Saddle River.

"I'm pretty happy with it," he was saying. "Four thousand square feet, cathedral ceilings in three rooms. Super, super master suite with a Jacuzzi. We've got three-and-a-half level acres, all backed on woods. We just can't wait to get in."

"That's great," Jennie said. She was watching Stephanie move across the room toward Joel. Stephanie said something to him and then they went out the door together; almost without thinking Jennie assumed they had left to spend the night together.

Jim Storvak was asking about the Sheldrake '80 grads who had died and Jennie told him. *Five car accidents, one from a congenital heart defect, two from AIDS, another from lymphoma, an ovarian cancer death.* Those were just the ones she knew about. In a class of 576, there were twenty-one she hadn't been able to find and it was possible some of those had died. But she had found it was the ones who had died *during* high school that people always remembered at reunions, the ones who had the in memoriam pictures at the end of the yearbook. From Sheldrake's Class of '80 there was one boy, Steve Allbert, who had died in a boating accident senior year, and Jennie was sure everyone there could still utter his name.

As those in Tara's class would always remember Erica Linders and Rachel Cleary. Jennie looked at Tara now, on the dance floor with Matt, and saw her looking happier, more full of joy than she had since the accident, though she was sure Rachel and Erica's names weren't far from her lips.

She wondered if what had lain dormant between Matt and Tara all those weeks was beginning to renew itself, and if it was something that could exist alongside Rachel and Erica. If whatever sorrow they shared about Rachel and Erica would not stifle anything that might be there on its own. She could only imagine that any kind of love affair they might have was already laden with far too much to carry. They were only sixteen—Matt not even. Together their ages did not add up to the age of everyone else in the room. *Thirty-eight.*

A twenty-year reunion was so different from a ten, Jennie thought, turning her attention from Tara and Matt to the roomful of adults surrounding them. By twenty years out of high school, people had to strain to even remember the old cliques and enemies; it seemed laughable now, pointless. And as a group they looked different. At the ten-year, the men had aged rather badly—balding, getting paunchy, but the additional ten years seemed not to have aged them at all. Women who were uniformly gorgeous at twenty-eight started to show indelible signs of age at thirty-eight—lines around eyes and mouths, skin that had lost its smooth freshness, the extra weight that babies often brought.

Thirty-eight. There had been the deaths, but most everybody still in the room was healthy. The divorces, if they had happened yet, had happened early enough to become distant memory, to be put aside as trial and error, wisdom gained, whole new marriages and families created in their aftermath. Most of them had young children, not teenagers yet, children who weren't old enough to terrify or disappoint them. Most of their parents were still alive, just reaching retirement age, maybe buying some airy condo in Florida or Arizona where they could go visit with the kids during vacation weeks. If the average life expectancy was now somewhere in the late seventies, at thirty-eight they were halfway there, on the brink of middle age. Maybe it was after they left this room that middle age would begin, because in ten years, by the thirty-year reunion—hadn't Jennie seen it?—so much more would have happened. Parents would age tragically, many would die; careers would stagnate; children would bring heartache by taking drugs, falling in with the wrong crowd or simply leaving home, going too far away and for too long. And spouses would be lost by age forty-eight—to breast cancer or heart attacks, boredom and other lovers. Even the lucky ones would face a relentless unsolvable jigsaw of demanding parents, children, jobs, lives.

Of all the reunions Jennie put together, the twentieth was her favorite. To Jennie, thirty-eight seemed a beautiful age, the most beautiful age, of still strong bodies and crowded, humming family life. And hope. It was an age at which you could still change your life, still find some way of undoing your mistakes.

"Nice party, Jennie Breeze." Joel's voice in her ear. Did that irony never leave him?

"I'm glad to see you didn't show up with a film crew," Jennie said. "You had me worried." She looked over his shoulder, searching for Stephanie.

"Is your dance card full yet?" Joel asked.

"I haven't danced at all," she said.

Smiling deeply, Joel held out his hand. "Well, then, let me have the honor of being your first."

"Ha ha," Jennie said.

Joel tugged her against him and she felt herself stiffen in his arms. His hands were warm, sticky even, and his eyes were small but bright. Like most everyone there, he had had too much to drink.

Joel nodded his head toward Matt and Tara and asked, "Who's the golden couple?"

"That's my daughter," Jennie said. "And her . . ." She floundered—
"the boy who works for me."

"So you brought them just to drive home to the rest of us how
flabby and wrinkled we've become?"

"Just a little dose of reality," Jennie said. "Not lethal, I hope."

She smiled over Joel's shoulder as she watched Matt and Tara dance.
Under other circumstances they might have been homecoming queen
and king, Tara's blond head next to Matt's darker one, both dazzling
white smiles not long released from braces. He was gorgeous and she
was a pearl. Both of these things Jennie knew, of course, but seeing
them as Joel might—beautiful, naive, desperately young—and yet
knowing what complications lay behind their faces, made her feel momentarily that there was no way someone her age, or Joel's, could
know anything at all about a boy and a girl aged sixteen.

"So," Jennie asked Joel, "have you found what you're looking for?"

Joel frowned. "Did you talk to Annabel Tiernan? She runs an or-
ganic farm in Vermont."

"I remember that." Jennie nodded.

"Yeah, and Wynn Pavlich went to Clown College in Sarasota,
Florida. I've been talking to him about a project I have in mind," Joel
said vaguely. "But for the most part, I don't know . . . everyone's pretty
crosstown."

"Sorry?"

Joel looked at her impatiently, paused for a beat or two. "You know,
crosstown blocks. In Manhattan?" Her blank look must have told him
she was terminally unhip because he proceeded to explain himself with
far too much thoroughness. "You know, in Manhattan, the fastest city
on earth, there are hundreds of crosstown blocks but only a dozen or
so avenue blocks. Crosstown blocks can be quiet, residential, pretty
unhappening, but if you want the buzz you just head for the nearest
avenue block." Joel looked around the room slowly. "There just aren't
many avenue blocks here."

"So you, Joel Tarn, are you an avenue block?"

"Don't think so. Maybe I'm a corner? The truth is, it's been twenty
years and I still don't have a damn thing in common with these people.
I just don't get what makes them tick. And if I hear the word *acre* one
more time I'm going to hurl."

"I know that feeling."

"Do you remember in high school always wondering who was going to *make it?* Who was going to be the famous actor or writer or politician? Did you do that—think, *which one will make it big?*"

Jennie smiled. "Sure. And it never occurred to us that maybe nobody would."

Joel nodded. "Exactly. You know what I've been doing with your sister?"

"What?" Jennie asked.

"Smoking hash in the parking lot. Same thing we used to do in high school."

"Steph brought it?"

"No, somebody she knew had some." Joel had to stop speaking for a moment. The song had changed to a faster one and they moved away from each other. Around them, people started to get rowdier, swinging hips and arms to Donna Summer. The deejay was really concentrating on the disco thing.

Joel had to yell in her ear now. "The thing is, neither of us has touched drugs in years. Something about being here brings it all back."

Jennie nodded, not wanting to yell over the music and not having anything to say anyway. They danced for a while and then Joel was yelling in her ear again. "I'm glad I came. If nothing else, to remind myself that these are just people. Not necessarily noteworthy because I knew them when I was eighteen."

"I see," Jennie said. She was caught between calling Joel the most arrogant man she had ever met and agreeing that he was completely right. He obviously wasn't all that thrilled with what he was going back to, but he had concluded that he didn't want to replace it with this either.

And then later, he did go home with Stephanie. Jennie saw them slip out laughing and she could tell by the way they leaned on each other that they were very drunk, or stoned, or both. She worried about them driving and followed them into the lobby, thinking she'd offer to drive them somewhere if they wanted. But they weren't heading toward the parking lot; they were instead at the hotel desk, asking for a key.

She slipped back into the reunion before they saw her. She felt foolish, dowdy, definitely crosstown. She was tired of being everyone's mother. How different Stephanie was to so easily accommodate this night with Joel. Stephanie didn't have to analyze what she was feeling, past and present, to reach some kind of decision. Stephanie would just do it. Because she wanted to. Because it didn't matter one way or another, except for how it would make her feel tonight.

Meanwhile, Jennie would wallow in her own monogamy. She was so pedestrian. She was a pedestrian, one-way, crosstown block. And yet she really didn't want to be *there,* she thought: in the elevator, on the way up to the hotel room with Joel. Though she wouldn't have minded being *there:* with Joel in her parents' house on that summer night almost twenty years ago. Because that, when it came right down to it, was what she envied: not Stephanie's easy pleasure, not the spontaneity that made her able to go with him while Jennie could not, but that first time, that one time, the feeling of being young and just making the acquaintance of all those emotions. A time when a certain song could mean the earth and an accidental touch in the hallways caused tremors for days.

Nor would she have minded being *there*—where Matt and Tara danced, not knowing, not even knowing that they didn't know, what lay ahead. Jennie let Matt and Tara dance for as long as she could because they looked so happy. It occurred to her for the first time that for all the damage the accident had done to them, for all they would have to deal with Erica and Rachel's deaths all their lives, they were young and strong in the world and they could get past this. This loss might fortify them, in some way, against the years to come and maybe now, just maybe, they would fortify each other.

It was nearing midnight when Jennie needed to pry Tara and Matt away from the dance floor. She took them across town to the wedding reception and asked them to stay in the car while she went in to find Chris. The day had exhausted her and her breasts were painfully full of milk. She needed to get home. She had been missing the baby for the last hour or so and realized that this evening was the longest they had been apart in Alison's life. Six hours.

After the quiet of the car, she wasn't prepared for the noise and commotion of the reception, the rowdy drunks dancing in groups, the band with speakers turned way up, playing something that wasn't twenty years old.

She searched the floor for Chris and found him dancing with

Frank's sister. He had a beer in one hand and was laughing like crazy, looking so disheveled and sweaty and totally sexy that after not seeing him all evening it was like arriving at a much-anticipated party and spotting someone new in a crowd that you had to find a way to meet. And then when Chris saw her, raised his eyebrows and raised his beer while dancing toward her, she felt a double edge of good fortune and melancholy because he was already hers.

"Hi, babe," he said. He gave her a long, wet kiss then whispered in her ear, "I'm pretty trashed. I better come with you and pick up the truck tomorrow."

"We're going to have to go soon," Jennie said. "I've got to get Matt home by midnight. And Alison—"

"One dance? I've been waiting all night."

"One dance," she said, going into his arms.

Though she and Chris hadn't had occasion to dance in months, it felt as if they knew what they were doing. They bounced around the floor waving at friends, laughing and shouting hello, and Jennie felt how real this was, this wedding, a celebration of only the best of intentions. Reunions suddenly seemed so tawdry by comparison. They were ways of measuring lives, charting progress, comparing now and then and him and her, usually tinged, at one end or the other, with bitterness. A wedding was a sending off, with all the brightest hopes for the future; a reunion, five hundred discontented reasons for looking into the past.

MATT

I T WAS THE senior prom he'd never have. Or the wedding.

Nostalgia in reverse—now he knew the term for it. Thanks to Nabokov. Thanks to Jennie who had given him Nabokov's *Mary* to read. Matt was sure that he never wanted to read another word by anyone but Vladimir Nabokov in his life. *Nostalgia in reverse:* to want desperately to go, not back in time to something you had and missed, but to go far away, to somewhere you had never been but craved desperately to go. He wanted a prom, a wedding, he wanted to dance all night with a girl he loved. He had never thought for a minute about these things before, but now that he knew his was a life that wouldn't contain them, he yearned with an ache that consumed him.

He didn't love Tara, but maybe he could. She had been in his thoughts last night as he went to sleep—Tara with her beautiful neck bones and the wisps of hair that dangled by the side of her face after so much dancing. It had almost felt like a date except they had never been alone and they hadn't kissed at the end.

He was an idiot. They couldn't go on a date. He couldn't even leave his house. It was miraculous that he had seen her twice in one week and that she had wanted to talk to him. When could it ever happen again? He was on house detention, and in a few weeks, he might be in jail.

Then it came to him. Church. Church was the only place he could go that Tara could go too.

He waited until nine o'clock to call. He knew Alison woke up early and somebody was sure to be up with her.

When Mr. Breeze answered, he said, "This is Matt Fallon. May I please speak to Tara?"

"At nine in the morning on a Sunday? I think I'd have to say she's still sleeping. I thought I was too."

"Oh. I'm sorry. It's just . . . I wanted to invite her to come to church with my family this morning. We usually go to the eleven o'clock service. We could pick her up."

"Well, I'll ask her. If she gets up in time, I mean."

"Thanks."

Mr. Breeze waited a moment and then asked, "Do you want me to wake her up?"

"No, just if she wakes up if you could ask her."

"Okay. 'Bye." Mr. Breeze hung up quickly and Matt wondered if he was upset by Matt's call or if he was just one of those dads, like Matt's, who was brief and uncomfortable on the phone. Last night was the first time Matt had ever met him and they had just said hello. Who knew what Mr. Breeze thought of him?

An hour went by and Tara didn't call. Maybe she was still sleeping. It was ten o'clock, then 10:15. Matt got ready to go anyway. He ironed his sage green shirt and khakis, gelled his hair. He mentioned to Mom that Tara might be coming, but she didn't call and he felt stupid for acting so rashly. He shouldn't have told her father about going to church. He should have just had him ask Tara to call him. Then he could at least have asked for himself.

Dad gave the ten-minute warning at 10:30 and at 10:35 the phone was for Matt. Yes, she wanted to come. Yes, she could be ready in time. His parents took it in stride as they did almost everything, and they went to pick her up.

Tara looked a little frightened getting into the big green van packed with children but she smiled at each one and repeated their names. Em immediately decided to own Tara and kept swiveling around from her booster seat to ask her, "Do you like elephants, Tara?" or "Do you like crocodiles? They have sharp teeth, you know."

When they got out of the van it just seemed like his family had absorbed one more child. Because it was summer and they had Sunday school only for the littlest ones, all of them but Katie and Em sat in a pew together, Tara at the end, next to him. *She's so small,* is what he kept thinking as they stood up to sing hymns. Her head didn't reach his shoulder. She was about the size of nine-year-old Peter, who sat on Matt's other side.

Matt asked her if she would come again next week and even before she nodded "yes" he counted in his head that there would only be five more Sundays before his sentencing. Five more total hours in his life to spend with Tara.

Except. Except. He could not leave his house but there was no reason she couldn't enter it. It had never occurred to him because he had never had a friend to invite over before.

"Do you want to come back to my house after this?" he asked her. "For an hour or two, if you want."

"Sure," Tara said. "Is it all right with your mom?"

When he asked, Mom said Tara could even stay for dinner, though he'd still have to do his part of the prep.

At Matt's house Tara sat on the deck with him snapping beans and husking corn.

"Wow," she said, "I can't believe how much food your family needs."

"Seven people."

"It's a lot. I always wanted to have a big family. I used to read all these books about big families—*The Five Little Peppers, Cheaper by the Dozen.* I hated being an only child."

"You're not anymore."

"I know, but it's not the same. She's so much younger. She doesn't seem related to me, she doesn't seem . . . close."

"I can remember feeling like that when my brothers and sisters were born. Well, not Brian, because I was only three and I don't remember that much. But the others, I'd get used to it and it would seem that our family was just how it should be and then we'd have another baby and it would seem so strange but after a while it would be just as if that's how the family had always been. Until the next one came along."

Matt was watching the way Tara was pulling the silk off the corncobs. Her fingers were tiny and delicate and she seemed to pick the strands off one by one and set them gently on the brown paper bag below, as if she had never done this before and now she had the rest of her life, a pleasant eternity, to complete the task.

"Do you play chess?" Matt asked her. Her patience, her precision, had made him think of chess.

"My dad taught me when I was ten but I've never really played with anyone but him."

"Let's try," Matt said. After they finished with the corn and beans he took the waste back to the compost heap and left Tara on the deck while he went in to wash his hands and find the chessboard.

When he returned, Katie and Em were showing Tara their hats. They kept leaving and returning with new hats on. Cowboy hats, sunbonnets, firefighter hats, nurses' hats.

"Your sisters are really adorable," Tara said.

Matt told the girls to go back in the house but they just walked a few feet away and sat down on the grass.

Tara set up the pieces and Matt was glad to see she put them all on the right squares, queen on her own color, knights next to bishops. She played more socially, moving a piece and then asking a question or just smiling, and he tried to adjust his play to do the same. He had been playing chess since he was four and he loved it—that combination of skillful play and unexpected maneuver. He tried to play more casually though, because he always hated it when you went over to people's houses and they invited you to play the game they were the best at.

Each time she smiled he smiled back, and each time she moved he nodded. But there was nothing to say, no way to remove those ten weeks since the accident, make it feel that this was just a day or two after he'd last seen her swimming at the Y. He saw how beautiful she was and how sweet, and he felt he should want her, but most of all he felt the futility of it all, the impossibility of starting over. When could he ever kiss her again? In the van on the way to church with all his family watching? Over the chessboard next Sunday, with Katie and Em watching their every move?

JENNIE

THE WEEKS that had passed since Alison's birth and the accident seemed to be all of a moment, all the same. The summer was, for Jennie, a long, hallucinatory corridor, one of those pointless dreams that is nevertheless dreamed over and over again. Perhaps it would even seem like a dream, this summer, when she looked back at it from a different point in her life.

Some things had changed. Alison had changed. When she hit three months, she became a new kind of baby. She could stay awake for four-hour stretches in the afternoon now and Jennie would plan outings with her—to the park to watch the ducks, to the pet store to look at the fish, to the library to look at the paintings that hung in the art wing. She was almost, not quite, big enough to go in the baby swings at the park. She was almost, not quite, big enough to go in the exerciser someone had given them as a baby present. She was still content in her bouncy seat or on the floor under her activity gym, but Jennie sensed that she would quickly demand more from the world.

She tried to remember what Tara was like at that age. She had done the same things with her, she supposed, and in the exact same places, but it had all felt so different then, so uncomfortable. Now, Jennie looked like all the other mothers; then, she had been so young, trying to raise a child in a town that simply did not have teenage mothers. She was always being mistaken for an au pair girl, and she hadn't always bothered to correct people.

Alison was three months old now, which meant Tara had made it to the three-month anniversary of the accident. Now that Tara was seeing Matt again, Jennie was vigilant: she worried about where the relationship might lead, but so far had seen only signs of happiness on Tara's face when she returned from Matt's house each Sunday.

Tara was at Matt's this afternoon; she wondered if together they were marking those three months since the accident. Jennie thought of Rachel's and Erica's parents and impulsively called Camille Cleary to ask if she might drop over.

She wished she had something to take with her. She had never been one to bake but she wished she had made muffins. Or a cake. She decided to drive quickly into town for some flowers but then couldn't bring herself to buy something else beautiful that was going to die too soon. In the gift section of the florist's she saw a candle and remembered that around middle school, Rachel used to collect them—goofy animals, the hippo with ballet shoes, a penguin in sunglasses. Jennie saw this pale peach column with flower blossoms embedded in it, baby's breath included, and she had it wrapped up in tissue to take to Camille's house.

Kevin was outside in the front yard, very listlessly doing something to the dirt around a little bush. Jennie sat on the ground next to him and he looked at her, a time delay in his response to her hello.

"Are you sure you should be out here working in this heat?" Jennie asked, hoping it didn't sound as if she were treating him as an invalid.

He shrugged. "I'm hardly doing anything."

When Jennie asked, "How are you and Camille getting along?" Kevin said, "I couldn't even say." He managed a weak, almost sickening sort of smile. "Camille's on the deck, I think," he said.

Jennie had seen it with Kevin and she saw it immediately with Camille too: for them, not a day had passed since they first learned of the accident, not a minute. Three months was nothing against what they'd lost. Until now Jennie had not realized how tangential her grief was to theirs. Even Tara's. Even Matt's was on the fringe, the tragedy striking close to all their lives rather than dead center, where Camille and Kevin were trying to survive.

Camille sat upright on a deck chair, an unopened book on her lap.

"I brought this for you," Jennie said, gently setting the candle on the book. "It reminded me of Rachel." Jennie was glad the tissue paper shed off easily so that it didn't seem too much like a gift.

"Ah," Camille said. Jennie saw her eyes still had that bruised quality. How many hours of these three months had she spent crying?

"Is there anything at all I can do for you, Camille?"

"Bring my daughter back? Let me adopt yours? Can you do either of those things?" Camille's voice was the voice of a devastated person trying to make a joke. She'd heard the same quality in Matt's.

"I'm afraid I can't," Jennie said.

"It's nice that you're letting me borrow her so often," Camille said. Jennie nodded, smiled.

"Has she told you what we're doing?" Camille asked.

"No."

"Come." The slow, pained manner in which Camille rose from her chair suggested that she had been sitting there, just like that, all day, and that tomorrow would be the same.

As soon as they were in the house, Camille turned toward the bedrooms. Camille's house was bigger than Jennie's but still small enough to have this hallway lead only one place.

Jennie didn't want to go there, did not want to see Rachel's room. *No,* she almost said aloud because she could anticipate the force with which it would hit her—the pillow on the bed, the shelf of trophies, the mirror tucked with postcards and dried nosegays. The Rachel equivalent of Tara's room. Jennie was sure she would scream if she saw it. She didn't want to get that close. *Don't. Take. Me. There. Please. Don't.*

But Camille turned before they got to the end of the hallway, turned into the den. On one wall was the computer desk and on the other a long table cluttered with paints and thick white paper soaked with watercolors, corners turned up. Jennie moved closer and put her hands on them. What she touched was something whose absence, specifically, she had not mourned.

Tara's watercolors. The way that in her gregarious, social fashion, Tara would plant herself at the kitchen table to do them while Jennie and Chris made dinner, washed dishes, folded laundry. She would chat away to them while she painted, covering pages and pages in an hour or two, often stacking them wet, each a draft of the next. Jennie had always thought artists were supposed to be solitary types, but Tara made her painting a family event. Jennie had always loved watching her do them, the happy concentration on her face, the tiny tip of her tongue jutting out of her mouth as she painted. Tara had stopped painting since the accident, but Jennie hadn't missed it so viscerally until now.

She moved the papers back and forth. They were drawings of children. Tara usually had trouble drawing people but these were lovely. Not small and round like Charlie Brown figures but tall, with long legs, elegant but wispy. Winning and vague, with a sunny vibrancy. It was obvious they were children. The curl of the hair. The triangle dresses. The colors.

"Let me show you," Camille said.

She sifted through the pages to find what she wanted, then placed it on top. *Rachel Makes a Friend,* the card said, and there was a picture of two girls and a big gray truck. A moving van.

An "oh" slipped from Jennie's lips.

"I've been in kids' publishing for twenty-five years—marketing, sales, subrights—and never once was tempted to write a children's book. Not even when my kids were little. Especially then. It's hard, writing for children. People think they can do it just because they *have* children but most of them can't. They're too close, somehow." Camille had switched over to a brisk, almost businesslike way of speaking, markedly different from the slow, strained sentences she had spoken outside. This was, Jennie supposed, the only way she could get through her days at the office.

Camille went on. "This," she said, "this just happened. Tara and I were talking about Rachel, about how they met, you remember? And we just began."

"They're really wonderful," Jennie said.

"These are just sketches of the cover. Nothing final. Tara's drawings are evolving nicely but my text leaves a lot to be desired."

"Thank you, Camille. Thank you for showing me."

Jennie's heart was feeding off these paintings. She wanted to gather them up in her arms, put her face against them, hold them to her the way she wanted to hold Tara. Jennie had spied on Tara and she was sorry for that, but she wasn't sorry for what she had seen. With Camille's help, Tara was finding her way through. *Why can't it be me?* Jennie fought against crying out. *Why can't I be the one to help?*

Tara was being cared for; that was the most important thing. Maybe as a mother you didn't always have to do it, maybe you weren't always the right one. You just had to do everything in your power to make sure someone was.

"Would you like to stay for a cup of coffee, Jennie?" Camille asked, then gave herself a reproving scoff. "Coffee, what am I saying? It's a hundred degrees out there. How about some ice tea?"

"Just water would be great. Thanks."

They sat in Camille's air-conditioned living room with their ice water, wearing out the topic of heat. Jennie asked about Sam, and Camille said he was spending a week with his best friend's family in Maine. They had planned on getting away, Camille said, all three of them, somewhere relaxing and cool, but she just hadn't gotten around to planning it and now the summer was almost gone.

"Can you believe it?" Camille asked. "School starting in a couple of weeks? The twenty-second of August. I don't know why it's so early this year."

"Didn't they used to wait until Labor Day?"

"The twenty-second of August," Camille said, ignoring Jennie's question, "is also the day Matt Fallon is going to be sentenced."

"Is it?" Jennie asked. "I knew it was soon but I guess I didn't know the exact date."

"We've been asked to prepare victim impact statements. Us and Chuck and Marilyn Linders."

"What are those?" Jennie asked.

"It's our chance to speak publicly. We tell the judge how what Matt has done affected our lives."

"Oh," Jennie said. Matt had told her he was preparing his own statement, but she hadn't known about these.

"I don't know what the hell we're going to say," Camille said. "I mean the idea that there are degrees of impact for what happened, how much were our lives ruined? I don't want what I say to affect the judge's decision about Matt Fallon's future. I feel the law should know what to do. But I'm glad we get to see him, to say something to him. I have found all the anonymity of this very difficult."

"Matt feels the same way," Jennie said. "I know he has wanted to talk to you since the day of the accident." Jennie was starting to feel uncomfortable, as if she had slyly come to plead Matt's case.

Camille spoke again. "I've talked to Marilyn. She'd send him to the gallows if she could."

"It's not hard to understand how she would feel that way," Jennie said.

Camille nodded. "Part of me does, yes, want that to happen. It's a matter of convenience more than revenge. If he were destroyed too, I wouldn't have to think about him ever again." She paused. "But as it is, I'll have to struggle with his existence for the rest of my life."

It's the same for him, Jennie wanted to say, but it wasn't right. She couldn't carry on a conversation about Matt with Camille, no matter how much forgiveness Camille had in her heart. Jennie suddenly felt suspicious; it wouldn't be Camille's fault, but grief could transmogrify that forgiveness at any moment, maybe into something that no longer had room for Matt or Tara.

Camille had begun to lightly cry and she seemed not even to notice. Jennie took her hand and they sat together in silence. Camille made no attempt at all to brush away the tears running down her cheeks. She must be so used to crying. For just a breath of an instant Jennie moved in the vicinity of what Camille was living with. No will to get off the couch. No will, especially while Sam was away, to do anything at all. Jennie could barely keep her own muscles from tightening and springing, from running home and clutching Tara, shouting with joy at the miracle of having her.

When Kevin came in from outside, covered with sweat and looking for a cold drink, Jennie got up to leave. She longed to return to Tara's watercolors, take just one more look, but there was no way she would be a glutton in the home of those who were starving. She just hugged Camille and Kevin good-bye, and slowly walked past the eleven houses that separated their home from hers.

MATT

THEY DIDN'T TALK so much when they were together, his family always around, Katie and Em finding every excuse they could to sit in Tara's lap, but after the third church Sunday they had taken to calling each other at night and that's when they talked.

It always started awkwardly, with neither of them knowing what to say. Tara would try to tell him about work or he'd bring up a book he'd read, but nothing seemed to lead anywhere until they turned their talk from what was happening now to what had happened *then*. In the past. Any bit of the past would do.

Once Matt began to talk about Oregon, it seemed there was plenty to tell her. He talked about his grandparents and cousins and friends, their old blue house, kayaking on the river, picking apples in the autumn and pressing them into cider. It was easy to talk about Oregon because that was locked away, separate from what had happened in Connecticut, like the boxes of Christmas decorations taken out each year, unaware that anything at all had transpired while they nested in the warm, dark attic.

And Tara, in turn, told him about her past. Her past with Erica and Rachel. She was the only person who both could and would tell him things about these girls whom he had scarcely known. He learned that Rachel was half-Jewish, that she had a thirteen-year-old brother, that she played the piano, that she had read *The Diary of Anne Frank* eleven times. And he learned that Erica wrote poems, loved to throw parties, was the star of Sheldrake's girls' soccer team and had hoped to play in college.

"Her dad really pushed her," Tara said. "I think that's why she kept doing it. She liked it and everything, but her dad would come to the games sometimes. He would take off work early on a Friday. She thought he didn't pay attention to her except when he thought she was going to be this big sports star."

Matt suddenly remembered what Erica's father had said the day after the accident when he showed up at Matt's house. *My dreams,* he had said. *You killed my dreams.* Not hers.

And he thought with bitterness of Erica's boyfriend, Jeff, who had treated her so badly and after she died worried only that she had done the same to him. He understood why Erica had spoken so fervently against men to him that night as they sat on the stoop. She hadn't lived long enough to meet one who would treat her right.

"Sometimes I feel that they're here," Tara said one night on the phone. "With us, between us. I feel that we're not alone."

"Are you talking about ghosts?"

"Not that they're ghosts." Her voice was small and far away. "Not that at all. Just that they're, they're becoming part of us or something."

"That we're taking them into our skin?" Matt asked slowly. It was something he could almost visualize if he closed his eyes.

"Something like that. Does it sound creepy? It's how I feel. I mean, I have other friends who knew them longer than you did, but because you were with them when it happened it seems that you're the only one who can understand."

"I don't know how much I can understand," Matt said. "I don't think I understand anything." He felt utterly arrogant for having had any connection to Erica and Rachel as they died. What would their parents think—those who loved them to the bone—if they knew the boy who had driven their daughters into a tree was talking now about how close he felt to them?

"It's just a way of thinking that maybe they go on too," Tara said. "Not just us."

Matt was thinking of something Jennie had said to him once and he tried to repeat it to Tara. "And also," he said, "sometimes that's the gift the dead can give to us—keeping us always just as we were when they died, which is sometimes a better way to be remembered than what we turn ourselves into."

"I guess I know what you mean," Tara said. He could hear in her voice that she didn't really. "Kind of. But it's pretty depressing. As if things will only get worse. It sounds like something my mom would say. Dad always says she's big into dwelling on past glories."

It made perfect sense to Matt that Jennie and Tara would look at things so differently. They were such different people. Tara was sunshine, even now. She was so nice to him, nice to everyone. Not that Jennie wasn't nice—no one had been kinder to him than Jennie—but he felt that kindness was there somehow in spite of what had happened in her life. With Jennie there were all these forces—regret, humor, hope—that made her a different sort of person, more variegated, more dappled than Tara's pure shine. He was sure it was because she was older, had had more things happen in her life, but part of it must be innate.

His life, he thought, would be more like Jennie's. Because of what he'd done, things would never be as simple as they were for Tara, who was a nice girl whose friends had died. And again he would feel the distance between them. Tara said she felt close to him, felt the presence of Erica and Rachel too, but Matt could only see the canyon forming by the blame that was his and not hers.

Things it should have been easy to tell her, like about his birthday coming up, or the latest Nabokov book he had read, were somehow impossible. He so wanted to tell her about his birthday, tell her that his heart started to quicken every time he thought of it, that he couldn't bear for the numbered years of his life to increase by one when theirs— Erica's and Rachel's—never, ever could. But he could never bring this up. For some reason he just couldn't get it out.

He wasn't sure if he was trying to fall in love with Tara or trying not to. There were reasonable arguments on either side. He longed to see her, but then when he did he didn't feel what he expected to feel. It was so hard talking to her, and each time he talked to her it was hard all over again.

When it seemed there was no way the two of them could go on, when it seemed there was nothing—*nothing*—to say, he was filled with despair because he knew she was his one chance. She had known Erica and Rachel, she knew him, she knew all he had done and still wanted to be around him. Who else in his life would offer him that?

JENNIE

A ND THEN summer was over.
The third Friday in August, Matt's last day of work—a date
they had agreed on some time ago and not spoken about since. There
was no reason to—the sentencing date loomed and both of them
knew it.

That Friday morning, Jennie was busy proofing the reunion book-
let for the St. Bernie's fiftieth reunion and Matt was working at the
computer when suddenly he said, "You realize I won't be here to help
you with this reunion."

"I realize," she said. She glanced back in his direction, but he wasn't
looking at her. He was no longer typing, his body suddenly rigid, his
face ashen.

"Matt?" she asked.

He seemed to be choking—not in a sputtering, gasping sort of way
but in the real way, as when something small and perfectly windpipe-
shaped prevents you from taking air in or letting any out. He wasn't
making a sound.

"Matt, are you all right, honey?" she asked. "Matt?"

She moved from the desk to his side, kneeling in front of his chair.

"No," he said, a strangled sound. "Yes, it's just . . ." He was alarming her but at least now he could speak. "I'm sorry, I'm sorry." He
spoke without looking at her. "It's just that . . . it's just that . . ." He
turned toward her, his face ominous. "It's . . . it's my birthday today,"
he said. "I'm sixteen today."

He wrapped his arms tightly around his own shoulders, trying desperately not to cry.

The minute she put her hand on his knee he collapsed against her and she almost lost her balance. Her arms went around him, half to comfort him, half to keep herself from falling over. His warm tears dropped one by one onto her hair. They were latched together; if either one let go they would both tumble to the floor.

You're so young, she wanted to say. *Sixteen is so young. You can make anything you want to of your life.*

She imagined he was thinking just the opposite: *I'm older. I'll get older year by year and they never will.* He would carry what he'd done through each year of his life. It would never, ever stop.

Matt lifted his head and whispered, "Do you want to come over to my house tonight?"

"What?" She pulled carefully away from him and sat on the floor.

"For dinner," he said. "You, Tara, Alison, Mr. Breeze. All of you."

"I'm sure . . ." Her voice sounded like a croak. She cleared her throat. "I'm sure your mom doesn't want a crowd."

"No, it's okay, really. We're having lasagna, corn on the cob, salad and this really great herb bread my mom makes. On your birthday you get to choose your favorite meal and that's mine." Just when Jennie had no idea how to deal with the devastated sixteen-year-old sobbing in her arms, he had turned into a six-year-old.

She couldn't believe he was serious. "Do you mean tonight?" she asked. "That's kind of short notice."

"Mom always makes enough food for two nights. She freezes half. Always."

"I'm sure Tara would love to come," Jennie said. "Why don't you ask her?"

"Because I'm asking you." There was something defiant in his voice. And the way he was looking at her. He had the most direct gaze of any teenager, maybe any person, Jennie had ever known. It gave you two options: cower and look away or live up to it, joining in its avidness.

"Come on, Matt," she said, trying to sound jokey. "Alison will probably spit up all over your birthday cake or something."

"Please," he said. "Please say yes."

She felt uneasy, but he was so eager. So sincere.

"Okay," she finally said, "but call your mom and make sure it's all right."

"I will," he said, already going to the phone.

. . .

O F COURSE she had to get him a present, but what could it be? As soon as he left that afternoon she took Alison with her to the mall. Presents for boys: CDs—but she didn't know what music he liked. Clothes—too personal. Books—of course. Where to start? She felt she had overdone it on the Nabokov and considered other Russians. Tolstoy, Turgenev, Dostoyevsky—they were all so long and depressing. Chekhov's stories might be a possibility—at least they would be short—but the first story in the collection she picked up was called "Grief" and on the last page a doctor was telling a man to say good-bye to his arms and legs.

She moved over to the American literature section, where everything seemed slim and cheery by comparison. Naive and optimistic. The problem here was that things that came to mind for someone Matt's age, like *The Great Gatsby* or Hemingway, Emerson and Thoreau, Edith Wharton—all of these he had already read. It was much the same for British literature unless she got him Trollope or Ruskin, which didn't seem like festive birthday selections.

She spent some time in the poetry section and then wondered about Proust. She remembered that when she first read Proust in her late twenties, she had so wished she had discovered him earlier.

It was ridiculous how much time she was spending on this. She had already been in the bookstore a half hour. Alison was fussy in her buggy so Jennie picked her up, flipping through books with one hand, trying to keep Alison's drool off the pages. She kept thinking what Matt might read into any book she gave him, what adult themes might surface that he might not be ready for. It was crazy: at the beginning of the summer she had handed him books blindly, thinking of nothing except whether she liked them herself, impressed over and over again by the sophistication of his readings.

She returned to the Russian section and picked up the hefty volume of Nabokov's stories. She hadn't read it and skimmed through, hoping there was nothing inappropriate for someone sixteen years old.

She deserted Nabokov and decided on the Proust. She bought a copy of *Swann's Way* and had it wrapped. She almost stopped the girl halfway through so she could write an inscription in the book but she had always been really bad at those and didn't want to have to agonize over what to write. She was being such an adolescent about this and was greatly relieved when the book was finally paid for and she was on her way back to her car.

Jennie assumed Matt had told Tara about his birthday, but when Tara and Chris got home from work she discovered it was news to Tara too. And then Tara wanted to buy a present so they had to drive to the mall again on the way to Matt's house.

After a half hour, she came out of the mall empty-handed.

"I'm not going," she said. "I can't find anything and I'm not going without a present."

"I'm sure he won't care. He's probably not expecting anything."

"*You're* bringing one," Tara said, in an it's-all-your-fault tone.

"The book I got can be from all of us," Jennie said, but she saw this wasn't going to work. Tara's expression did not lighten at all.

"I wish he would have told me," Tara said, "so I would have had time to get him something really nice."

"If you want, you could give him the book yourself, honey," Jennie said. "It's all right with me." When Tara nodded Jennie ripped off the tag and handed the wrapped book to Tara. She was happy she had decided not to inscribe it.

It seemed to Jennie that as soon as they rang the doorbell at Matt's house a dozen people were there. Once they had been led through the house out to the back patio she was able to actually count and saw that there were only seven of them, including Matt and his parents, Grant and Belinda. The girls were Katie and Emily, curly haired and adorable, and the boys, long-legged and grinning, were named Peter and Brian. Matt seemed leagues older than the rest of them.

Belinda Fallon was different than the glowing earth mother Jennie had expected. She was at least ten years older than Jennie, thin, wiry—and smoking. That surprised Jennie most of all. She wouldn't have expected Christians to have addictions. Belinda wore a Museum of Natural History T-shirt and jean shorts and looked from the back like one of her sons. She was energetic, quick, a little nervous. Matt's father, on the other hand, was an oasis of calm. Grant Fallon was big, dark-haired and quiet, but when he smiled it was Matt's smile and Jennie could see exactly where Matt had learned how to look people in the eye.

The adults and Matt and Tara sat on the lawn chairs and talked while the older girl, Katie, passed around vegetables and dip, looking as if she had been solemnly appointed to the task. The two boys seemed on a campaign to entertain Alison and brought out every toy they could find to shake over her head and make her laugh. She looked in danger of being overstimulated, her head darting back and forth, legs and arms motoring. The kids were all friendly and talkative and dinner was much more comfortable than Jennie could have imagined, all of them describing *their* favorite birthday dinners, and how old they would be, and when.

They stayed outside all evening, despite the heat. The kids didn't even seem to notice and after dinner, Chris was hustled into a game of soccer with Grant and the boys. Matt and Tara joined in after a while; they had kept their distance from each other all night. Having an audience was not what they needed right now.

Jennie remained on the patio with Belinda while Katie and Emily took turns holding Alison, with Belinda carefully supervising.

"I guess now would be the time to thank you for everything you've done for Matt," Belinda said, a little nervously. "Not that any thanks would ever be enough."

"You don't have to thank me for anything," Jennie said. "I've been really lucky to have him this summer."

"Well, it's done him a world of good. He was such a mess after this accident." Was she attempting to sound light, using the word *mess,* rolling her eyes? It seemed as if she were searching for the right tone. "Of course something like this would have affected anybody," she continued, "but Matt's so sensitive. It was almost too much for him. We were beside ourselves trying to figure out what to do. I can remember scouring the library for books to help him, but they're all about the loss of a parent, loss of a sibling, stuff like that. Nothing about what he's been going through." Belinda sounded matter-of-fact now, as if Matt were a problem she was trying to solve.

Jennie nodded. "I probably looked at all those same books myself."

"And the minister has come by frequently but to tell you the truth, nothing has helped him as much as this job. It's just given him a purpose this summer." She smiled, though she looked a little puzzled, wondering if she had adequately explained herself to Jennie.

"A distraction," Jennie said.

"More than that, Jennie. So I thank you." Belinda lit up a cigarette, gave Jennie a sheepish look. "Can you believe it? I quit smoking almost twenty years ago but picked it up again this May."

May fifth, Jennie thought. "He's a great kid," she said aloud.

"Isn't he?" Belinda agreed quickly, pride showing. "I know it's terrible for a mother to say that but he truly is. I've known hundreds of kids, thousands. I worked as a teacher for ten years." She took a drag off her cigarette and Jennie eagerly awaited her next words, feeling a little voyeuristic. "Matt's just different," Belinda said. "Was from the beginning. He's the reason we started home-schooling, you know. We're not some sort of separatists like everybody thinks." She grimaced, rolling her eyes again. "Neither of us had ever even heard of it before. Matt was in preschool and he was bored. Day in, day out he would just go off in a corner—four years old!—and work by himself. I thought he must be withdrawn, but that wasn't it. He made friends and he liked to play, but he taught himself to read at four and while everyone else was playing dress-up he was reading books, writing these little stories, building elaborate structures with blocks. I tried another preschool but that made no difference. He just liked to work by himself and at his own rapid pace so I decided to teach him at home." Belinda cast her eyes across the yard, where the children ran after the soccer ball. "I'm not sure it's going to work with all the others. Some of them have a little bit different personalities. There don't seem to be any more geniuses among them."

Jennie's head snapped toward Belinda. That genius comment—was she serious? Jennie searched her face, looking for a roll of the eyes.

"We'll see," Belinda said. "It's funny how your first child sets the pattern and the rest of your kids just have to follow."

Jennie still wasn't certain what to make of Belinda's words but she could suddenly feel Matt's anguish at letting his family down. No matter how slight your disappointment as a parent was, your child was sure to feel it a thousandfold.

"I always loved big families," Jennie said. "Would like to *be* in one, I mean, not *have* one."

Belinda laughed. "People always think we must have had this master plan—have a brood, teach them at home. Truth is, we had the children one at a time and there just happened to be so many at the end. After I had Matt, I thought it was the worst idea I'd ever had. I didn't know a thing about babies. And the sleep deprivation—I'm sure you can relate."

"Yeah, I'm still there," Jennie said. "It becomes your major personality trait. Exhaustion." They looked at each other and both broke into laughter. They were on the same footing again. Maybe under different circumstances they might become friends.

"I was sure Matt would be an only child," Belinda continued conspiratorially, "but things seemed to get so much easier after he was two, so we decided to do it. And then Brian was so easy, a cherub, so I had a third."

"Three boys!" Jennie said.

"Again, I thought that was it. But then I was pushing forty and I knew that would be my last chance before shutting the system down and we just wanted to do it." Belinda shook her head and laughed. "We just wanted to. Maybe we're crazy. Then somehow we ended up with two more. Now I really am done. I mean, I'm forty-six. I don't want to set any Guinness records." Belinda was quiet for a while and then asked, "How about you? Are you planning for more?"

"No," Jennie said. "This will be it." Belinda nodded attentively, as if expecting Jennie to talk about her own family planning, that curious sixteen-year gap between Tara and Alison. People always wanted to know, always expected a sad story of infertility or multiple miscarriages, but the truth was Jennie had wanted to concentrate on her own education before having more children. Taking care of Tara, working and going to college and then grad school had been so taxing; Jennie had felt her life was lived on a treadmill for years and years. Chris had always wanted more children and Jennie promised him that once her master's was finished they would have another, and they had. And now Jennie's goal was to get through these first couple of years with Alison and then start on her Ph.D.

She didn't tell any of this to Belinda. She was pulling back, becoming more reserved about her own life as Belinda talked more familiarly of hers.

"Those two are getting quite close," Belinda said, nodding out toward the yard.

Jennie turned to look. It was starting to get dark and the soccer game seemed to have disbanded; Brian alone was left kicking the ball with his father. Jennie saw Chris pulling coins from his pocket to do magic tricks for Peter, Katie and Emily and across the yard, Matt and Tara were sitting together under a tree.

They were in the darkest part of the yard, the part shaded by trees, the part where you would first spot fireflies as the dusk turned to night. Matt held Tara's hands in his, in what looked to Jennie to be a gesture less of affection than of examination. He was looking at her palms, not reading them—he was no fortune-teller—but running his fingers over the lines, tracing each vein, curling and uncurling her fingers with the greatest of tenderness.

What if they're falling in love? she thought, not for the first time but this time with more fear and regret.

Suddenly Matt glanced up from that dark part of the yard and his eyes looked straight into hers. And stayed there. His eyes fastened on hers while his hands held Tara's. That's when she knew how much she wanted those hands he held to be hers, that girl, that sixteen-year-old girl, Tara, her daughter, to be her.

She tried to breathe and couldn't. It was calamitous, what was happening to her. She could barely get up.

"Excuse me," she mumbled to Belinda, and went inside the house. She walked through the kitchen searching for a bathroom, opened a coat closet by mistake, and then the door to the basement stairs. She finally found the powder room. She had barely shut the door when a loud, wracking sob came out. She threw herself down on her stomach so the tears would drop straight to the floor without reddening her eyes, without touching their rims or lashes. It was a trick she had taught herself in high school, a trick to use at a party when you needed to steal away to the bathroom alone because you had learned that the boy you liked liked someone else.

What was this? A summer of grief and exhaustion, of mothering and looking back, all coming together in one look thrown across the yard from him to her. She was knocked over by it, weeping and coughing on the powder room floor. For what? For Matt, for herself, for what her life hadn't been and what his might never be?

And because it was good-bye, that look. She hadn't expected to be in Matt's life forever, but she had wanted the time she spent there to be of some use. Now he was leaving and she had given him nothing a fraction so valuable as what he'd given her, by being, for a summer, hers.

When she stopped crying she sat up and leaned against the door, putting pressure against it with her back because she did not even want to think about having to open it and go out. She waited and waited for this feeling to be over.

Across from her, taped to the powder room wall, was a long narrow poster, a timeline of the Civil War. Jennie studied it for a long time, all those dates breaking the turmoil into battles and eras and marches. Jennie had always loved those kinds of charts. They were so neat and orderly, the turning points marked clearly, the philosophies and actions of the major figures summarized neatly in boxes to the side. You could do that with history, but only long, long afterward.

MATT

I T WAS THE LOOK. Just that look, caught from where he sat across the darkening yard, under the tree where the lightning bugs gathered, holding Tara's hands, talking to her, for some reason, about God.

He was telling her something he had believed a long time ago, before this summer, before the accident that had changed everything he had ever believed about God and about himself in a way that kept him from knowing if he could ever go back to the way he had believed before. He had started to think that maybe Mom and Dad and his Sunday school teachers and all of Christianity was just a way of everyone getting their stories straight, of giving the children something to believe in so the idea of belief would at least be planted.

Right after the accident he believed God had gone. But then—just today or maybe yesterday—it had come to him that it wasn't God who was gone but his way of looking at God. He had always been told that all men were sinners and that he was one too, but he had never really seen himself that way. Well, maybe in some neat little way he would take Brian's piece of cake and confess his sin and it would be over. Now he was looking at God through the eyes of a sinner and that made everything different. He just hadn't known where to look for God because the alignment had changed. He was looking in a different direction.

Maybe all summer long he hadn't wanted to see himself that way, so all the Bible verses and stories that had ever meant anything to him had become incomprehensible. He had found more meaning in Nabokov, in any of the books Jennie had given him to read because their words were new to him. It was not so painful to read them with a sinner's eyes.

And then suddenly, after he realized this, God had come back to him. His trust in God. He felt God there again, underneath every-thing, and for that reason he began to talk to Tara about God. He was telling her that the beauty and texture of her hand, the flesh and mus-cle and tendon of it, all the bones, the veins seen and unseen, were enough to know that God was there, that she was a miracle, and he, for all his flaws, was too. He had had this demonstrated to him once somewhere in childhood, maybe at a church retreat, and he had be-lieved it the way he believed all things then: To know the power of God's love for you, all you had to do was look at your hand and see how much a God who had put so much into a single limb of a single human body adored the creatures he created.

He could almost feel himself returning to God as he held Tara's hands; it was some second, solo round of confirmation.

For the first time he almost felt he could forgive God for not killing him too. It was something about Tara—if she had been spared, why couldn't he be too?

But it was his fault. Not hers. That's what made the difference. Was it because it was his birthday that he was trying to find some justifica-tion for himself moving another year?

And that was the moment when he looked up, wondering what people would think they were doing. Mom was holding Alison—she could never resist a baby—and Katie and Em and Peter were watching Jennie's husband do a magic trick with a coin. No one was watching, and then he turned his head to look straight into Jennie's eyes.

It wasn't what she said with the look but what he received.

The movement inside him was tectonic. He was holding Tara's hands but he wanted to shake them free and float over the yard, over the children and their toys, to take Jennie's hands in his own.

But Tara was saying something to him.

"What was that?" he asked.

"I love you," she said. Tara had said, *I love you* and he had said, *What?* He opened his mouth before he could think of what to say. For-tunately she rushed on. "You don't have to say—that back. Or any-thing, even. I just wanted to say it to you."

"I . . . I . . ." He truly couldn't get any words out. He couldn't even construct a thought. What could he say? What was the thing he was feeling? He loved her. He loved Jennie. It came as this surge of feeling except that surges were momentary and this one wasn't subsiding. It was like a geometry proof that you puzzled over for days and finally, when you knew it, it seemed so simple. What he felt for Tara, anything he'd ever felt for anyone else, he now knew how to define because he had this.

He didn't understand this at all. He had hardened his heart, and this is what it had come back with.

JENNIE

"**I** WANT TO GO AWAY," she told Chris that night as they were undressing for bed.

"You don't mean a vacation, do you?" he asked wearily.

"I want to *move* away," she said. "Far away. California or Colorado or Michigan or Texas."

"It's a nice fantasy, Jen, but we've been through this before." He stopped talking to pull his shirt over his head. "The slight problems of money, housing, jobs."

"If we sell this house and move somewhere cheap . . ."

"California's as bad as Connecticut."

"Okay, Iowa. We can rent an apartment above a bakery in some midwestern downtown. Iowa City. Ann Arbor. Champaign-Urbana. Hell, we could even buy the bakery. We could just start over, away from everyone who knew us in high school." She heard how frantic she sounded, how demanding. *You must help me change my life.*

"Like our best friends?" he asked. "Like my brothers?"

"*Your* best friends, Chris." Jennie unbuttoned the buttons of her blouse and then took it off, tossing it on the huge mound of dirty clothes in the corner.

"What about Tara? You can't ask a sixteen-year-old girl to leave her friends."

"Her two best friends are gone," Jennie said, then turned to the dresser to take off her jewelry. She was moving quickly, sloppily, as if under the influence of some drug she'd never taken.

"Which is why you can't possibly uproot her now. And now she's got this boyfriend, if that's what he is. . . ." Chris hung his shorts on the clothes tree to wear the next day, pulled off his boxer shorts and kicked them on the pile.

He turned to her, completely naked, as she also was. It was strangely embarrassing to face each other this way, using these tones. She searched for her nightgown under blankets and pillows on the bed.

"You don't want to throw your business away any more than I do," Chris said.

"That's not true. I don't like reunions anymore. I don't want to do any more reunions." Jennie could hear how petulant she sounded but at the same time she was telling the truth. It was a completely misguided line of work for someone like her. Always looking back, always trying to re-create the past for others as puzzled about the way their lives had turned out as she was. She wanted to just turn it off, go forward with her life.

After a pause, she said to Chris, "You don't even like landscaping. You can do something else."

"What? Work at McDonald's? Every reasonable job in the world wants you to have a damned sheepskin to hang on the wall."

"*Damned sheepskin.* Where did you dig up that phrase? You sound like some rough Brooklyn character in an old black-and-white movie. Marlon Brando. Why don't you get the *damned sheepskin?* I'll work on my Ph.D. and you can get your B.A. . . . ."

"And we'll live happily ever after in college town dreamland."

"We can work too. We can live cheaply. We can plan our schedules to alternate so we can take care of Alison and we can get these part-time jobs." Jennie was being seduced even as she created it, the romance of the struggling academic life. It wasn't a dream. It was something they should have done years ago.

Chris was on the bed now, in the shorts and T-shirt he slept in, while Jennie still stood in the middle of the room, unwilling to give this up until she could get Chris to say something, anything, that would give her some kind of way to run away. *Let's leave tonight,* she wanted to say. *I'll drive first.*

"I just can't believe you want to walk away like that," Chris said quietly, from the bed.

"Walk away from what? I could close this door and never look back. If you and the girls come with me I wouldn't want a damned other thing from this house."

She was not being petulant now. She didn't want to live anymore in a town where she was first and foremost Jennie Northrop, the teenager who got knocked up and ruined her life. Most of all to herself.

"I don't want to put it off," she said, finally softening her tone. "I don't want to make any strategic plan. I just want to do it. Please, Chris, just say maybe. Say, 'If it means that much to you.'" She felt the wildness in her eyes, the heat in her face and neck and arms that made her want to pounce on him, to physically demand that he agree to her terms. She couldn't bear that his answers were so slow, so lethargic and disengaged.

What if she told him? What if she said, *I'm scared to death of what Matt is making me feel, this passion and regret and envy?* What if she confided in him like a best friend, which after all he was, instead of a husband, which he was too?

Chris said, "Why don't you write it up and I'll sign it in the morning." He adjusted his pillow, pulled the sheet halfway up and turned his back toward the fan to sleep.

MATT

A LL NIGHT HE LAY awake thinking only of her, of tracing the line of her smile with his finger and unclipping that lopsided barrette, the thick gold one with a chip in it, so heavy and shiny it made him think of a solid gold brick. He would spread her dark hair over her shoulders. He would kiss the point of each cheekbone, and then that mouth which he always saw slightly open, always ready to spill her next thought.

These were the things he wanted to do, and it was not without shame that he felt them, but he let himself feel them, all the way through, again and again, all night long, in this S-curve of wanting and needing and having that led from the depths of his buttocks up through his spine and stomach to the hollow of his throat.

JENNIE

THIS BEAST, this wild thing that staggered and lurched from her chest to her brain each time she pictured Matt's face, thought of his smile or his wrists or his voice—it had been with her two solid days. It demonized her; she was inhabiting an adolescent's skin.

She had felt like this before in her life. Only once or twice. Only briefly. You see some brilliant, gorgeous poet you've just heard read meet his girlfriend, equally brilliant, equally gorgeous, afterward. She hands him a book and, with captivating indifference, he pulls her to him. You want to die from wanting that so much.

Or the deeply tanned free spirits draped over each other in the airport lounge, the ankle bracelet, the tarnished silver earrings, the sandaled devotion of youth. That gives you a pang; however strong, it's only a pang, like you might feel during a certain scene in a movie, but the difference is, you don't know the people. They are strangers, the feelings fleeting, and even if you remembered the incident later you couldn't remember the faces exactly so the feelings couldn't strike at you again.

MATT

TARA MOVED A KNIGHT, her usual opening move, and after Matt advanced a pawn, she moved one of hers. His bishop, her knight again, another pawn move and she said, "I'm sorry I said that on your birthday."

"Uh, you don't have to apologize," he stammered. "Uh, it was . . ."

"It was stupid. I was just . . . I don't know, thinking about how . . ." She looked down, clearly so embarrassed at the memory of saying *I love you* that she couldn't meet his eyes.

He looked down too, wishing he wasn't the one causing her embarrassment. Just last week he had wanted to lean across the chessboard and kiss her.

Tara was waiting for him. He had to think of something to say.

He had at first thought of calling her to cancel today, but what could he have said: *I have somewhere else to go?*

He finally said, "You shouldn't think that way about me. I'm not free."

"You don't know that. You have to wait until Tuesday, see what happens. It might be okay." She smiled a smile of comfort. "I think it will all be okay."

"It's not just Tuesday," he said. "It's everything. I don't want to put you through anything. I won't let you go through anything on my behalf."

"I'm not going to go through anything I don't want to go through," she said earnestly.

"No, I really mean it." The force in his voice must have surprised her. She backed away. More gently, he said, "I don't want to pretend to go on if we can't. If *I* can't."

"Then we'll wait," she said, as if some problem had been solved. "We'll wait until Tuesday and see what happens."

"Okay," Matt said slowly. "We'll wait." Excruciating words. He felt the sick pool of a lie in his stomach.

Two more days. He found himself almost wishing that Tuesday would bring a harsh, unforgiving sentence. Tuesday would be his way out, the only way out, a much better way than telling the truth.

JENNIE

S HE HAD TO GET OUT of the house. There had been thunder-
storms all weekend and she had been inside all weekend, striding
around in a panic, not sleeping, silently stalking Chris, trying to make
him flee with her.

She went to the window to check the sky, thinking maybe she
would take Alison for a walk if there was no sign of rain. But the
minute she gazed outside she saw Tara coming up the driveway, arms
full of—her watercolors?

Tara had gone over to Camille Cleary's house, but now, less than fifteen minutes later, she was back.

Jennie held the door open for her. "What happened?" she asked.
"Camille's not home?"

"She's home," Tara said coldly, brushing past Jennie to her room.
Jennie waited for the door to slam, but instead she heard only the sheaf
of paintings being thrown to the floor and then Tara came straight
back to the living room and dropped onto the couch.

"I'm not allowed over there anymore," she said.

"What?" Jennie asked, moving immediately closer. Tara made a
small space on the couch for her and Jennie sat down. "Why?"

"I told her," Tara said. "About me and Matt. She says it's too hard
for her to know about us. Too painful."

"I can't . . ." *believe it,* Jennie didn't finish. She was furious at
Camille. How could she take Tara in, welcome her and help her, and
then send her home with her paintings as if they were just cluttering
up her house?

"I better go talk to her," Jennie said, but Tara grabbed her wrist.

"No, Mom," she said, calmly. "It's okay. I understand. I mean, it must be so terrible for her to know . . . about us . . . about me and Matt, when Matt was the one, you know . . . the accident?"

Jennie took a good look at her daughter. Her face was placid, with a hint of a smile.

"Camille's grieving," Jennie said uncertainly, "and I guess grief does unexpected things—" In her mind she was storming across lawns to Camille's house, seizing her by the shoulders. Knocking her to the ground.

"I *know* that," Tara said, gently interrupting, rolling her eyes ever so slightly. "It's really okay."

Jennie put a hand on Tara's cheek, studied her round, sincere eyes, her forgiving mouth. "You're a smart girl," she said quietly.

"What can I say?" Tara smirked and Jennie gave her daughter a hug. This time, Tara did not pull away instantly. She let Jennie hold her.

"Come for a walk with me," Jennie said. "I was just about to take Alison—"

"No, thanks. I'm going to call Matt."

"Okay," Jennie said. Tara sprang from the couch and back into her room and Jennie, not quite trusting Tara's easy forgiveness, silently invoked Matt, this boy who consumed her, saying, *Please, please take care of her heart. I'd pay any price for its safety.*

MATT

FOR THE SECOND TIME that summer, he broke the terms of house arrest. The day he had ridden his bike up to the tree on Connaught Road had been unmeditated, but this time had not.

He left his house after midnight, after he was sure all of his family was asleep. He went out the sliding glass door in the back and walked to the garage to get his bike. He was aware of the risks. To be caught on the eve of his sentencing in the dark of night, away from his house— that could make things worse for him. But he didn't care. He had to go, and he took the familiar ride for the first time in the dark, passing only two or three cars the whole way there.

He felt as if all summer long everyone had been waiting for this sentence, as if that would determine everything. But now he felt that it was he who should take action first instead of waiting, always waiting to be told.

A certain part of his life was ending, now. Would end tomorrow, anyway, and he wanted to take care of some things tonight.

It was Jennie he saw first when he glided into the driveway. He could see her through the front window, open because of the heat. He could actually hear her humming as she walked Alison back and forth, trying to get her to sleep. His heart strained with love and he watched her in the moments before she saw him. He smiled at her, but she looked as if she'd seen a ghost.

She came out to him quickly, shutting the door behind her.

"What are you doing here?" she whispered. "Do you know the kind of trouble you could be in if the police found you?" She clutched Alison against her, backed against the door to the house.

"I know," Matt said.

"Why are you here? Matt? Do your parents know you're here? You've got to go back home."

"I've got just over ten hours until I have to go to court," he said. He was less than a foot away from her, six inches. He would barely have to move his head to kiss her.

"Are you here to see Tara?"

"No," he said. "Yes." He almost thought he would kiss her. In the dark he could take that last step toward her and do it before she even knew. It would be his only chance.

"She's asleep," Jennie said.

His throat gurgled with a strange, nervous laugh.

"Matt," she began as a whisper and that was enough for him.

"I love you," he said, and then instantly, "I'm sorry, I'm sorry," suddenly terrified, suddenly feeling the breadth of her friendship between them.

"Matt." She said his name gently, but as if it was the beginning of a long speech he absolutely refused to hear.

"Don't say anything," he said. "I didn't think I would . . . I'm just sorry." He dropped his chin over toward one shoulder. He should have kissed her. To have that kiss instead of those words hanging between them would be far more valuable. There was no way now he could have both.

"Matt," Jennie said, "I'm the adult. I . . ." Nothing in her voice was certain.

"No one's blaming you," Matt said softly. "I'm the one who did something wrong." He held out his hand to her but she didn't take it.

"No," she said.

"I'm grateful," he said. He covered his eyes with his hands as he searched for a way to explain. "I've never felt this before, and now I know what it is. It's not just some passing . . ." He felt it all well up inside him. He felt he would love her for every moment of his life. "It's not lust. I know what that is. You don't have to tell me." He dropped to the ground, sitting on the front stoop.

Keeping her distance, she joined him.

"Everyone wants to know why I drove a car into a tree when I wasn't even drunk," he said. "I'm telling you, just you, that I wasn't looking at the road because I was looking at her. I was reaching for her and I probably didn't even care who *she* was." He wanted to do this once, to just tell it once. "I'm saying 'her' because I don't even need to tell you which one it was. It doesn't matter because it didn't matter to me then. Anyone would have been all right. I just wanted—"

"You're sixteen," Jennie interrupted.

"It is a sin," he told her. "That's why—"

"It's not *why*," she said. Her voice was parental. "It wasn't some punitive accident to tell you what was wrong with you. Surely you must know that? I'm not religious at all and even I know that's not how God operates."

"I'm not blaming God," he said. "I'm blaming myself." He was able to look at her now. She was gravely listening. "You're right. God doesn't punish you. All this time I've been asking Him to, I've been hoping He would but that's not what He does." He tried to find the right words. "God gives you two things," he said. "Well, He gives you a lot more than that, but He gives you two main things. He gives you free will, and He gives you forgiveness. He says, go and make your own choices, do what you will with your life, and if you make mistakes I will not punish you, I will forgive you. But I figure that's kind of a punishment in itself."

She was quiet for a moment and then asked, "Why?"

"Because it isn't easy. You have to use the free will wisely and you have to learn how to accept forgiveness. And I haven't been able to do either of those things."

Jennie was shaking her head. "But you've tried. And you are trying. You're too hard on yourself."

"I think it must be kind of like growing up, learning how to use those gifts." As he said this, he felt grown up. He felt there was no way she could look at him as a boy anymore.

"It has nothing to do with growing up," Jennie said. "I'm sorry to say. It's not a rite of passage. You take little steps but everybody struggles with it all their lives."

"Little steps," Matt said. "That's what I mean. Because I never thought I'd ever know what love feels like. I thought I'd ruined that with what I did, how I treated . . ." He trailed off, afraid to use the words, afraid, almost to remind her who he was. He smiled at her.

"But now I know what love feels like. So don't tell me I don't know the difference between love and lust, Jennie. Because now I do."

She went for so long without saying anything and then he realized she was crying. He reached out to her but she held the baby between them like a shield.

"You have to go home, Matt," she said, sniffling. "It's so dangerous."

"I thought I'd never see you again," he said.

"You'll see me again." She put her hand on his arm and, though surely he was imagining it, her eyes were the saddest eyes he'd ever seen.

"Can I ask you something?" he whispered.

"Anything."

"Will you come tomorrow? Will you come to court? I would feel . . . it would be so much better if you were there."

She hesitated and then said, "Of course I'll come."

Forget about tomorrow, he wanted to say. *Let's run away tonight. I know you have a life, but this could be better than life.*

Instead he bent down and kissed Alison's moist head.

"I need to talk to Tara," he said, without meeting Jennie's eyes.

"What do you need to tell her?"

"That I can't feel about her the way she wants."

Jennie gave a heavy sigh. "It would be better," she said, "if you didn't tell her tonight. She's sleeping, she's got to go to school tomorrow."

"I have to," he said. "I need to tell her in person and I need to tell her before I go to court tomorrow."

"You can't," Jennie said. "She needs to sleep."

He heard the determination in her voice, almost hated her for it, then loved her.

"Okay," he relented.

"Tomorrow," Jennie said. Her voice took on an imploring tone. "And choose your words carefully, Matt. She's already lost so much."

JENNIE

FOR INFANTS, each day was like a rebirth. They opened their eyes upon waking and took in each sight, each color or shaft of light or face with the delight and exploration of the first time. Everything was new again; they had been sleeping.

Who knew what was in the darkness of infant sleep? Maybe it seemed as long again as the time before they had been born. Maybe memory wasn't so ingrained yet, and almost everything they had learned about the world was forgotten during that long night's sleep. Alison had still been inside more than twice as long as she'd been out.

Jennie watched her wake up that morning. She hadn't done that very often because usually it was Alison who woke Jennie with fierce cries of hunger. But last night, for the first time in her life, she had slept through the night.

Chris joined Jennie in the bedroom now, looking at Alison bat at her mobile, occasionally letting out a little shriek to tell everyone that nothing in the world could make her happier.

"Good morning, little girl," Chris said. He bent down to kiss her and she gave him a smile.

"When are we supposed to change these?" Chris asked, fingering the black-and-white cards on the mobile. "When does she begin to see colors?"

"I'm not sure," Jennie said. "I'll have to check the book, but I'm sure it passed us by."

"I always imagine everything changing in one fell swoop, like the black and white to color that happens once Dorothy hits Munchkin Land."

"She slept all night, Chris," Jennie said.

"I know. Did you see what time it is? It's past eight o'clock."

"Oh my God. Tara! She's got school today, she's—"

"It's fine, don't worry. I got her up."

"You remembered about school?"

"Not really, you caught me." Chris grinned. "She had a phone call early."

"A phone call?" Jennie asked sharply. "Who was it?"

"Matt."

"Damn," Jennie said. "Is she all right? Was she upset?"

"She seemed okay," Chris said. "The bus just picked her up."

Jennie fought the panic, the absurd urge to get in her car and chase the bus, trying to catch a glimpse of Tara's face to see if it was tear-stained.

But no. After Chris left and she fed Alison, Jennie went into her bedroom to get showered and dressed. It was after she turned the water off that she heard crying coming from the other room.

"Honey," she called, grabbing her robe and running. "Tara?"

She was on her bed, face down, hysterical.

"What happened, Tara? Honey, what happened?"

"Momma," Tara cried, turning to Jennie and seizing her, her whole small body latching on to Jennie's. It was minutes before she could do more than sob and gasp.

"I ran all the way home," she finally said. "I couldn't stay."

"What happened, honey?"

Tara breathed fast and loud, her face distorted from crying and trying not to cry. Jennie tried to keep hold of her, to rock and pat her, and Tara alternately fought and surrendered to Jennie's arms.

Finally she spoke. "They . . . weren't . . . *there!*" This last word came out as a shout, followed by new tears.

"Oh, Tara." Jennie smoothed her daughter's hair, rocked her on her lap.

Tara nodded. "Mommy, I miss them so much."

"I know you do, sweetheart," Jennie said, and that became what she chanted over and over while she held Tara for the next couple of hours, as Tara cried and rested, screamed, coughed and, occasionally, talked to Jennie. *I know, sweetheart, I know.*

There was a time when it still would have been early enough for her to make it to court in time. She could have gently shifted Tara from her lap and said, *Sweetie, I have to go. Matt's expecting me in court.* But she didn't. She couldn't. It was a betrayal of Tara's heart that she wouldn't enact. She felt the last possible moment pass as a small, devastating death, but she didn't go. He would be in court, he would be listening to all the words Marilyn Linders and Camille Cleary had for him, he would hear what the judge had to say, and though he had asked her to be, she wouldn't be there.

She was appalled by the casualness with which she had taken on the burden of his life, made him someone who needed her, who asked for her, who even . . . loved her. And now she was letting him go. Because, when it came down to it, she could—no hard choice at all. All that he made her feel was nothing, nothing compared to diving in and trying to save Tara. Her child. Hers.

EPILOGUE

S HE DIDN'T COME. While the court psychologist told the judge that based on her assessment, yes, Matt had felt extreme remorse, despair, that yes, he had entertained thoughts of suicide (how Mom cried at this), she didn't come.

When Erica's father read his victim statement, saying, "You put our daughter's dreams to rest violently, not gently," she didn't come.

When Erica's mother said, "You made a stupid choice and for that Erica paid the ultimate price. There is no punishment severe enough for what you did," she didn't come.

When Rachel's mother said, "We can forgive you, but we can't forget, will not forget, for any day of our lives what we have lost," she didn't come.

And then Matt read his own statement, tears falling on the pages he had brought.

There is nothing I can say to take away what I did or to take away what you're feeling. If I could go back in time, I would. If I could trade places with them, I would. If I could do anything to make your pain lessen, I would spend every day of my life doing that. But I can't.

All I can say is how sorry I am. I should never have driven that car. I regret so much the decisions I made that hurt not me, but them, and you.

I could make a promise to you that I will never be so stupid again, never sit in the driver's seat of a car when I'm not capable of driving. But what would that matter to you? Your daughters are gone and anything I do cannot bring them back.

I will promise you that as I live my life I will never forget them. I will honor their memory in everything I do, every decision I make. I will try to choose wisely because they'll always travel with me. Always, because I won't let them go again.

That was it—the four short paragraphs that had taken him twenty or thirty hours to compose. The words were nothing in the courtroom, flimsy and useless as the paper that was now damp and wrinkled as a tissue in his hands.

He looked at all the faces in the courtroom, those he knew and those he was seeing for the first time today—Erica's parents, Rachel's parents, Rachel's brother, the same age as his own—and he thought that he had for his life now things he would never have imagined or expected any boy to have. And they were permanent things: for the whole of his life, every day, until its end, he would also carry with him someone's father and mother who could never forgive him; someone's father and mother who miraculously had; a teenage girl who loved him though he wasn't able to love her; and a woman who taught him how to recognize love without accepting his. Though he would never have asked for any of these things, much less all of them so soon, they were perhaps the attendants he would need if he was to try to live the way he had promised to. Never forgetting. Choosing wisely. Never letting go of the memory of the two girls he had killed.

The judge read his sentence: Five years probation, eight hours of community service a week, and no driver's license until he was twenty-one.

"It's the best possible scenario," Finchley whispered. "Because he saw how much you've suffered he didn't want to see you suffer more."

Matt shook his head. It didn't matter. He looked toward the back of the courtroom. Mom put her hands together in prayer. Dad gave him a sad smile and a nod. And behind them, the door didn't open. No one else came in.

ABOUT THE AUTHOR

NANCY WOODRUFF, born and raised in Chicago, received an M.F.A. in writing from Columbia University, where she was awarded the Henfield Prize/Transatlantic Review Award. She has taught at Columbia University, the State University of New York at Purchase and Richmond College in London, where she now lives.